THE MEMORY ROOM

THE MEMORY ROOM

Mary Rakow

COUNTERPOINT

WASHINGTON, D.C.

The author gratefully acknowledges the following for permission to quote from the following copy-
righted works. From *Paul Celan: Poet, Survivor, Jew,* translated by John Felstiner. Copyright ©
1995 by John Felstiner. Reprinted by permission of Yale University Press, New Haven. From *Selected Poems and Prose of Paul Celan,* translated by John Felstiner. Copyright © 2001 by John Felstiner.
Reprinted by permission of W.W. Norton & Company, Inc. From "[To Stand]", "[Once]", "Think
of It" by Paul Celan from *Poems of Paul Celan,* translated by Michael Hamburger. Translation
copyright © 1972, 1980, 1988, 1995 by Michael Hamburger. Reprinted by permission of Persea
Books, Inc. (New York). From *Paul Celan, Breathturn,* translated by Pierre Joris. Copyright © 1995
by Pierre Joris. Reprinted by permission of Sun & Moon Press. Excerpt from "A Tale Begun" from
View with a Grain of Sand by Wislawa Szymborska, translated by Stanislaw Baranczak and Clare
Cavanagh. Copyright © 1995. Reprinted by permission of Harcourt (New York).

Library of Congress Cataloging-in-Publication Data

Rakow, Mary.
   The memory room / Mary Rakow.
   p. cm.
   ISBN 1-58243-172-8 (alk paper)
   1. Women — Fiction. 2. Redemption — Fiction I. Title.
PS3618.A44 M46 2002
813'.6 — dc21

               2001047243

FIRST PRINTING

Jacket and text design by Gopa & Ted2
Typeset in Sabon and Galliard

COUNTERPOINT
P.O. Box 65793
Washington, D.C. 20035-5793

Counterpoint is a member of the Perseus Books Group

10 9 8 7 6 5 4 3 2 1

L.R.B.

Grato Laetoque Animo

"The world is never ready
For the birth of a child."

Wisława Szymborska,
"A Tale Begun"

CONTENTS

I.

A Thousand Darknesses

Introit	1
Confiteor	45
Peregrinatio	75
Laceratio	101
Lamentatio	129
Fundus	155

II.

Into the Straits

Deus	185
Corpus	193
Laborare	217
Memoria Excidere	249
Artes Liberales	269
Delectatio	297
Latere	307
Requiescere	329
Musica	351

III.

Solstice

Ars Magica	361
Libertas	377
Ignominia	383
Infirma	393
Fractio	403
Poeta	417
Pictura	431
Credo	443

IV.

Come the Sabbath

Mobilis	453
Appetitus	465
Salvus	473
Ratio	481
Rosa	489
Benedictus	495
Notes	507
Acknowledgments	511

I.

A Thousand Darknesses

INTROIT

I wonder, on this first day of October, why I can't solve the simplest things.

It was the new student, the one from Cambodia
who found me crouched in the corner,
when the doors finally opened
and the light came back on.

So slowly, he put his books down next to me.
Carefully, lifting me out.

His expression saying, He would never tell.

"Anyone would panic stuck in an elevator," the Department Chair said, tenderly, but I thought, Not like I did, they don't. Seven times I stood before my students, white as a sail, unable to remember my thoughts, my hands gripping the podium's edge.

Seven times in one year.

"I need an immediate leave of absence," I said. He was not surprised. His large office with its pictures of Loisy, Newman, a framed photo of himself with four other seminarians, when they were young, in cassocks, leaning onto each other.

The brilliant grillwork of a gate.

"Can you stay for the reception, at least?" he asked. "You're the one he'll want to talk to." And I thought, It can't be worse than my students today, their wide and vacant eyes, their faces like empty plates.

Past the curtain, St. Ignatius stood in marble on the empty lawn.

Fog

through the plate glass windows formed droplets on the
eucalyptus leaves high above
above the faculty, alumni, the Bishop,

while the scholar from Boston stood near me
pouring sherry—

but I could not recall

the title of his book, his name, or the journal that published
my favorable review
because

he wore a charcoal sport coat with small raspberry flecks
and with it a shirt of minute houndstooth, red

and all I could think was, Red next to raspberry.
Red.   Reduced.   Mute.   You,
who have eyes to see this chasm between hues, you,

you could see me.

The red dress came into our house on a child-sized elephant hanger in a plastic bag. The woman at the door did not know it was a crime to interrupt my mother's piano practice. My stomach hurt with the silencing of the keys.

Her quick steps down the hall. "You might as well have this." She dropped the red dress on my bed. "It'll be too small for Cheryl anyway." Rolling the bag between her palms. Unable to get the plastic tight enough.

Everything about the dress was different from clothes at our house. Puff sleeves ironed with a crease at the top. Pleats pressed into the sash. The fabric soft and old, balled threads like a cotton sheet. Inside one arm, a mending line stitched in red, not black. Red, to match the dress.
From a different world, I thought, a different kind of mother. A voice that never came back to our door.

I wore the red dress everyday.
Retrieved it from the dirty clothes. Wet my hands to iron it against my chest.
The first dress that belonged to me without being Cheryl's first. That summer before kindergarten. That summer I was four.

My mother made up a song for it.

> *"Barbara's got a red dress, red dress, red dress.*
> *Barbara's got a red dress all day long."*

6.

Boxes from my office still piled high in the car.

we hung our harps among the willows

What if no one came?

Dolores Mary's birthday gift here on the night table by my bed.

"I thought this might have a better home with you,"
she handed me a book covered with brown paper and
overlapping strips of tape.
"I can't make heads or tails of these poems," her voice dropped,
as if a failing. "Gerald was the smart one in
the family, not me."
Her fingernails trimmed to tight ovals, calcium moons sailing
to the edge. Next to the stiffness of her veil, a fringe
of gray curls, soft as sheepswool.

7.

How did she know Celan's words would come at me like this?

threadsun   starhard   icesorrowpen

bearing the marks of destruction.

I rake my fingers through his soil.

cleftrose   *black milk*   *word-moon*

Grain left on the ground. Gleanings.

He is Boaz. I am Ruth.

8.

Bedroom to bathroom to the bed to the bath.
I haven't always been like this, stuck in my bed!

These walls should bear me witness.
But they refuse.

At twenty I was strong.

    Those four weeks in Italy after college, hopping from
    region to region like a sparrow.

    So easily I left behind the hard wood of Protestantism—
    bird flight! free!

Catholicism was everywhere.

      "Here!" they said. "Touch this!"

      God's body
         in the eggplant's aubergine skin.

I ate their salads—garlic, vinocotto, mint—I ate their legends too.

William the Hermit who was served macaroni stuffed with dirt.
When he blessed and ate it, the dirt became ricotta cheese and
meat, inventing the miracle of cannelloni in the year 1253. They
said it was in Parma that basil leaves were first crushed with
pine nuts, olive oil and the sweet milk of ewes. Creating pesto.
Fifteen centuries before the birth of Luther.

I had an appetite. I ate cabbage and pork soup for St. Anthony
in Savoy. Lemon fritters on St. Joseph's Day, the sweet custard
on my tongue.

I'll drive to Sorrento's Market.

I'll buy Lambrusco wine from the birthplace of Verdi, Toscanini,
its delicate violet scent. I'll fill my cart with squash, tomatoes,
peppers—the good foods from the ground. I'll walk beneath that
other light, pale cheese glow. Dark olives in a barrel, oregano
floating on the top. That certain smell of brine.

My thoughts will clarify. I'll coalesce.

God will be right there, on the shelf with truffles from the town
of Gubbio where St. Francis tamed the wolf.

The cashier smiles but points that I've misbuttoned my blouse.
Things aren't the same. Newspapers stacked unevenly by the door
are sliding to the left. Long scuff marks on the floor. Milky smell
of almonds in a bin. But what about that scholar from Boston?
Or that student from Cambodia—what did he see? Nougat candies
in small boxes.
But what about the veal?
Why didn't that bother me? That slaughter of the young?
Or those Sicilian fishermen harpooning swordfish while they spawned?
What of that? Fresh ricotta in a mound, its sickening white silky moat.
Holding my sherry, what should I have said? My stomach, nauseous.
My head.
Tapenade samples on a cart. Rows of salami hanging above the cheese.
Their mahogany skins, tight nets of string. I am too permeable.

And what about those turkeys with red pomegranates on a spit?
The woman ahead won't make up her mind.
The butcher swings down a salami.
Marble slapped to meat. She hesitates.
Blood on his apron. The salami rolled under his palm.
My bones are too exposed. He presses with his knife. "Hold still!"
He cuts the string. But the slant of her shoulders! The whir of the fan!
"Hey lady..." There is no air.
Cans fall off the shelf. My purse.
Silver all around my feet. I can't get out.

"Lady, I can help you now." On every surface
—cans, glass, shelves—the image repeats.
Held down, released, cut from string.
Where is my car? There's not enough skin. The sun hurts.
Why's that man honking? I'm in the crosswalk. I'm doing it perfectly.
My shoes are right between the lines. "I can't find my car!"
The woman sweeping looks up. Scowls, points her broom.
Down the street. The only parked car. Mine
Right in front of Sorrento's. I run.

II.

It comes.
I lock the doors. Hold my waist. It comes just the same.
Rising from the bottom of a sea. Great ship cutting the surface
of the water. Sheets fall fast away.

> *I'm sitting on my bedroom floor, tearing white paper*
> *into snow.*
> *"Why aren't you dressed?" My mother's words, crisp*
> *as sugar cubes.*
> *She doesn't tie my sash this time. She doesn't button*
> *the back of my red dress.*
> *A picnic table in the living room. "Up there," she points.*
> *"Lie down. No. At this end. Hold still!"*
> *She pulls clumps of my hair.*
> *Snap! The scissor sound. Snap! Snap!*
> *Above my head her wrists, the pale blue of her veins.*

It is over.

Withered grass.

Wet palm marks on the steering wheel.
My hair. Still on my head.

The dashboard, radio, speedometer,
clock. All the same.

Just the way I left them.

I make it to the bed.

> *You I could hold*
> *while everything slipped from me*

I count what I know:

—the letters of Gregory the Great
—castle gardens at Leeds, Russell Page, flowers around a moat
—the first line of the Periodic Table
—my new lipstick color
—Bach's Cello Suite no. 2
—the island of Burano, its lace-making school
—Josephine Bremen, age 70, who lives next door

The clock on the night table moves its three hands.
Enough motion for the two of us.

I sleep.

14.

Five days. Bedroom to bath.
I catch my reflection in the mirror by mistake. My lips could be on my forehead. Both eyes on one side of my nose. Jumbled blocks of wood.

Maybe Cubism started this way. Memory re-arranging a face.

During the night, a down feather worked its way through both pillowcases, the satin liner and the outer cotton case. A single feather leaving the others behind, pressing through both layers of tightly woven thread. I cry.

> *"Of course you can play a cello!" Daniel said. "Your father was*
> *a nut!"*
> *So we bought a student model.*
> *My father said, when I was young,*
> *"Girls shouldn't sit like that in public," by which he meant,*
> *Don't spread your legs.*

I climb the stairs.
Unzip the leather case.
Wooden torso, full of breath. I tune.

First note, long and solitary. Brown tassel-cord. It moves across the room.

Touching the other side.

arms holding you become visible, only they

15.

But now it comes into this room!

"Why aren't you dressed?"
She doesn't tie my sash.

Bright print of the chintz.
The breeze that tries to lift it from the sill.

I loosen the hairs of the bow. Fold the metal stand.
Slam the door. Sit on the stairs.

Outside, the oblivious moon.

She tosses my head between her palms.
Back and forth. Back and forth.
"I'm making you pretty for Daddy."
"Hold still!"
Her long auburn hair falling down toward me.
She doesn't mean, Hold still. She means,
Stop staring at my hair.

So I stopped looking at the one thing
I found beautiful on her.

16.

I don't bathe or brush my teeth. I don't get out of bed.

These bedroom walls should show a counting, a tabulation of the things I've done.

The neighborhood Christmas parties each year, my three decorated trees, a croquembouche, the harp. On Valentine's Day a mother-daughter tea hosted with Josephine. Egg hunts on Easter, a rented tent, blue and yellow iris at each table, foiled rabbits by each plate.

17.

The morning sun pulls me out. I tie my gardening shoes. Not the new ones with the rubber soles, but the sturdy ones I wore when Daniel moved to England and I dug my trench.

> *"You could have gone with him. You could've leased the*
> *house . . . .*
> *I was angry with Josephine.* "England suits you, Barbara.
> Talk about gardens!"
> *I stopped digging and looked up at her.*
> *"Physical movement doesn't fix a thing Josephine."*

Three feet wide and four feet deep, around my property like a moat. I set in ficus nitida, five truckloads, one hundred and thirty plants in all. I made a wall of green.

Shechinah   Peace

How well I came know the handle of my shovel, the press of metal blade against my shoe.

18.

I oil the clippers and set the ladder against the hedge. I want to say, "Something horrible happened when I was four." But today my words fall hollow to the ground, hitting the ladder's edge.

I move the ladder closer to the street. Why can't I remember Daniel's eyes? Were they gray? Blue? The marked indifference of these leaves.

> *"All you believe in is color!" We were fighting. It was a Wednesday. "You've got skeletons in your closet, Barbara, that's all I'm saying!"*

> *"Shut up Daniel!" I yelled. "You're drunk." But what I meant was, It's over now. You've come too close.*

I trim harder.

> *Just the lilac of his shirt, his faded jeans, when we stood in the airport terminal and he asked, "Do I look okay?"*

Branches pile up on the grass.

> (*If I were like you. If you were like me.*
> *Did we not stand*
> *under* one *trade wind?* . . .)

This is not peace.

19.

I bring out the tallest ladder and climb it to the top. Telephone poles, the Convent roof and beyond, the Church. Proud tower of bells. That place where hard words stand.

I should take my memories there. Living stone. Thorax. Heart.
Leave my words inside her walls. She'll graft them to her thigh.
Then I will be done with this.

requisit   *pacem*

She'll take these memories and dissolve them in her veil.

20.

"Barbara, long time no see!" Monsignor Kilmartin smiles, eyeing my left hand where he wants a wedding ring to be. "How's work? Tell me about your students."

"There's something I have to say. Here. Out loud." A pencil snaps in my fingers. Did I take it from his desk?

"Relax, have a seat." He pushes the crystal golf ball paperweight to the blotter's edge.

Good mother, hide me in your veil

"I don't know what's happening. A memory. Something . . . ."
"Are you crying? What on earth . . . ."
"Something happened when I was four . . . ."

"He's here Monsignor," Alice opens the door. "Oh, excuse me Barbara."

"Blast it! You've come at a bad time, Barbara, that's all. Today our new Associate arrives. Here, let me be brief." His hand to his chest, fingers smoothing his black lapel.

"Let me tell you something as your Pastor," he stands, touches my shoulder. The memory can play tricks. Believe me, I know." He glances up at the clock. "You're a bright woman, Barbara, no question, but . . ."

"This isn't ordinary memory, Father!" He adjusts his belt, moves closer to the door.

"There's a lot of this going around. People say they're remembering things. I'm not saying you're doing that. But you see it. Families break up over things that could never have happened. Divorce. Lawsuits. It's gotten out of hand."

voice-rift   worm-talk

"You're troubled, I can see that. Can we talk another time?" Artificial flowers in a vase.

blindness-bell   disenfranchised lip

"Here," he opens the door. "Let me introduce you."

Hide not thy face far from me

"Barbara, don't rush off!"

21.

The Convent gate open. Driveway, clothesline, empty strings.
But the lawn's too pungent smell. And there is too much red.
The camellia bush is in full bloom. Ahead of time.
Scarlet bleeding on the leaves.
I pull off a bloom.
Another.

> *Faster, faster, my mother cuts my hair.*
> *Her breath in rapid puffs.*
> *Tight opening between her lips above me.*
> *Sour smell coming through her freckled skin.*
> *Her forearms. Her dress.*
> *Pulling my hair.*
> *The more she cuts the more I think,*
> *She's peeling me like a potato.*
> *Cutting everything off. Not just my hair.*
> *She'll take my arms, my legs.*
> *All my moving parts.*
>
> *Then I won't be a girl anymore.*
> *I'll be good.*
> *Smooth. Like a potato.*

22.

"Barbara, is that you?"

> My cheek cold against the grass.
> Past my nose, the scuffed toes of brown shoes.
> Ankles thick as tree stumps.
> The legs of Sister Helene.

"What are you doing?"

> Higher up, her shoulder, head.
> On the garage roof, the satellite dish framing
> her face like a nimbus.

"Jesus, Mary and Joseph!"

> Torn petals on my arms, my legs, my skirt.

She lifts a petal from my neck. Presses it to her lips.
Looks to heaven. Makes the sign of the cross.

> My palms, blood stained—
> like a branding.

23.

I carry my favorite recordings upstairs. Casals, Rostropovitch,
Bylsma, Ma, Du Pré.

Lay the cello on the guestroom bed, the CDs on the pillow next to
its neck.
Pull the shade. Lock the door. I should throw away this key.
Sit in my prayer room.
Weep.

24.

"You might want to talk to someone Barbara."
The Department Chair helped me to my car. We loaded boxes.
I didn't answer. I slammed the trunk.

I find my hammer in the garage.

Enter into his gates with thanksgiving
and into his courts with praise.

Psalms, what do they know?

25.

I knock the first plank off the wall.

This altar I built when I first moved in, before unpacking
pots and pans. On the wall that faces west, the Church.
Smallest room in the house, but centrally located and
hidden like a heart.

I knock the other plank.

These silk cloths I hemmed for each season of the year.
Green for Ordinary Time. Purple for Advent and Lent.
White for Easter. Red for Pentecost. As if time could
be shaped.

I pry out the nails.

"You're a bright woman Barbara, no question."

I parsed my day in three-hour intervals, reciting the Liturgy
of the Hours like a monk. I drenched these walls with
Psalms.

"Barbara, is that you?"

I pry off both support beams. The good loud sound. The hammer's
clean claw end.

Jesus, Mary and Joseph!

Bang the wall for their release.

Rip it apart, verse by verse.
Rubble. Dust.

Plaster on the floor like hosts.

(. . .
Did we not stand
under one *trade wind?*
We are strangers.)

I'll throw no more Psalms upon this air.
Oversized chrysalis, I sit, my folded wings.
Four volumes of the Breviary silenced in their cardboard sleeves.
No seraphim.
No live coal carried to my lips.

This day I've made obscene.
This day that begs for nightfall like a coat.

Outside, a geranium reaches toward the sun.
Past its soft pink bloom, a sparrow hangs on the tree bark,
holding tight.
I didn't see him until he turned his head, exposing
his gray and creamy throat.

> *Once*
> *I heard him,*
> *he was washing the world*

On the littered floor, I sleep.

28.

Morning light comes through the shutters. Outside, against my door, sunflowers wrapped in paper and rough string. Who put them there? And inside the paper, what? Something ticking between the stems?

I watch them for an hour. The flowers do not move.
Make coffee, another hour. Three, four.
The paper wrap fades in the afternoon sun.

Finally, midnight casts blue shadows onto the paper, the stems.
I hold my breath. Open the door. They fall across my feet.

29.

Inside, a note from Josephine.

> Barbara,
>
> You aren't practicing? I miss my nightly serenade!
> Heard you quit work. Is this true? Call me.
>
> Josephine
>
> p.s. Sister Helene says she found you in a trance.
> But then, we know how she exaggerates.

I cut the stems. They're too short. I can't arrange them in the vase.
Butchered. The stupid dripping stems.
I'm a barbarian.

A thickening. Walls closing in.
I throw them in the trash.
My father in a lab coat
It's something in the color. There's danger in the hues.
Apples on the counter.
Yellow in the banana telling me I'll choke.
Chrome in the toaster, that I'll burst in flame.
Pink in the azalea, that the earthquake will come.
My mother presses down my cheek
Color through my rods and cones. I close my eyes.
Red glow through my lids.
I tie a dishtowel around my head.
It doesn't go away.
My father doesn't see
I find the trash bags. Go from room to room.
Throw in small things first. Pillows from the couch,
their mauve, their silver blue.

It slows.
It starts again.
He doesn't see my cut off hair
I grab towels from the bath.
I'm making you pretty for Daddy
Tear the drapes. Their hideous floral print.
The bedspread. Needlepoint footstool.
More trash bags.
Candle   Heat
Prop open the refrigerator door.
Dump all the bottles in, the colored foods.
Leave only clear. Green. White.
Barbara's got a red dress, red dress, red dress
The freezer shelves. I can't stop it.
There's still the curtain over the sink.

I tear the sheet off my bed. A cocoon of white.
This time I'm not going to come out alive.

> *My father doesn't see my hair.*
> *Lying on the picnic table. Napkin on a dinner plate by my*
> *head. Dental tools on the napkin, in a row.*
> *His voice is sing-song.*
> *"We're going to do something important for science."*
> *Stoically, he folds back my red dress.*
> *Hard, my mother's hand pressing down my cheek.*
> *Hard, her other hand gripping my ankle.*

30.

I put a sweater on over the sheet.

The long and empty night.

The second hand, slender, sweeps across
the numbers of the clock.

Soft and steady like a duster.
Covering a girl with soil.

31.

At last, the sky shifts from black to deep teal blue.

It takes seven minutes.

The sun lays its golden arm, courteously, across my sill.

32.

There was a story in the newspaper. I saved it in my box.
A young man was killed in a car accident. His father, after ten years,
entered the garage where his son's car was stored. He removed the
personal items and sold the car. The mother remained in the kitchen.
She could not move. Even after ten years.

I take off my sweater. Unwind the sheet.

The kitchen floor is strewn with garbage bags, stuffed and over-
flowing, as if a burglar came in the night. I drag them to the curb.
All down the street, the houses look the same. Trash bags, cans,
papers set out. So many people sure about the coming of the trash
truck. So many people sure about the coming of the morning after
night.

Three straight, uneventful days!

Maybe this is all I needed. House rinsed of color. Stimulation.
I could write an article on this. Tell others, so simple a solution!
And, if things get worse, I'll just remove the color from my garden.
Imitate Beatrix Ferrand, leaving only the lush and simple white.

I wash my hair. Dress.
Take my car in to be serviced.

I sit on the plastic chair for a full hour.
I am doing it as well as any other customer.

> *"We were normal!" I yelled. "Stop bothering me."*
> *Driving to Daniel's farm we passed a woman burning trash in*
> *a tall can. I made him stop the car. I paced the shoulder of the*
> *road. It was my mother I saw standing there. My mother thirty*
> *years ago. Her wedge-heeled sandals propped against the*
> *incline of the hill.*
>
> *Thin folded-over socks, sun reflecting off the dainty buckles at*
> *the ankle. She poked the incinerator with a stick and stood back*
> *with caution. Flames rose high above the rusty edge. It was the*
> *first time she burned clothing in the can.*

"Might as well get rid of it," she said, because I wouldn't wear
the red dress anymore. She found it hidden in the closet
under Cheryl's coloring books.

I leaned against the swing set pole until the flames died away.
Slid down to the grass thinking, I'm just like the soap girls I
make with bubble bath. I set them on the bathtub rim, but they
always slide back down into the water, totally erased.

35.

I find the broom and sweep the plaster from the prayer room floor.
Celan's words could fix these walls. Scarred and wanting.
Black paint from the garage, a wide brush, the short ladder. I pry
off the lid. I make the letters neat:

brightnesshunger   *perjury-poem*

The brush widens as I press. Paint runs down my arm.

icethorn   *smokemouth*   *almonding*

I paint words on all four walls. Ceiling. Door. The window casing.
Letters on top of letters.

deep in the refused

The words drip down like oil.
They soothe me like a gilding.

I paint until the room is solid black. A shawl. I pull it close. Around my shoulders. Over my mouth. His words, near! near!

Below my ladder, the Seine.
I watch him climb the ledge.

copper glimmer of the begging cup

He jumps.
It holds him in its narrow straits.

A prisoner in her cell writes a plagiarism on the walls. A poet's words instead of her own. He lies with her on her narrow cot. She smells his body, soaked with the Seine.

Three hours until dawn.

At last, the first glint of gold on the balcony's edge. The sun, showing itself. Revealing its decision. Great gift. The sun that remembers when red was just a color. Just a crayon in a box.

I pour a cup of coffee. Unfold the concert program from my evening purse. Yo-Yo Ma played the First Bach Suite, then a new work by David Wilde, "The Cellist of Sarajevo."

Composed to honor the cellist who played at the site of the bombed bakery. Every afternoon at four o'clock, in full concert dress, mortar and machine-gun fire, his folded chair, silk tails falling to the dusty road. A requiem for the dead.

I saved the clipping from that bombing. Years ago, when I still read the papers.

I find it, frayed and yellowed, in my box. Bakery, bombed. The flustered birds.

It was the girl on the left-hand side of the photograph that made me keep it. A teenager, perhaps fourteen, her jutting jaw, the downward crescent of her fastened mouth. Pulling back her hair. Fingering, with her other hand, the coins she'd tied to the corner of her scarf.

I set her picture on the table next to the program of Ma's playing.

I want her to know that in Los Angeles, halfway around the globe, no one stirred in the hall when Ma played Wilde's "Lament in Rondo Form." We were startled in unison. Like strangers, immigrants, carried in a boat. Newly landed in a harbor, I was exhausted. Rags over my knuckles, my wool coat wet with fog.

I want to say, This is how notes travel. Like a key sewn in the lining of a coat.

We emptied our pockets, our small treasures, a locket, a letter, a key. Leaning against gunny sacks on a different shore. Waiting for our new names to be penned in ink.

I bring the photo and the program closer, so their edges touch.

Perhaps,
the young girl went to buy a loaf of bread. A simple errand. After hearing the blast, her mother finds her. Twenty-two others in the bakery, dead. She thinks, My daughter, not even wounded! And weeping, draws her down onto her shoulder. Thick arms, her wrinkled neck.

Already, handkerchiefs on the faces of the dead, a fluttering of white.

But the girl does not see this. She is saving herself. Making herself blind. And it is not the tilting racks, rye breads rolling on the floor, the wedding cake behind shattered glass, not someone else's blood splashed across her checked skirt like paint that made her do it. It is the woman to her left, propped against the wall, who rocks her child, not seeing that the baby has no head.

The girl falls into the texture on her mother's arm. Caught in the sweater's weave, garlic, onion, marjoram. The fragrances of home.

Perhaps,
for three days the young girl doesn't eat. When touch and appetite return, and speech, and sleep, she still does not see. Her father snaps his fingers before her face, talks too loud. On the tenth day, hits the table, calls the priest.

No one asks her if she wants to see.

On the fourteenth day, the girl smells paraffin and beeswax in the night. Her mother whispering prayers. Matches struck, one by one. She counts them. Twenty-two in all.

Candles set on small tables and chairs around her bed.

When the candles burn their way and there are no more in the drawer, her mother does not buy new ones. The girl wakes to find something cold and wet on her eyes. "It's just a compress," her mother says, but the girl smells sour earth, cow dung mixed in. She feels bits of eucalyptus leaf sharp against her lids, the bits of straw. Her mother pats it down. "It's just a compress," she repeats, an urgency in her voice like a tangle, and the young girl thinks, Now even my body does not belong to me.

A young American doctor with instruments in his backpack finds nothing in her eyes. She feels his fingers on her cheekbones and wants to stay in that warmth of skin on skin. She holds his hands there, considering how touch is better this way, without sight interfering. She wonders if he knows this.

She would like to tell him what she preserves in the darkness she's created:

The memory of a hair ribbon her boyfriend returned. Apricot satin against the mat, when she opened the door and he was not there.

The autumn mist shrouding the Mary window of St. Margaret's Church, fringed blue gray like a shawl.

Her father's back, looking out from the balcony, coffee in hand, waiting for an answer from the sun. Copper sunlight on the telephone wires, the train station, the domed roof of the mosque.

Her grandmother's cramped hands, pickling cucumbers lowered into a vinegar bath, one by one. Marking the arrival of summer.

Grains of sugar suspended in the clear flesh of a just-peeled pear. Sweet taste of fall.

Aspen trees in winter.
The gilding of chocolate on cherries in a tin hinged box.

A lipstick kiss she put on the bathroom mirror, the heart she drew around it, the initials of his name.

39.

With thin needle and a fine thread I sit in my now-black room and bind the edges of the frail photograph. Then the pages of the program. I sew the two together like leaves, sheaves, the bakery girl and Ma's playing. It takes the afternoon.

I want to tell her, I haven't experienced the explosion of breads. But I know how a melody, a lament, can be heard inside one's head. Bearing down with its own necessity.

This chain of laments can link us across oceans. Notes lifting up the wreckage.

In the back yard, next to the hedge, I hold the new slim-stitched book. I pray for myself and for the teenage girl.

The simple words of the invitatory Psalm still on my lips, even though I spit them out. Better sung antiphonally, I recite both our parts,

> *Lord, open my lips*
> *And my mouth will proclaim your praise*

"Are you moving?"

It's too early in the morning.

"All those trash bags on the curb?"

Josephine lives next door but like a woman in a lighthouse. From her parapet she watches the night sea fold itself to foil.

"I'm not moving."

"Let me bring you some persimmons, then. I've got a bumper crop."

I wait in my pajamas on the stair. Front door open to the morning light. A crow on the telephone wire drops to the grass. A squirrel, noticing me, freezes on the trunk.

*"What is it you really want Barbara?" Josephine asked when
Daniel moved to England and she invited me over for drinks.*

"I want to be seen."

*"Aren't I seeing you at this very minute?" she smiled. Her
cigarette holder high in the air, ebony with a fine chased silver
tip. She sighed. "Honey, sometimes you're just too brainy
for your own good."*

"There you are!" she waves, her wide-brimmed gardening hat, its
orange bobbing ball fringe. Standing over me, the thin gauze of her
Mexican drawstring blouse, bright embroidered flowers fading at the
neck. The skin on her face is pale and luminous like an abalone shell
lit from behind.

"Here," she hands me bright fruit tied in a tea towel. "They're
high in vitamin C." She scrutinizes my hair.
Will I eat persimmons now? The peculiar way people eat who are
old? Prunes? A refrigerator filled with little jars?
There's too much red in their skin.

From beneath the fruit she lifts a business card and places it in my
palm, folding my fingers around it like a coin entrusted to a child.

"I know you don't go in for these things, but my cardiologist says
he's top drawer." The coolness of her bony hand. "Call him, Barbara. You look like hell."

Her tall straight back as she walks away, old running shoes tipping
in at the ankles. Bangle earrings, large wobbly feet.

Long, the clatter of crows on the wire.

I put the card back under the fruit. Take it out again. A psychologist with enough degrees behind his name. But that is not the crucial thing. It's the card itself.

Formal clean black letters engraved on clear white stock.
Crisp, elegant, even calm, against the rough weave of the towel.

It would be nice to have someone to really talk to. Like a good tailor.

A person skilled in the art of mending and alteration.
He'd have a small shop, a rack holding a hundred spools of thread.
Each spool given a name: Hawk Brown, Tuscany Red, Pansy Yellow, Flemish Blue. Apprenticed in another culture, his craft ancient and time-honored, private and guild-tested.
He'd have his vocabulary for body types, stitches, ways to finish off a seam.
He'd know the difference between lace from Belgium, lace from Spain.

I'd stand on a small platform, his mouth full of pins.
A rainy boulevard past his window at my fingertips.
He'd turn my hem, touch the insides of my legs. Run his hand up and down there, toward a nomenclature, a way of knowing.

He'd teach me a language for all the things that I leave blank.

We'd examine all the moments of my life without shame or titillation. Against a mingling of shop smells, coffee, damask, silk.

There would be plenty of time for marking and sorting. And in the marking and sorting, I'd regain all that I have lost.

This skilled person, this tailor, with his drawer full of labels and his very good, large heart.

45.

How many days since I've had a meal? Josephine is right. I can't live on white vinegar, white pepper, fennel seed. I'll go out, I'll buy some lettuce, potatoes, milk.

High in the empty cupboard, the Morton Salt Girl in her yellow dress. Walking against a midnight blue. Her wide umbrella. White salt rain. Crystals from her salt box flowing out behind.

We moved into the new house.
My mother ordered Morton Salt Girl raincoats for me and
Cheryl. They came with matching hats.
But Cheryl called herself a scientist and wouldn't play.
So Georgie wore her raincoat. Elastic tight under our chins.

"That's a girlie raincoat," my father said.
But I told him, "You'll be okay, Georgie, wear it anyway."
And he did.

The business card. The salt box.

> *We played into the night.*
> *Lying in the gutter filled with rain, pretending to be boats.*
> *Sailing down the steep hill on our stomachs,*
> *pushing our hands off the gray wet curb.*
> *I led the way.*
> *Georgie's face on the soles of my wet shoes.*

I'll take the innocence of Georgie with me. I draw up a grocery list. Go.

Just ahead, at the intersection, a woman standing at the bus stop raises her arm to strike her child. I speed up. But she doesn't strike, she hesitates, holds her arm in the air, fingers taut. The girl jumps up and down, whimpers, rubs her mother's leg.

"Excuse me!" The mother doesn't turn. "Pardon me!" She looks away. "What are you doing?" I yell. The bus approaches, opens its doors. The woman yanks her daughter up the stairs.

> *Georgie stopped wearing his Morton Salt raincoat.*
> *I heard him crying in the night.*
> *In the morning he dragged a chair to the kitchen window.*
> *He cut the head off his teddy bear. Threw out the body then the head.*
> *Tan stuffing drifted in the air.*
> *After that day, he would not leave his room.*

And now this produce section has miniature zucchini? baby beets?
I've been coming here for fifteen years. When did it get so fancy?
And worst of all, these pansy heads. In plastic boxes. Violet, yellow.
Cut at the neck. Their faces looking out.

I tried to hide Georgie when he was new.
Stood on a chair, lifted him from his crib.
I hurried, before her music stopped.
Notes vibrating the floor boards.
I carried him to the clothes chute. Put his legs in first.
His squirming tie-up shoes.
"Good-bye Georgie." I pushed him down.
Arms up against his ears.
I pressed his head.
His flat curls between my fingers and thumb.

I didn't save Georgie.
I start the car.
Nothing coheres. Birds by the lamp post,
their separated wings.
Flower heads in boxes.

I drop the groceries on the floor.
Run up the stairs.
Enter his gates with thanksgiving
Grab the cello by the neck.
Georgie, you'll be okay
Hold it over the handrail.
Wait.
She didn't tie my sash
I let it go.
Stop looking at my hair

Slowly,
like a scarf.
Lord, open my lips
Chandelier swinging.
Explosion of rye bread
Splash of bulbs.
Crash of marble against wood.
Girls shouldn't spread their legs

Cello splayed open on the floor.

48.

I lean against the railing until darkness rubs my skin.

49.

Morning somehow finds its way.

Sunlight through the window touches
the broken things below.

Neck, fine tuners, scroll.
Fingerboard, disconnected strings.

I weep.

50.

I find the card from Josephine.

I make the call.

51.

His voice is calm.
I make myself say the words,

"I threw my cello over the railing.
It was the only good thing left."

52.

A certain empty slice of time.

"Do you think I'm a crazy person?"

"No. I don't think you're a crazy person."

Hanging up, I notice he has an accent from Missouri.

CONFITEOR

"Can we sit without talking?"

> *Black milk of daybreak we drink it at evening*
> *we drink it at midday and morning we drink it at night*

"Yes," he answers without hesitating.

Even in his tone he doesn't ask for an explanation. I don't have to say, I must feel the texture of this air. The exact silence that surrounds you.

We sit the entire hour without speaking.

I watch him and he watches me.

The silence feels good. He seems comfortable with my emptiness. He doesn't need me to make this time meaningful for him.

I feel free to be of no consequence.

2.

At the end, he asks if I want another session. He suggests next week at five o'clock.

"I can't come at dusk," I confess. "To be here, I need the full strength of the sun."

3.

For six Tuesdays we do not talk. We just sit.

It is all I want.

4.

"May I ask you a question?" It is our seventh week and my first time speaking. "It's personal. It's about this room."
"Sure," he smiles.
"May I touch your walls?" He nods.

With two fingers held together I trace a line around the room. My fingertips record a sequence of textures: wood door, plaster wall, clothbound books, glass sliding door that opens to a deck, plaster again over the couch, and last, the cool handle of the door.
I make around myself an invisible closed loop.

Our feet shall stand within thy gates, O Jerusalem

"I'd like to do this every time," I say, "if I'm going to talk here."

And I think see something good, there, in his face.

48

5.

The next session he wears a different shirt and tie. Different slacks
and socks. Only his shoes are the same as last week.

But through my fingertips, the sequence on the walls stays the same.
Despite the seven days.

6.

Each week I trace my loop around the walls.

within thy gates, O Jerusalem

His shirts and socks and ties change. Varied permutations of color,
pattern, texture brought together on his body. Simple elements carefully observed, composed, held.

As if a person might be similarly understood.

7.

He invites me to look at something outside in the pond, just past
the deck.

"It's a fresh water trout," he says. I look through the glass door.
Small fins on the side of its body move rapidly back and
forth, yet the fish remains in the same place, hovering in
shallow water, a bright patch of light. Every few minutes it
turns to face another direction, but the body, fluttering its
small fins, stays over the same spot.

"What's she doing?"

He does not look over at me. Does not make me have too much of him.

A man lives in the house he plays with his vipers

"She's guarding her eggs. Aerating the water. The mother and father take turns."

your goldenes Haar Margareta
your aschenes Haar Shulamith

"I'm sorry," I head for the door. "It's too hard for me to see."

If she would just eat half the eggs it would be easier.
Less beautiful, less pain.

8.

At the beach, I unroll the window to let in more air—

round rock on the corner of his table where the patterns of
opposing grains meet, coffee mug with its photograph of his
two small boys, the older with his arm around the younger,
their neatly parted hair,
crystal vase with seven clean cut antherium,
the pressed cuff of his slacks—

I don't know if it's the careful placement of each object or this warbled air coming across the dashboard, that draws me in from tenderness to something mournful.

The day we met, Daniel was wiring echeveria to a wreath of
succulents on his front door. Silver grays and pewter blues.
Subtle gradations of color. So unlike my garden with its
demanding pinks and whites. So unlike me.

I moved toward him with steady steps. Thin arms under
his flannel shirt. Brown corduroy pants flapping around
his narrow legs.

That morning I'd read in the paper that a man was murdered
in broad daylight, at a gas station. Bystanders were motionless,
too stunned to act. The killer drove away
in the slain man's car.

Daniel asked me to hand him wire cutters from his tool box
and I thought, Today there is murder and
there is the careful wiring of echeveria.

9.

St. Francis greets me at my front door. Giotto's St. Francis Preaching to the Birds, a gift from my first students.

His rough brown robe, the smooth curve of his back deeply bowed
to his meek audience. Two ducks, a royal rooster, doves and black-
birds with red bills. His arm outstretched ardently toward them, finger raised, begging their attention. Determined that they, even they,
not lose a thing.

within thy gates, O Jerusalem

10.

This time after I trace the room, he wonders if he can ask a few questions, which is fine with me.

"Have you ever been in therapy before?"
"No."

"Do you have any concerns about it?"

It's not hard to look him in the eye.

"I don't want to fall in love with you. I don't want any more losses."

11.

The fountain on the pond generously offers its silvered plumes.

"Is there some reason you didn't fill out my questionnaire?"

> *A man lives in the house he plays with his vipers . . .*
> *he grabs for the rod in his belt he swings it*

"I left it blank except my name."
"Yes."

> Closed in that waiting room. No windows. And on the
> radio a violinist ruining Dvorak's "American" Quartet.

"All your questions are loaded."

Are you on medication? Have you been in therapy before?
Have you ever been hospitalized for mental illness?
Parents? Siblings?

"None of that matters. We looked perfect from the outside."

Black milk of daybreak
we drink and we drink

"What you need on your clipboard is a question about memories.
How they cut open a life."

"I notice that you've stared at the scissors on my desk most of the
hour."

Exactly. Two blades joined at the hinge.
The way a life could be.

The next session, ducks gather on the pond. In jagged patterns,
male and female, they work themselves into pairs. A male mallard
forces a female under water and holds her there. Like a drowning.

"What is he doing!"
"They're mating."

His tone is matter of fact. Like a person used to viewing violent ways.

"Would you like to go out on the deck?"
"No!"
What I mean is, If I'm going to be this close to nature with you, I need the protection of the glass.

Pine needles scratch the backs of my legs.
Pine needles mounded to make a bed.
An isolated campsite.
Georgie and my mother on a hike to see the Falls.

My father tells Cheryl to guard the road.
Pine needles scratch my neck, the backs of my ears.
My father presses down all his weight.

Finally he stands.
He zips up his pants.

Branches behind him make a fagoting of green
and I tell myself,
It doesn't matter. I'm not even here.

The female mallard comes to the surface, shakes her feathers, and darts off on her own.

I am sixteen. My father opens my bedroom door.
The hallway light hits the sag of his skin at the jaw line,
the part of his body that never touches me.

My head is weighted with fever. Blankets piled high on my bed.
I shake. My face wet. My dripping hair.

I lift myself off the pillow before he takes another step.
I yell that he stop. Right there. At the threshold.

It is the first and only time I yell at my father. Then I laugh.
I mock him for the smallness of his frame.
He says nothing. He doesn't move.
Then he backs into the hall and closes the door.
He never again enters my room.

14.

"Last week you mentioned memories," he offers.
This session moves in slow refrain.
He doesn't see that I'm asleep.

He waits.

So I begin:

"When I was sixteen my father started making lamps."

It was the sixth "new" house. Pink recessed lighting,
a double flagstone fireplace, curved drive, parkway
where neighbors walked their horses under eucalyptus
trees and fog.

What I should say is, He started making lamps right after I
stopped him.

A man lives in the house he plays with his vipers

"He made dozens of them."

> *Working late into the night, alone in the garage.*
> *My mother regulated their placement and population.*
> *Like a breeder who, reaching into a cage, destroys*
> *unwanted eggs.*

"Each lamp was functional but at the same time superfluous."

> The way a mustard plant in summer combines rape seed oil
> with leaves destined as fodder.

"At first he made lamps from figurines."

> *An Indian head, an Egyptian god, a pyramid.*

"Then they got uglier and more crude."

> *Redwood branches from camping trips, scraps of manzanita.*

"The lamps had less and less to do with illumination. In the end,
they were all the same."

> *Wall models with a single redwood branch projecting up*
> *and outward to a bare bulb at the tip.*

"He made about ten this way, then stopped."

15.

"Do you have any idea why he started?" he asks, innocently.

He doesn't know my family.

"My brother Georgie got two lamps because he was never home."

"My older sister Cheryl got three."

> He doesn't know me. That if necessary
> I would have installed locks on my bedroom door.

"No lamps ever came into my room."

> *he grabs for the rod in his belt he swings it*

The sun maintains its post but the fountain hits the water's surface, fracturing the leaves.

16.

This time the ocean moves away. I roll up the window tight.
Two businessmen walking on the pier fall behind a film of gray.
What was I thinking? I saw the fountain break those leaves.
we drink and we drink
That plane overhead won't reach Hong Kong.
It'll pierce the sky, leaving flower-bursts of blood.
Good-bye Georgie
Those pier pilings only look strong. They'll collapse any second,
killing the surfers and all the fish.

breeder destroying eggs
His ducks have probably drowned by now.
play death more sweetly
Cheryl made to guard the road
I drive through the traffic light. Slam the front door behind.

"Is this an emergency?" the woman asks on the phone.
"I don't know!" I scream back at her.

I trace the perimeter of the house. Bushes. Ferns.
Crawl space vent.
It's all leaking out.
Death is a master

I wrap in a blanket.
Sit on the living room floor.
Press my back against the wall.
It's sliding away.

17.

"I shouldn't have talked about the horses!" I cry into the phone.

"I shouldn't have talked at all. I ruined the office."

"You didn't ruin the office."

    His voice is like a rowboat settled flat.

"Is your round rock still where the two grains meet?"
"Yes."
"And the ducks?"
"They're fine."
"And you? Are you still in the same blue shirt?"
"I'm still in the same blue shirt."

Still, I say it,
"I need to come and see."

18.

"I'm glad you made it."

"You're wearing the same shoes."
"Yes."
"Even though I talked about my father."
      Rock. Mug. Scissors. Fountain. Pond. Ducks.

"Yes" he says,
      as if it were a simple thing.

19.

    Death is a master

I collapse in the car.

Josephine and I finished canning her summer peaches.
I rested my head on her tabletop. Rows of jars with gem-colored
fruit. The garbage pail filled with thready pits.

Inside thy gates, O Jerusalem

The announcer on the radio says the piano that belonged to
Vladimir Horowitz, Steinway number 306925, is making its USA
tour. Months in advance, people have signed up to play for twenty
minutes on the instrument alone, undisturbed. In Chicago, a taxi
driver bought a suit and a set of dentures just for his time with the
concert grand.

The taxi driver, the mother trout, the silence in the room.
These are the things that matter now.

20.

"I put something in your mailbox," Josephine is coy on the phone.

A Catholic convert like me, Josephine supports local
churches, the synagogue, by buying large blocks of tickets
to their raffles, car washes, concerts, bazaars. She says it's
her way of being ecumenical. Inside one of last year's Rosh
Hashanah cards, in my mailbox, two tickets for
Mendelssohn's "Elijah" at the Methodist Church.

"You should get out Barbara . . . dress up . . . take a friend." She
pauses. "There must be someone . . . ."

The programming doesn't make sense. "Elijah" should
be sung in Holy Week, not now, in the Fall. Elijah mounts
his chariot to heaven without dying first. It's music for
Spring, for the lengthening of days. Spring, with its milks
and mosses.

"It's not much notice," Josephine adds, "but I figured you not
working . . . ."

It would be foolish. Like setting a plum on a railroad track,
expecting it to stay whole.

"Thanks Josephine, for thinking of me again."

I was thirteen when I first heard the "Elijah."
Eighty voices and fifty-two musicians in a football stadium
downtown, at sunrise. Their sound broke the pre-dawn air.
My Shoe Make-Up dyed high heels and a purse dyed pink
to match, my first pair of pantyhose. And best of all,
no parents.

The sound moved up the bleachers to where I sat. As if
to correct something deep inside. A ragged coastline.
Some ripped apart thing I felt but could not name.

The splintered bench snagged my stockings but I didn't care.
Elijah was coming toward me
like color out of black.

I oil the hedge clippers, I'll find my answer in the leaves.

> *"Here, Cheryl, you take soprano." My mother handed us sheet music. "Barbara, take alto this time. Hurry! Meet me here when it's over."*.

> *Swagged in evergreen, three balconies of the Music Center filled quickly with strangers humming, finding their seats. Shoulder to shoulder. A thousand voices maybe more. The "Messiah Sing" at Christmas. We made a crystal-breaking sound. Holly on the chandeliers.*

Two mourning doves dart out from the hedge. What would St. Francis tell them? I have no words for birds, no promises, no certainties in my brown wool.

I could say, Sometimes I think flying is possible. And they would laugh their birdy laugh, so obvious who among us is the unbeliever.

Yet, I have learned to be useful. I tend this hedge, this arboretum, making sure there are branches and leaves enough for nesting.

And in this way, I salute the true believers, saying, I see your brocades and your crosiers. You, the bishops of the air.

22.

Shadows lengthen on the lawn.

The choir will be volunteers, the musicians mediocre. It will not be wonderful. I can listen and not be moved.

I wash and put my tools away, inside, find my good black dress.

How else will Mendelssohn get here, to a city not his own? to a different time? Unless music stands are fanned out on a stage and singers assembled, unless someone comes to hear?

How else will Mendelssohn come from Germany, with his notes tinged by coal, ashes and the sparrow's gait?

I set out my silk purse, shoes, my spray cologne.
I sleep well.

It must be the rise and fall of the tides.
Invisible pull of the moon.

The moon, so rich in mercy.

23.

The Methodist Church sits on the corner of two quiet streets.
A modified Spanish architecture from which all adornment has been washed away, a lampshade dipped into a water bath, spiders and dust, unwanted things left behind.

The consistent moderation makes me nervous. I roll up the windows. Sink lower in my seat. What if I'm seen? What if I forget my name?

> *"How do they do it?" I asked Daniel because I'd read that*
> *migrating butterflies often fly 500 miles in a single day.*
> *He touched the small of my back, saying,*
> *"They move toward the heat."*

I lock the car and walk inside.

24.

I'm early, the first person here. Velvet cushions listless on empty pews.

There are no niches. No side altars. No darkness.
I feel overexposed.

I need to fall into the tangible. The lush dichondra of all that is secondary—a black fringed shawl, the soft tip of a sable brush, a palette knife scraping pigment against wood.

This emptiness feels miserly. As if to say,
There's nothing holy here, Barbara, unless it's you.

25.

In stained glass, a dove and an empty cross. I miss St. Margaret with her breath, her wheel. St. Barbara with her tower.

Blood and imperfection.
Leprosy beside the gilded frame.

26.

An open Bible is displayed. No relics, no bones, no hair, no
tongue.
Nothing linking me to deserts in Syria, the catacombs in Rome.

I need a real altar.
A place where violence is performed
and regularly observed.
A place where violence has a chance
to become something else.

The timpanist tunes outside on the walk. This was a mistake.
Even the candles here are supervised.

How will this sanctuary hold Elijah and his chariot of fire?

27.

The conductor raises his baton. A soprano steps forward, but hides
behind her score. She hasn't bothered to learn her part, and sings as
if nothing matters. As if Mendelssohn couldn't see violet and weep.

I escape to a better place.

My grandmother's bed. Pale green afternoon light.
The mattress high above her smooth waxed floor. Slender
polished mahogany posts, pineapple finials, their dark
and dustless grooves.

At last the woman sits down.
Silence spreads itself over an ordered field.
Straight and even rows of neatly baled, still-green hay.

The tenor begins. From the first note his voice surprises me. Rich
and compact, he lifts the lament like flight! Airborne! Then brings
the stream of notes back down, carefully fitting them like a rug
curved over the bones of a small animal. Turning, quickening all the
skins of my body, opening their fibrous pores, their threads, spreading woof and weave. I want to dance across the pews! Apricots roll
from a tabletop, spilling, pink fleshed, their surrendered seed.
This air thrust into the skins that clothe my body like saffron silk,
saffron silken editor, keeper of bees, finding all that is worth saving.
O Jerusalem!

This familiar, holy turn.
Great rotation of the silver wheel.

28.

My prayer room, its warm black touch.

Journals I no longer read, piled high: *Cistercian Studies, Journal of
the American Academy of Religion, Theology Today.* Only art and
architecture magazines make sense now. The things that I can see. In

one photograph, a man's dresser: colognes gathered on a silver tray, small pyramid of leather boxes, bronze lamp with a matte black shade.

The soprano and the tenor side by side in the same concert.
My father's lamps and the round rock.
The bakery girl, a baby's blown-off head.

How does it all belong?

A photo of Joseph Beuys' "Vitrine I." The vitrine holds five objects: two brass cymbals standing on end, an iron head, a seashell, a Siberian lynx coat.

It shows exactly why I cannot teach. I can't say, "The lynx explains the cymbals, the iron head explains the shell." Only, "The objects in the box are real. They'll resolve themselves or fail to. That is the work now."

How does it all belong?

My grandmother making her own bar soap the same day men walked on the moon.
A wide aluminum tub set outside on two kitchen chairs under the tree. Her tiny Canadian hands holding the long-handled wooden spoon.
Carefully. Carefully. Stirring in the lye.

"I went to a concert Sunday," I say, excited, after tracing my loop around the walls.

Bright light through the fountain, a crystal chandelier.

"How did you feel about it?"
Does he think he has to lead me into such a self-examination?

"I'm insulted by your question."

He re-crosses his legs.
"Duly noted."

The fountain sheltering a pair of ducks.

"I didn't fall apart," I finally say. "Most of it was awful. Except the tenor."

"And if you had fallen apart?"

at midday and morning we drink it

"If I had loved it too much?"

"Yes. If you had loved it too much."

How do I begin? In this room
where there is just his decency and my raw edges.

"Next time I'll bring in something for you to see."

30.

Six hours until my session. I climb the stairs. Put in the guest-room key.

Why press hard against a tender thing?

I lift the shattered cello from the bed. Silk tied around its broken neck. Tuning keys. Coiled strings. I bundle the broken pieces in a sheet. My hands are shaking. My palms. I tie it with ribbon.

Time is unwilling. Three hours, still.
I've destroyed something innocent.

I lay it down on the back seat of the car, fasten the belt.

31.

People return to the parking lot, crossing the bridge over the pond. They've seen the dentist, the accountant, the tutoring office for children who cannot read. They carry purses, bags, briefcases. No one carries a corpse wrapped in a shroud.

I find a payphone and leave a message on his machine. "Can you meet me on the bridge? I can't be seen with what I've brought."
Fourteen minutes until my session. Ten. Three. Finally he comes to the bridge.

Quickly! Quickly!
From a burning building a fireman carries the child.

32.

Sheeted body across my lap.

your aschenes Haar Shulamith

"I notice you're not looking at me, Barbara."

33.

"This used to be my cello."

"I'd like to see it."

"It's not an instrument anymore. It's parts."

"I'd like to see the parts. Whenever you feel ready."

I untie one black ribbon, the next. The wrinkled cloth on the floor, spread out like a sail. I lay the pieces in a row across the sheet.

"I lifted it over the railing."

O Jerusalem!

"Then I let it go."

34.

—"Barbara?"

The hour is over.

One by one, I fold the pieces back into the cloth. Making the corners neat, like a color guard. Thick, the quiet in the room. Only the hushed sound of cloth laid onto cloth.

He reaches out his hand. He helps me up from the floor.

> *Walking next door to Inez' house. Holding my mother's hand.*
> *Steep, the cement stairway through the ivy bank up to the street.*

"Thank you for showing me your cello."
"It's not a cello," I repeat.
And I am not Inez.

Inez gave me pop beads. Pink, yellow, powder blue. She snapped them together around my neck. Her hands were gentle against my chest.

We stand by the door.

within thy gates, O Jerusalem

"I broke my cello."
"I know."

"I broke the thing I love most."
"I see that."

A tear from behind my sunglasses falls onto my cheek.

"You can see that?"
"I can see that," he says. "Absolutely."

35.

Sometimes to be seen is the same as being saved.

36

"Barbara cut her hair for kindergarten," my mother told Inez, brightly. "Just like her sister Cheryl!" She lined the sailor boy salt and pepper shakers straight on Inez' table, then looked away, out the window, down the hill.

Inez lifted me to her kitchen stool. Pulled a plastic cape from the drawer. Pale pink with a print of black poodles and Eiffel towers. She twirled it in the air, then lay it on my shoulders. Her cool hands on the back of my neck, fastening the stiff ties.

She stood close, her fingers moving through my hair. Her nails were long and frosted pink. I wanted to put my face against her angora sweater, touch the polka dot scarf knotted at her neck.

She worked through my stubbled hair, lingering, resting her palm on my head, turning it slowly, left to right, as if this helped her think. No one had ever touched my hair like that before.

"How about a Pixie?" she asked, bringing me out of my haze. I didn't know, until then, that haircuts had names. Light, the clicking sound of her gold-heeled sandals on the linoleum. Slowly cutting a few hairs at a time. Here, there. Here, there. Close to my face, the skin of her forearms smelling like sweet peas.

"There we are!" she smiled, holding up a hand mirror, lifting my chin, for me to see. "Aren't you a pretty girl?" she sasked, and I thought, All she's looking at is me.

PEREGRINATIO

Josephine calls, asking me to join her on a trip to the Santa Barbara Mission. "They're having a healing service. Trying to get Junipero Serra canonized." My stomach hurts. "They need miracles."

> The Church requires three documented proofs of Serra's intercession. Not ten miracles. Not five. Three. Like counting beads. One of the absurd things I like best about being Catholic. I hear her light a cigarette. The click of the lighter. The cough.

"Do you pray to Serra?" she asks, waiting for my reply.
"No. But I have a photo of his bedroom on my bulletin board."

> A rope-strung bed, blanket, small table, a candle, crucifix on the wall. Intrinsically satisfying, the way a life could be.

"Maybe he could be canonized for the aesthetics of his room," I say. She laughs.
"Will you come?" her voice softens. "It's important to me, Barbara."

> *You're an intelligent woman, no question.*
> Monsignor Kilmartin with his rattling chains. Chastity belts clamped over every orifice. Ears, eyes, mind, heart. Saving himself for himself. Afraid to be broken. Afraid of me.

"I'll go for the drive. But I'm not getting anywhere near the Church."
"Suit yourself, then." Her voice plucky once again.

2.

The walls of my prayer room are cool against my cheek. Dark seed at the center of the house. I stretch out my arms. Press my whole body against words cast into the boughs.

> *We hung our harps upon the willows in the midst thereof.*
> *For they that carried us away captive required of us*
> *a song . . . saying, sing us one of the songs of Zion.*

I drove to the Santa Barbara Mission once, alone.

> *By the rivers of Babylon, there we sat down, yea we wept*

I heard singing from a distance,

> *voice-thread*

I left the Mission and followed the sound to a quiet street, succulent with stillness like ripened fruit. A heavy cup of gold vine lay across a grape stake fence and further down, a lattice portico where wisteria could have been. I heard,

> *"God, come to my assistance.*
> *Lord, make haste to help me"*

The sign read, Monastery of Poor Clares.

> *Up the bread-step.* Through the *door-crack.*

The chapel was delicate as spun sugar.

> *breathcrystal* buried deep.

I found them behind the grille.

Their unbarred voices

Their from-silence chant.

> *Easterword*
> Rising.
> *Songfast*
> Free

3.

"My neighbor, Josephine, has asked me to go to Santa Barbara," I announce after tracing the walls. My neck stiff. My cold arms.

"Your saint's city," he smiles.

Two mallards snap at each other on the deck.
"Barbara's not a name I chose."

> Patron saint of safety during thunderstorms and fire.
> Betrayed by her father into martyrdom.
> I rip off a thread dangling from the couch's seam.

"It's for a healing service. The last one I went to was hideous. The priest was signing people up to go to Lourdes."

> Smelling salts, rosaries, feeble liquids. As if God prefers a swoon.

Slim capped tins of borax. Ointments in jars with purple
crystal lids.
Clogged lungs. Fog caught in angora. Lap blankets. Zeal.
Crutches piled on the shore like matchsticks.

"It was everything I hate."

As if I should make some trans-Atlantic crossing. Sit on
a rattan deck chair. Wrap my crippled legs in a mohair
throw. As if another time, another place, is more powerful
than my own.
As if I need something more holy than the sun.

"I hate that kind of healing. Even if it works."

I walk across the room to him, my voice raised.
He has to understand exactly what I mean.

"I only want healing I can understand."
He pauses.
"Of course."

"I don't want you to save me. That's really what I mean."
He smiles. Why?

"Good," he says, an eagerness in his voice.

"So why are you going, then?" he wants to know.
"To be close to the Poor Clares, I guess. They're nearby."
He gives a questioning look.

"They're a contemplative order, cloistered. I like the hidden
orders best."

"They don't give retreats, teach, that kind of thing?"
"No."

Blood in soil. Yeast in flour.

"They just pray."

Aaron's rod takes root, bearing ripe almonds

"I visited them. Twice."

He waits.

A fishing net is thrown wide over the sea, saltwater moves through the knots and string, salt touching the pain.

I tell him the story of my second visit:

I drove to Santa Barbara when everything was new. My house, my teaching job. I parked outside the Monastery of Poor Clares. The singing of Daytime Prayer had ended. I closed the windows to hold in their sound. The empty plane of afternoon shaped with an in and out, singing and silence, breath in a body.

In the rearview mirror I saw a man in baggy trousers approach the Monastery on foot. He carried a bag brimming with lemons. He opened the gate, climbed the stairs and disappeared into the building attached to the chapel, his face downcast, creased, as if pulled into the future against his will, as if pulled by a leash fastened to his brow. His body looked soft and crumpled like his trousers and I thought, He would collapse into one of his pants' pockets if he could. His suffering as tangible as an attic exposed to day.

I got out of the car and followed him in.

The foyer was small. He leaned against the metal turn—a tall enclosed lazy Susan by which things can be passed back and forth, while the Extern, on the other side, remains unseen. The man spoke to her in whispers, cradling the brown bag to his chest.

"My daughter's still missing. It's three days now," he said.

The Extern must have known him even before he spoke, hearing the pace of his footsteps, the way he closed the foyer door. Perhaps waiting for him to speak she ran her finger along the edge of a holy card taken from her neat stack, carefully considering what she would say to him, what word. The card with its picture of the Holy Family, gray lettering and a prayer printed on the back. Perhaps as she did this, she smelled lemons through the metal turn.

"Do you know today's Gospel, the Prodigal Son?" she asked him with great kindness. I felt like an intruder. "The father saw his son returning when he was still far off," she said, "because he never stopped watching for him."
Compassion. Like music. The only sound, then, was the father weeping.
"Of course we will pray for your daughter," she said. "We haven't stopped."

He set the bag of lemons in the turn, spun it, and watched them disappear, then waited, as if he had done this before. Perhaps yesterday. Perhaps the day before that. From the other side, a holy card. He stared down at it, then put it in his pocket.

Through the narrow window I watched him pause on the outer steps, looking at the garden. Tears on his cheek. The agapanthus border in sapphire bloom.

All of his losses at one time. His daughter, the lemons, the simple yellow of the fruit he'd clung to like a conviction.

4.

A eucalyptus tree, roots anchored beneath the building, reaches a single branch out over the water like one great arm.

"Did you speak to the Extern yourself that day?"

> Bare feet, rough clothing. Praying every three hours of the day and night.
> Their lives like empty urns.
> Unafraid of every flying bird. Strong enough to receive every satchel, every shamed detail, every pornographic filament. Empty enough to wrap a stranger's sorrow in brown wool.

"I brought dahlias from my garden. An armful. Pink with soft yellow throats. I begged her to pray for Cheryl and Georgie."

> *Dayhard   Nightlong*

"Because I couldn't help them anymore."

These are old tears.
I cry until I'm through.

5.

"Barbara, we have to end now," he says. "We've run out of time."

"I have to ask you a favor."

The fountain, what will it think? But if not now, when?

"May I leave my cello here, with you, when I go to Santa Barbara? In case I don't come back?"

A mother buys a coffin for her child.
She selects the pretty one.

"That's fine. But why wouldn't you come back?"

He has no idea how my world works.

6.

Bob has left three bags of soil on my front porch, a receipt, and fertilizer for my acid-loving plants. "You'll need this. Bob." I fold his note and put it in my bra.

I slam the shovel blade against the bag of soil. It fails to cut. My gardening jeans so loose they fall onto my hips. Where's all my weight? I cut the bags with a knife.

Fold the living soil into the garden's natural sand. Sand sieve. It all seeps through.

7

"I should have buried it," I say, after tracing my loop, the broken cello on his couch.

> *I buried my pop beads in Inez' yard, reaching under the fence, digging with my spoon.*

"What did you say?"
"I should have buried my cello."

A piece of bark hangs loose from the eucalyptus tree.

"Cellos are pretty nice above the ground."
"Nothing above the ground is safe."
"It will be safe here Barbara. You'll see."

> *We hung our harps upon the willows*

I'm not ready to let it go. This hour moves too fast.
"Are you looking for something special?" he asks. I step back from the glass. Marks from my hands and forehead on the sliding door.
"I was looking for the mother trout."

8.

I wait for Josephine to call, saying she's ready to go.

Above my door Christ hangs on his iron cross. Some say, "This is the One who takes away the sins of the world." But I say, It's not a special thing to carry in one's body the sins of the world. Georgie threw his teddy bear out the window, cutting off its head.

To have scars, holes in one's palms. This is not salvation.

9.

"Hop in, Honey," she waves, backing out her 1964 Thunderbird. I slam the heavy door, and we glide onto the street.

Lush aqua interior, soft broad white leather seats. Door handles, window trim, knobs on the dash, all in heavy chrome. Majestic weight, I love this car. Slow, wasteful, regal. A vehicle, a Sabbath.

"I feel like I'm going to the Prom."

"You always say that, Dearie," she smiles.

Josephine has buried five husbands, the last, a man ten years her junior. She is wearing driving moccasins of ivory suede. Her hands loose on the steering wheel, its glamorous, wide-flung shape. A dozen pairs of evening gloves scattered across the dashboard like roses.

We cross the city and the first set of hills. Drop into the valley. Farmland, lettuce, citrus orchards, grapes. It feels good to move through open space, where everything that approaches can be seen for miles. Even my arms are warm. Sunlight through tinted glass.

"Why don't you pull out that lunch for me, Barbara?"

She's packed small sandwiches of white bread and apricot preserves. I fold back the wax paper, it creases like shattered ice.

"Is that all you brought?" she glances at my jicama sticks, celery and white cheese. Eating, she does not slow down. Eighty miles per hour and the Thunderbird without seat belts. I watch the road.

"You've gotten thin as a rail, Barbara. It's not your look, you know. You can be a regular Gibson Girl. I've told you that." She reaches for her cigarettes. "This way, you're no better than a Twiggy." She struggles to fit the tip into the holder's pearl handle. "That doctor of yours," she inhales deeply, "doesn't look to me like he's doing you much good. That's all I'm saying."

I want to be alone.
"Is he smart enough for you?"
"He's smart enough Josephine." These aren't the things that matter now. "And he has a clean heart."

10.

A tractor kicks up dust in the distance. Daniel's farm, not far from here.

Touch, voice, tongue, kiss, arm, thigh, breath—right here, in this scent of lemons on the hill, the artichoke's thistled bloom.

He promised to protect me from the tree- and barn-loving snake when he boasted that he had three skins, three earlier sheddings, coiled on the mantle made of river stones, and I said, "No. I will never sleep there!"

"Snakes are symbols of regeneration, you know that," he hollered back at me from the porch when I stayed frozen and determined in the truck.

"I don't give a damn! Just kill it or I'm going home!" He carried a shovel, yelling curses at the snake, in jest, forbidding it to appear during my stay.

"The house too!" I yelled, wanting him to go, room by room, banging pots and pans, but he refused, saying he'd already done enough.

During dinner, which was spaghetti and hearty and good, I jumped with every sound the house made as it cooled and creaked, until I finished the bottle of merlot single-handed and only then tried to follow, with more complete attention, his theory about the exact date of the manuscript the museum had just purchased for a quarter million dollars. A great coup, being five hundred years old and in superb condition.

The soap suds in the kitchen sink were gentle on the backs of my hands when he made patterns there like finger painting. Cold air on the mud porch when we brought in kindling and logs, his tall black rubber boots on a rack, and three different sets of flannel liners.

"You'll love this book," he said against the firelight. Thin gold leaf pressed onto the morning glory vine running up the margin, but instead of considering medieval manuscripts I watched the firelight play on his collection of toy metal trucks that skirted the hearth.

"I'll make us oatmeal in the morning," he offered and I thought, I'll never get through this night. But the bed was high like my grandmother's, four maple posters with finials and a spread of quilts, boxes crowded underneath the bed, falling open with papers, journals, notes. The lamp he made at camp as a child, its parchment shade laced together with leather string. And I felt comfortable there with him.

The wallpaper in the corner above the bed was darker than the walls, and I thought, Not enough life goes in and out of this house. Holding the headboard I wiped it clean with my lace camisole while he was in the bath, and tucked it in my suitcase, filthy, wrapped inside my socks.

Steam escaped when he opened the narrow bathroom door, and I spread my hair across the pillow like rays of the sun, to say, Come here. Come quickly. Come touch my hair.

But it was the stroking of my neck, my back and down my spine he did instead, drops of water, and then my hipbone when he turned me to face him again, the towel at his waist. The quiet night. The bold blank window without drape or shade. Long flat branch of the apple tree and past it, the line of daytime hills made silver by the moon.

When we stared at the ceiling, after, with its pattern of cracks, he said, again, "Come to England," and I got up and pinned my hair.

"I care too much about my students," I said, back turned, but what I meant was, I can't be with you. I can't look at all you want me to see. But if I could graft my heaviness onto you, my hip, my breast, the weight of my dark hair, my head too large for women's hats, if I could graft my heaviness onto you, then you wouldn't leave me like the wind.

In the morning we ate oatmeal coarsely ground, lumps of brown sugar from a tin, coffee beans from the freezer next to a plastic bags of herbs. I sat next to him, our elbows touching, hip, thigh, that patch of skin, hairless, a blank stretch at his side.

We loaded the boxes in the truck from closets, dressers, from under the bed. Disintegrating bindings, notebooks, another magnifying lens, a lamp. Returned them to his office in the bowels of the museum, where manuscripts are handled with cotton gloves, and the rooms kept cool enough and dark enough to extend the life of animal ink, gold leaf and vellum.

"You're awful quiet," Josephine yells, leaning across the seat. She doesn't believe in air conditioning. The valley is hot, the windows opened wide, the loud rush of air. At the far end of the field, migrant workers line up beside a truck.

"I'd like to work a few weeks in these fields," I holler back to her.
To be a pair of hands. Develop stronger arms, a sore lower back. Inhale the toxins. Learn to use a bathroom without toilet paper or walls.

"There'd be lessons. I'd change in some irreversible way."
She fumbles, puts out her cigarette, tightens the scarf over her ears.
"You romanticize everything Barbara," she calls back, shaking her head.

I2.

The Mission parking lot is full of chartered busses.
"You remember, I'm not coming in . . . ."
"My memory's sharp as a tack!"
She slams into the curb.

She rests her head against the seat.
"Are you all right?"
"Just a little tired," she sits up, sprays heavily with perfume, freshens her lipstick, blots it, wipes her brows. She checks herself in the fold-down visor mirror with its light, then the rearview mirror on the dash. A pocket mirror in a velvet pouch is lifted from her purse, holding it outside the window she sees her reflection in the light of

the sun. Last, she pulls a large mirror from under the seat, battery operated bulbs light up on either side.

"You look wonderful Josephine."

I have seen her perform this ritual many times. Still, it pulls me gently toward sleep. So certain her reflection will be there in each mirror, every time she looks.

"Good luck."

"You'll be okay out here?" she wants to know.

"I'll be fine."

She crosses the parking lot, looking anxiously left and right. Pausing on the stairs, she smoothes her dress down over her breasts, repositions her belt, walks in.

13.

Warm, here, inside the car.
Nearby, the Poor Clares.
A copse of notes behind their vellum walls.

We hung our harps

They reach into the willows.

Mercy-tall

They pluck the strings.

He shouts play death more sweetly

Their purity hurts.

he shouts scrape your strings darker you'll rise to the sky

My cello, bound in its sheet.

    My father built thin shelves in our bedroom closet for her music.
    She never put it there.
    She lifted the window.
    Turned the cardboard boxes upside down.
    Sheet music flew into the air, opening its wings.

14.

Ushers close the Church doors, my arms, my legs, my waist.
Memories stitched to my body by slender black knotted threads.
They sail across my body, a regatta of small boats.

    The closet shelves were too thin for toys.
    I hid inside. Safe from my mother in daylight, my father at dusk.
    Licked dinosaur decals and pressed them to the empty shelves.

If I go inside those walls my sutures will not hold.
My skin crosshatched
with tender scars like yearlings.
Priest's cope, Easter light, embroidered on my skin.
Cloves of pungent incense pressed into my palms.
I am that Easter candle.
The smell of melted wax rises from my cheek.

Walls laid out like a cross.
I am that building of mortar and saturated stones.

15.

Half past the hour. The missionary priest will be launching his sermon soon. Between the pews, an expectant, bristling air. Josephine craning her neck, listening for someone's crutches to fall.

I stretch and walk part of the Mission grounds. It doesn't matter if I go inside the walls. The Mass lodges inside me. A cuddy boat stuck in mud.

Thick-arched hallways, rooms cordoned off, a glass case, vestments burdened with pearl. Visitors click cameras, voices hushed, busy respecting the past.

smokemouth to smokemouth

As if the Church were an invalid, memories clutched inside her purse.
As if she has no living water. No living bread.

16.

Communion. I can hear the shuffling feet. Nagging voices say, "This is Jesus, the Crucified. Be careful! Use two hands! Don't chew! Don't hide it in your pocket. Don't drop it on the floor."

As if the Crucified couldn't land on linoleum
and live.

17

The Mission's modest cemetery, down the hill.
Simple markers in the ground. Roses tended, pruned.

Here, the Mission feels alive. Bare canes will bring
a commotion of color against their strong leathered leaves.

I sit on the crusty soil. Wear my feathered mask.
This last place of color. Opening. Gate. Mouth fringed
with blood-specked fern.

I smell the breath of animals that pass. Insect guides,
their sure-psalmed wings.

Property blessed, this dirt. Countless openings
where life seeps through.

The whole mantle of earth perforated
with pinholes of grace. Portals of wheat.
Dots of blond-wafered light.

Up the incline, a young woman exits through the Church's side
door. She stands on the portico, looking at the sky.

Her appearance frightens me. Her elbows, even from this distance,
point the sleeves of her white blouse. Her skirt drapes loosely from
her sharp protruding hips. Her face, skeletal. Cheek bones below
sunken glassy holes.

Why does she stare at the sky?
Why does she want to disappear?

your aschenes Haar Shulamith
you'll rise then as smoke to the sky

I move closer to see her, hold fast the cemetery gate. Does her body still menstruate? Has she grown that downy hair under her blouse? that animal protection?

I want to say, I see you! I see you standing there, your arms, your legs, your neck and hair. Come home with me. Sit in my garden, see yourself in the leaves. They are fragile, small. But they know the breeze that moves them.

19.

Mass has ended, the thin woman goes inside, front doors flung wide open.

Other women gather on the steps, talking to the priest. They untie their sorrows one by one, draping their stories across his shoulders like so many scarves.

Their husbands are already in the cars. They see the palpitation. One man looks back to the Church steps and frowns. Perhaps he is thinking, This missionary will be gone soon enough. Then my wife will come back.

Everyone more celibate than they want to be.

One woman strokes the priest's arm lightly once, then pulls it away. Perhaps she thinks, Under the satin, his skin is smooth like soapstone. He bends toward her touch that marks the inside slats of his body, the empty barrel.

Perhaps tomorrow, in another Rectory that is also not his home, out the window over the kitchen sink, a bird will land on an oleander bush, swaying its clustered ivory blooms, and he will touch his arm in that same spot, remembering her and think, An approximation, this touch I can allow, an approximation, but precious like an amulet.

Church, you old woman.
Your drab, wrinkled skin, your
forgetfulness. I smell
the sea litter caught in your salmoned hair.

But sometimes I also see in you
what compassion can assemble.

An open tray with pomegranate and the fish's silver side.
All that can be forgiven.
Brute and the endangered caught in your ragged veil.

Josephine walks slowly toward the car, her mouth drawn down in anger.

"What's wrong?"

"He's a No-Show." She slams the door.

"Who's a No-Show?"

"Remember this?"

She slaps an issue of *Harvard Magazine* onto the seat. In the back pages under "Crimson Classifieds," an ad is circled in ink.

"You don't remember helping me with this?" She fumbles for cigarettes. "Let's get out of here." I offer to drive.

"I had a gentleman. He sounded so good. Sharp. Made his money in oil."

"He was going to meet you here?"

"Don't look at me like that. At my age, love's a miracle. Trust me!"

She dabs perspiration from her forehead, the back of her neck. Her ruby lips are quivering.

"It's his loss, Josephine. He must be a moron." She reaches over and I hug her. Her hair smells of White Shoulders perfume. Tears in the loose folds of her lids.

She falls immediately to sleep. The sun leaves the branches of the trees. Dusk hour. When everything blurs. And good dissipates, piece by piece.

She looks small. Her head against the window, compact, like a dried fruit. She is not wearing gloves. Stones from her rings fall into her dangling palms.

She is fading away. And I can't stop her.

Glad to be on the highway, I pick up speed. That oil man, why
didn't he come?
Why don't people do what they say?
It will be safe here, Barbara, you'll see
The road is empty. Not even trucks.
My cello is not where it belongs.
God come to my assistance
What if he threw it in the pond?
Lord make haste to help me
And that woman on the stairs, floating up to the sky.
That father with his lemons and his daughter? What about her?
Nothing above the ground is safe
He doesn't understand me. Neither does Josephine.
It's too hard.
Cellos are pretty nice above the ground
The hills are behind us at last.
But what if his cleaning person took my cello home?
She found my red dress under Cheryl's coloring books
She burnt it in the can
What if the ducks needed the ribbons for nesting and he put it on
the deck for them to pick and choose?
What if a client asked too many questions?
I can't keep things together.
I need to see my cello. I need to see it now.

"You drove like a bat out of hell!" Josephine wakes with a start. I've hit one of the towers of newspapers stacked in her garage. Papers fall onto the hood. She looks at her watch.

"You didn't even play your classical station either, thank God!" She seems fully refreshed.

"Come inside awhile, Barbara. Let's toast Mr. No-Show."

"I've got to get home, Josephine."

She rubs her eyes.

"Willy-nilly," she shrugs.

"Thanks for today," I say, handing her the keys.

24

I can't catch hold. Even the moon.

My cello's not on the guestroom bed. I can't touch it. I can't breathe.

"Everything's fine," he says, returning my call.

"The cello?"

"The cello's fine. Just the way you left it."

"The ribbons?"

"They're just the same."

"And the ducks?"

"They're fine."

"I can't do this!"

"Can you tell me what's wrong Barbara?"

"I saw a woman at the Mission. She's going to disappear. And Georgie, it didn't work putting him in the clothes chute. And Josephine is going to die."

"What's happening right now? Where are you?"

"I'm sitting on top of the twirl-around slide."
"Okay."

"My mother is far away, past all the grass, leaning against the new car. It's a Studebaker. It's turquoise and shaped like a rocket. She's in her suit with the kick pleat in back. And her brown high heels. She took Cheryl and Georgie on the plane. But she couldn't take me. That's why I got the Junior Stewardess pin."

I am crying.
"Is there anything else?"

"She had her glasses on and everything. But she didn't see."
"What didn't your mother see?"

"I was almost five."
"When you were almost five and sitting on top of the twirl-around slide, what didn't your mother see?"

"She didn't see that I was keeping her alive!"

"And how were you keeping her alive?"
"By not telling what happened when she was gone!"

A trap door slides back over a hole.
I can't remember the rest.

LACERATIO

I

He sips his coffee, looking at me over the rim of his mug.

Who will bring me into the strong city?

The cello next to his chair.
Each time I look at a thing it feels like my last.

"You didn't put the ribbons on the deck for the ducks to pick and
choose . . . ?"
"No. I didn't do that."

"You didn't throw it in the pond . . . ?"
"I didn't throw it in the pond."

"The cleaning person didn't take it home . . . ?"
"It stayed here the whole time."

I lay the cello on the floor. Unwrap the long white sheet.
Turning. Turning each piece.
Broken neck. Open mouth. Tuning pegs. Coiled strings.

"Daniel didn't mind wearing gloves to handle manuscripts. He
didn't mind the dim lighting or the coolness of the room."
"You've mentioned that before. How careful he was handling
texts."

> *The fifteenth-century Book of Hours. Purple vinca along the
> gold leaf grid.*
> *St. Michael with his peacock-feathered wings.*

"You didn't mind keeping my cello safe for me."
"That's right. I didn't mind."

The rod of Aaron takes root, bearing ripe almonds

2.

"Can we open the sliding door?"

The stillness of ordinary things.
Duck, fountain, his matching socks.
Without the tinted glass, the sun is brighter than I thought.
We sit next to each other on the rug, just inside the metal frame.
The cello in between.
A man in hip boots fixes the fountain.
Ducks swim about.
Nothing special happens.
It is just right.

There is a river whose streams make glad the city of Zion

3.

"On the phone you mentioned a very thin woman."

I crouched among the roses' bare canes.
Ferns specked with blood.
The entourage passed me by.
Moth and beetle in gold wing.

"She frightened me."

The *shadow-break* of her hand upon the rail.
unvoiced
deep in the refused

"She reminded me of all the times I want to disappear."

My Grandmother's oyster white breadbox, the rounded
roll-back lid.
I pulled it over me like a roof. Warm and humid.
Perforations in the metal. Enough holes for breath.

"You said you were keeping your mother alive. You were four.
Sitting on the twirl-around slide."
"I don't know what happened when she was gone."
The man in hip boots wades away.
"If you need to remember, you will."

4.

Mail is piled high on the kitchen floor. Christmas cards and bills. A
greeting from Father Paul. He jokes, again, about my turning all the
portraits in the Seminary foyer backwards to face the wall. "Yes," I
had confided. Sixteen Cardinals, three Popes. "There was just too
much red."

A birth announcement for Sister Helene's niece. They've named her
Heloise. She's the youngest member of our parish now. Next week
she'll be Jesus in the crèche.

A card from neighbors down the street says they missed my Christmas party. What should I say? "Come, let me show you what dental tools can do"?

Fudge wrapped in foil from Sister Dolores Mary.
A pink variegated poinsettia from Josephine.

Christmas colors side by side. Green, a comfort. Red, an affliction.

> *"I love it, Daniel." He gave me a red sheath of merino wool.*
> *Deeply cut at the breast. Straight as an arrow.*
> *"But does it come in another color? Maybe black? Kelly green?"*
> *"You never wear red, Barbara. Besides, it's a Christmas party.*
> *You'll look great!"*
>
> *He was right. I looked good in it. But my arms trembled and*
> *my stomach ached. I drank three old-fashioneds just to put it*
> *on. After the party I threw it in the trash.*
> *"The dry cleaners ruined it," I lied.*

Carolers approach, even to my darkened house. I recognize the voices, a few kids from the youth group. "O Holy Night" they sing, then laughing, go on to Josephine's.

They'll run across my lawn, stuff soda cans in my hedge. A lucky carelessness. The way life ought to be.

5.

In the drugstore, a woman looks at Christmas cards, a stroller by her side. It's not a baby in the stroller, it's a child, six, seven, maybe eight years old. She's covered him completely with a blanket. All I can see are his boots. They dangle to the floor. Even his head is covered. Even his face. And I can't see him breathe. I watch the pattern on the blanket but it doesn't move.

They shed innocent blood, even the blood of their sons and daughters

His body is too still.

My arms freezing, even in this coat. I pretend to look at birthday cards. But then she leaves the store. I follow. What if I pull the blanket off? She could be kidnapping him, right here. He's so quiet. She could have drugged him first. No one stops her. No one cares.

Mothers can get away with anything.

My teeth chattering. I hold my jaw. I can't find them! They've completely disappeared.

I have his card. One in each purse. Each jacket, each coat.

But I haven't told him that when I see a school bus I'm sure it will explode.

Each time I come home, that I'm sure someone will be dead across my floor.

That first quick breath each time I open the front door.

"Yes, it's an emergency! Yes, have him paged."

That mother's fooling everyone. Dead in his cowboy boots.

I can't do this. I can't be here anymore.

The payphone finally rings.

"Barbara?"

"There's a baby. No, not a baby. A boy in a stroller. And he's covered up and I don't think he's breathing. And his mother just took him away. I didn't stop her. Nobody in the whole store did anything to stop her!"

"Do you think the boy is in danger?"
"I don't know! That's the trouble. Maybe I'm just like Inez. Maybe I missed the clues!"

My body won't stop shaking. Nose dripping. Tears all over my face.
"What clues? What did Inez miss?"
Nothing stays together.

"Barbara, tell me what Inez didn't see."

"She didn't see the cuts."

Voice shatters the cedars of Lebanon

"My mother said, 'You can't wear shorts to Inez' house.' But all I had was shorts and my red dress. She took new long pants out of a bag. Jeans. They were stiff on my legs."
A man walks by the phone. I turn my back. Face the wall.

"Inez didn't see the cuts on your legs, under your new long pants?" he asks.

Breaking the cedars
Breaking the cedars of Lebanon

"Inez never saw anything."

I cannot stop.

"I want you to try something. I want you to imagine what should have happened that day. What would have happened if Inez saw everything."

It is hard to imagine something good.
"You can make it any way you want. You can put anyone in the scene. A policeman, yourself as a grown-up, me."

"Inez would have called the police."

"And what would the police have done?"
"The police would have stopped my father and my mother."
"Good," he says. Time starts to slow.

"Inez would have told the police that she should be my mother instead."
"That's good. Anything else?"
A hammock settles after being stirred by a great wind.
"They would have let me live with Inez forever."
There is a silence in the phone.

On the sidewalk, a small black bird with a yellow beak comes close to my shoe.
He is not afraid of me. He comes closer still.

"Sometime I'll tell you everything," I say.
"I'd like that."

Soft blanket on my skin.

"I have one more thing."

"Okay. Then I have to go. I have a client waiting."

"Will you believe me?"

Time should be long. But he answers right away.

"I'll believe you Barbara."

6.

At home I throw the mail away. Lock all the doors. Go back to bed.

> *We wept when we remembered Zion*
> *We hung our harps among the willows*

I'll sleep until the season's through.

The cards. The birth. The fudge.

> *Who will lead me into the strong city?*

> *I'll believe you Barbara*

I'm not with any of these.

> Somewhere in the corridor, the soft folds of time between childhood and birth, there must have been a moment when I cried out freely. Cried out, without at the same time thinking, Now there will be an exchange of skin.

7

The neighborhood women gave a baby shower for Inez. She said I could come. Five women sitting around her kitchen table, smoking cigarettes. My mother staring at the door. I'd never seen her with other women before. Corn chips, olives, a dish of butterscotch candies. Next to the candy dish, a twig tree mounted in a Styrofoam base. In the branches of the tree, tiny naked plastic babies and rolled dollar bills tied with ribbon, pink and pale blue.

When it was over, Inez untied a plastic baby and gave it to me.

trees of Lebanon
full of sap
stork abiding in the fir

8

I pass the phone booth where yesterday all that's here and now, fled, left my fingertips, slid to the right. Today, nothing moves. Pavement, walkway, grass.

Back into the drugstore, the aisle with tablets, pencils, fine-tipped pens. Wide sketchbooks, pages blank. I fold back the cover. A bright rectangle of white.

In the office, inside my loop, I could draw my way instead of using words.

9.

I set the opened tablet on the dining room table. This is how I'll spend Christmas. The house, empty. No tree, no wreath, no harp. I watch the tablet as I vacuum, mop the floors.

Digging out of prison with a silver spoon.

Morning, midday, dusk. The four corners of the tablet stay rigid, uncompromised. They maintain, perfectly, the full ninety degrees of their joined sides.

10.

For two days and nights the white rectangle on my glass table doesn't change.

11.

I open the box of crayons. Spread them on the white, the good colors—pinks, yellows, greens.

There are seven different colors for red: Mulberry, Maroon, Red Violet, Fuchsia, Brick Red, Magenta, Violet Red.

I keep them closed tightly in the box.

I know how they would bleed across the white.

12.

In the waiting room the walls are too close. I can't make a pleasing face. My features won't compose. People read magazines.

Did they see me eye the vent? Do they know how hard it is to resist going there? Through the vent and gone. Between the metal louvers. Dust would coat my back.

I pace out in the hall, go to the bridge. It doesn't help. When will he come?

This stupid tablet, this box of crayons. I'm not staying here forever. Like a goddamn fool.

"Barbara?" I jump. Crayons almost lost over the rail.

13.

I trace the walls, tie myself in.
"I have to tell you something. I have to draw."
I sit on the floor. Take out a red.

He sits at the edge of the chair, his shoes close to my hand.
I draw a girl. Flip to another page. Switch the crayon to my left hand.
Now I'm free. I don't care how it looks. I'm drawing like a child.
Stick figures come out fast. Legs. Hair. Eyes.
Faster, faster. I slam the cover, hand him the tablet.

"Here." He opens to my drawing. I watch his eyes.

> I am that drop of rain that hangs, quivering,
> before it falls off a line.

"You have to ask me questions. It's the only way I can do this."
Outside, the pond is already moving away.
He's too slow.
"Just start!"
"Is this you in your red dress?"
"Of course it's me! I'm four."
"And these two larger figures, are they your mother and your dad?"
"My father's in the lab coat." I rock against the rug because it is the only unmoving thing.
"And the yellow on the floor?"
"That's my hair."
I scrape. Carpet against my thigh. Faster. The good burn.
"My mother peeled me like a potato."
"And the gray things that look like sticks?"
"They're dental tools. To make designs in clay."
He takes too long.
"Hurry up!"
"Did your dad cut your hair too?"
"No!" I scream. "He liked girls to have long hair. I already told you that!"
Rub my face against the rug. I can't get low enough. Can't get it to hurt enough.
To hurt more than what's going to come.
"My father did science on me with dental tools. He put them in the candle one by one. He said they had to be clean. He said we were doing something important for science."

"And your mom?" Harder, harder against the rug.
"She pressed my cheek against the wood. She held my leg so it
wouldn't move."

Cool sizzling burn. Again. Again. I rub. It takes me in.

"Barbara." A hand on my head. "You need to stop that now.
You're going to hurt yourself."
Everything inside my body is red and hot and hurts.

"Can you open your eyes?" This is a voice I know.

Toe of a shoe. Kleenex box, a soft white plume.
"Can you look at me?" Cuff of a pressed pant leg. A knee.

Tablet on a lap. His fingers on the red.
"Can you look up to my face?"

    The severed ear listens

Past the tablet, a chin. One blue eye on either side of a nose.
Fence posts. Line in between. I hang there.
Wet and heavy laundry, sheets barely held by pins.

    Who will bring me into the strong city?

14.

Christmas Eve, Monsignor Kilmartin and the other priests are vesting in gold and red.

I'm in a different red. I'm four years old. Everything inside my body hurts.
I'm doing something important for science. And I have no hair.

It's midnight. The Church proclaims its "Glorias." Says, "Don't fast now. Feast! And if you pray, do it standing up. In the joyful position!"

> *How can we sing in a strange land?*
> *Our harps among the willows*

I'm with that other congregation, the diaspora outside the walls.
Past the shadow of the dome. We hide under our coverlets.
Matelassé making its mark against my cheek.
Nothing else feels proximate. Just this fabric on my skin.

> *Put up your knees, hold still!*

My father holds the first tool in the flame. My mother presses my cheek.

> Memory plays round and round.
> Ma's performance and the bakery girl.

> Of course Wilde composed his lament in rondo form.
> The way pain bears down, over and again.

15.

Past midnight now. Everyone is going home.
The night is long. I do not sleep.

Outside, shade from the moon covers the azaleas, moss on the
walk.

> *The Lord swept the sea with a strong east wind*
> *Egyptians followed in pursuit. The water covered Pharaoh's*
> *chariots and his charioteers. Not a single one escaped.*

I would let Cheryl and Georgie cross unharmed, dry shod.
Myself cross safely too. Enter kindergarten like every other child.
Long hair, ivory legs, my favorite dress.

Then I'd let my blood flow out
over my father and my mother. Bloodied water.

> I am that Sea.
> Opened. I am that Sea
> of blood and drowning.

16.

"Do you remember that woman who was very thin?" I ask.
Rows of Christmas cards, some presents, lined next to his desk.
"Yes. The woman at the Mission who reminded you of the times
you want to disappear."

Sitting on the rug again, I bring the tablet down from the couch.

"There was the corner above me," I begin. "The napkin folded on the plate. A candle by my waist. A line of white light where the two walls joined."

Put up your knees   Hold still!

"I went into that line of white. I tried hard to think of good things. Birds, milk, grass, sky, my swing set, my new dancing doll. But then everything I thought about turned blue."

My mother pressing down my cheek

"There were eight dental tools. I was not awake for all of them."

I look up.

"Was that the first time you tried to disappear?"

starbright   northtrue

"The first I remember."
This session when time does not move.

17.

Crayon in my left hand, I draw a girl standing upright in a red dress. With a blue crayon, I make a line across her body.

Dividing it in half at the waist.
Upper and lower.

cleftrose

"Did you ever feel like this?" I ask.
"No. But I know people who have."

"It's a girl cut in half at the waist."
"I see that."

brightword   Witness.

"When I woke up, I felt my stubbled hair, then my legs. Inside each thigh, going up from the knee, was a red line, like thread. I touched one leg and the line widened out, because it wasn't thread but blood, and I thought, These aren't my legs. These legs belong to some other girl. Too much hurts. It can't all belong to me."

the severed ear listens

"My mother was in the kitchen. She called out, 'Clean up that dirty hair.' So I lowered myself onto the picnic bench, slowly, then the floor. Everything hurt. I put on my socks. Then my shoes. But I couldn't buckle them. I couldn't get the patent leather flap to go through the buckle. I couldn't make hands that were mine touch feet that belonged to that other girl."

Tears fall onto the tablet, puckering the white.

"It was an idea that didn't work. I couldn't make that girl. All I could make was a line through my waist that no one sees but me."

By the rivers of Babylon we sat down, Yea, we wept

18

Already, today Marie is putting her Christmas, Hanukkah and New Year's cards into plastic bags to store until next year. Unlike other shopkeepers, she never has a sale. I like the way the value of her items always stays the same.

"How was your Christmas?" she asks, but what she also means is, Why didn't I print invitations for you this year? Not for Christmas? Not for New Year's Eve?

"I've been too busy to entertain," I say, and, generously, she accepts this. She opens cartons with items for February, May, June. Stuffed bears dressed as bride and groom, a guest book of hand-pressed paper bound in white silk, a wreath of dried hydrangea, freesia, daffodil.

Who will bring me into the strong city?

I choose Scent of Spring room spray and a box of honeysuckle soaps.

19.

Marie's items wrapped in tissue paper and tied with satin string. I carry them with me, I climb the stairs, the attic is full and organized.
Boxes hold Christmas wreaths, the summer hammock, bamboo tiki lights. At the far side, under the eaves, the brown box I am look-ing for. Worn and poorly sealed. Inside, items from high school, dried

corsages, diploma, my cheerleading pin. At the bottom, my first art book. A tart smell rises from the leaves. Dust gathered in the crimson knots of binding thread along the spine.

> The photograph is exactly where I left it.
> My whole body shakes.
> I hold it to the light. Me and Cheryl sitting on Inez' lawn.
> Our legs spread wide.
> I'm wearing my red dress. My curly white blond hair.
> I slam it shut. Too hard to see.

> *They shed innocent blood, even the blood of their sons*
> *and daughters*

I re-open the book, take out the photo, retrace my steps, close the attic door.

20.

This time, after tracing my loop, I take the chair that is closer to him than the couch. I went to show him something small. He stares at the envelope on my knees.

"Do you think the best thing about a girl is her hair? It's a real question. My father always said, 'The best thing about a girl is her hair.'"

"No. I don't think that." My stomach hurts. I hand him the envelope.

"Shall I open this?" I nod.

"It's me with Cheryl. Before science and the haircut. In my red dress. With my blond hair. You can touch it if you want to."

He takes out the photograph. Holds it carefully, at the edge.
He doesn't speak.
The lines in his face drop lower from a weight.
I shouldn't have brought it in.

"The good thing is I met Inez."
He looks at me.
"Are you trying to cheer me up?"
"You're sad. I can see it. It's the picture."
"You don't have to take care of me, Barbara." His voice is calm, like always. "It's not your job."

He studies the picture for a very long time.

"This is you before you made your split at the waist, then, isn't it?"

all, all-visible

"That's me before I broke."

I empty another box of Kleenex. Throw it in the trash.

"Now do you think I'm a crazy person?" I gather myself up. Dark glasses, the check.

"No. I think you're brave." He hugs me briefly at the door.
The smell of starch caught in the fibers of his shirt.

21.

Something is very wrong. I drive faster.

It felt right at the time. The smell of linen, the starch in his shirt.

But it is not okay. I pull off the freeway.

Dial the phone. The gas station attendant seeing me stops sweeping, leans against his broom.

a man lives in the house he plays with his vipers

"This is Barbara," I leave a message. "I won't be coming back."

I drive faster, over the speed limit by at least thirty miles.

22.

It's impossible to trim this stupid hedge. I rake the clippings off the lawn.

The phone rings, and rings again. I play back the message. A second time, a third.

The timbre of his voice has changed, a half-step higher than usual.

I take off my gardening gloves, stiff with dirt. Throw them on the floor.

So what if he hopes we can talk about this?

He says I can page him. Not to hesitate. I pace.

Put away the ladder, the clippers. Sweep the drive.

When the sun has fully set, I return his call.

23.

"I don't want you to hug me when sessions please you! That's not what this is about for me."

I yank leaves from my shoe.

"I don't have to be some crazy person sitting on the floor drawing like a baby then getting some reward, a hug like a goddamn seal thrown a stupid fish!"

I feel his concentration.

"On the first session, I asked what we should do, and you said, 'Some clients hug, others shake hands.'"

"And we shook hands," he says.

"Right. So why did you hug me today?"

"With some clients I end sessions that way. But we have to be clear on what we're doing. I screwed up. I'm sorry. I'm glad you called me on it."

"You're glad?"

"Of course!" he laughs. "I dropped the ball. You hugged me when you came back from Santa Barbara. As soon as you saw your cello."

I don't believe this.

But he was standing by his desk. It was the blue shirt. I did hug him. I hugged him as soon as I saw it there, next to the plant.

"I forgot I did that."

"We should have talked about it at the time. That was my fault."

"I don't want to hurt everything I care about."

"You're not hurting a thing. You're being protective. This very is important."

With long needles, the fishermen repair their nets.

"I only want touch I understand."
"Absolutely. Me too."

In the pond, when the moss has moved away,
the carp are plainly visible.

*I sat on my Grandmother's horsehair upholstered couch. She
served cocoa in hot chocolate cups, violets hand-painted on the
rim. Then she propped her narrow bare feet on the ottoman,
facing the t.v. She buffed her toenails. The long silver buffer, its
tight spring holding the chamois in place.
She gently shook bright pink powder from a tiny can, and
spread it across the chamois with the backside of her nail.
None fell onto her black Japanese pajamas.
She watched her show and I watched her.
"Isn't he marvelous, Barbara?" her voice almost trembling at his
good looks, the lawyer who rescued his client each week, without
fail. I liked that he was good.
She smiled, "He wins every time!"*

24.

The moon falls between the branches of the pine.

Barbara's got a red dress, red dress, red dress

What was it like to be a child, to have lived through that night
when all things were divided? The firstborn, even the cattle, dead.

There was a great cry in Egypt,
for there was not a house where one was not dead

Perhaps,
a young girl, wakened by wailing heard through the walls, tries to decipher a pattern. Outside, death everywhere—but not exactly random. Screams only from the clean houses, the ones without the blood.

She dresses quickly, running to the house of her best friend. The next morning her father and six brothers find her, arms fastened around a tree, in her hand, the friend's bird cage, emptied of stiffened wing.

At dusk, in the weeks that follow, perhaps she feels a nervous agitation. At night, she does not sleep. Wandering under the moon, she learns the different night sounds, the moaning of wind across the desert, the spider who lunges forward on the sand. She knows the calls of the nocturnal birds.

Days and nights become weeks.
She eats figs pressed between flat bread, warm goat milk from a pouch, handfuls of olives, tasting them for salt, licking the oil dripping from her wrist. With her tongue she feels how thick her skin has become, not like the others. Hair on her camel's back, its blue moonlight a bristled comb.

Weeks blur into months.
Another brother is born. Still, she doesn't sleep. Apricots melt on her tongue. Her skin pales to blue. They call her, The lost one, The short girl, The one who fails to thrive. No one expects her to marry when she comes of age.

A full year passes.

Her mother takes dates from a lidded basket, her father sharpens the slaughtering knife. She doesn't understand how blood coming from an animal can seal a thing. She refuses to hold the basin, to dip the hyssop. She refuses to stain the door.

She runs into the desert, latch of the empty birdcage still banging at her thigh. She wants to say, Deliverance comes to no one this way.

Perhaps,
it's not until her first child is born that she understands why she doesn't sleep.

The rod of Aaron takes root, bearing ripe almonds

The fear of sleep because she doesn't want to wake. Her body remembering what the mind has left behind. Thirty years to remember that night when she was eight. Cries through the walls. The lament of her neighbors, the barking dogs. The thud of cattle falling to their sides.

Thirty years to remember that she left the house and ran. The rolled back eyes of a dead horse. And on the stair, blood like pomegranate juice from the lips of her best friend.

25

This old wicker chair, blue moonlight in the weave. Pleasing, how it slowly tatters from the sun and nighttime dew, naturally crumbling into the grass and soil.

I open Dolores Mary's fudge. In my pocket, a note from Josephine:

> You missed my New Year's Eve party!
> Father Dennis wanted to meet you.
> Why didn't you come? I wore my Bill Blass.
> Lots of compliments! Happy New Year!
>   Love, Josephine

Who will bring me into the strong city?

Wrapped in a blanket, I hold my presents and fall asleep.

LAMENTATIO

I

This early February morning, the sky is gray and close at hand.
The narrow leaves on the pepper tree shake as if under tufted silk,
holding a tent up with the curve of their backs.

All the garden is covered with incipience like dew, and I am going
to the art museum to see the victory of St. Michael over evil. His
message perches like a three-winged seraph on the edges of my
world, where things slide back and forth without warning.

Like a pilgrim, I carry my empty vial.

Before I leave, the fog turns to rain. I take off my high heels,
nylons, my suit. I can't resist. The bricks are wet under my feet.
I sweep pine needles from the court, skim leaves from the pool,
hose off my shovels and rakes. They drip dry under the trees.

I let the rain cover me, like always, since childhood.
It comes down onto my bare skin saying,
"Stop, Barbara. Feel this. Feel how touch can be."

Drops accumulate and slide off the wet cedar shingles, but the
eaves underneath stay dry. Wet and dry, the same wood, proximate,
contradictory. With experience like this, I wonder how we achieved
the idea of monotheism.

Left to my own devices, I'd envision little jealous gods, mandarins
in charge of petty spheres of power, ruling their private microclimates.
Small gods who'd dry themselves off under my eaves, brushing down
their coats. One in wing-tip shoes, the other a Chinese gardening hat.
They'd gossip and pickpocket. They'd cause flukes to happen.

"Barbara!" Josephine waves, adjusting the buckle of her transparent rain boots, holding a plastic grocery bag over her hair. Seeing me, she does not say, "Why are you soaking yourself in the rain?" She's seen me plenty.

"Can you help?"

She's joined the Altar Society and they need old clothing to cut to squares for patchwork quilts. "It's for the parish bazaar," she beams.

"When did you join the Altar Society?"

"Fiddlesticks. I'm late." She dashes off, hurrying to her meeting.

My affection trails after her like a scarf.

3.

The museum is empty and the guard has no one to supervise but me. I should ask, Do you know the same dark alcove where the world's evil is subdued?

I make my way. St. Michael on his pedestal in the narrow windowless room.

Lit from above, a dim spotlight warms the mahogany walls. He's carved in linden wood, gold and carmine paint chipped from five centuries of touching.

He startles me again with his simplicity, his small dimension, no larger than a cat. Yet, in spite of this, he fills the room, emptying it of all that is superficial, even thought.

I imagine him in his original home, perhaps a rural church in Germany, cool and dark inside, a quiet weekday afternoon. The heat and smell of melting wax, the humble light of votive candles casting their crescents at his feet.

I walk around him, stunned, again, by what is left behind. I know the iconography, the white rearing stallion, spear plunged in, the blood. None of that is here. No spear, no sword. Even the audience is gone. The princess who should be watching from her balcony, the proud king holding the keys. Here there are no witnesses. Not even herbs, not even twigs.

Just the dragon, surrendered, underfoot. The archangel, not a warrior but a child. Armed with nothing but his innocence, as if to say, This is enough. In this alone, evil can be overcome.

Like always, I'm uncertain. Again, I ask, Until I believe you, may I rest beside your leathered shoe?

4.

I sit on the floor. The guard watches from the hall. I re-read Daniel's postcard, sent in an envelope, grateful that he remembers how I hate strangers reading my mail.

The photo shows a mass of rhododendron beneath a shingled dovecote.

Wymans Garden, Sussex.

B—

Taking Emily to gardens on my days off. Wymans was
our first. She sat with her headphones on the whole
time. Wouldn't get out of the car. What the hell—the
forsythia
were great. You never write.

D.

The gallery lights blink closing. Outside, the sky is dark.

Of course Emily is angry. To lose a father, then to have him back again. Of course she'll punish him.

In my glove compartment, stationery, stamps, a good pen. I write,

> Dear Daniel,
>
> I just visited St. Michael.
> Your Van Gogh is still behind glass—damn vandals!
> I miss you. Miss your hair—smelling of anise.
> I'll write more, soon, I promise.
>
> > Love, Barbara

I don't mail this one, either.

At home, I seal it in a paper bag and throw it in the trash.

5.

The office is the same, but inside my loop there is a change.

My stomach hurts.

"Your hair is shorter."

"Yes," he answers.

"What does it mean, that your hair's shorter?"

"That I'm getting ready for a trip, I guess," he smiles. "Don't worry. We won't miss any sessions."

> Taking everything away? All I've told him carried in that pocket, in his cuff? All I've stored behind the knot of his silk tie? Dental tools between the laces of his shoe? Doesn't he know his shirt carries my memories plaited in its weave?

"I've got a presentation in Santa Clara over the weekend," he says, "that's all."

> Fragments of my body left in another city? My arms? My separated legs? The memory of my red dress left in some hotel room by the sink? Inez left beside an ice bucket? Georgie in the ashtray? Cheryl forgotten by the phone? Santa Clara means a plane trip. He could crash. All my parts scattered, five hundred miles away. Or worse, up in the air. I might as well be dead.

"You should have said something." I don't sit down. "And your plant's almost dead."

"The plant will be fine, Barbara. I'm coming back."
I head for the door.
"How can you be sure?"

"Can we talk about this?"
"I don't need to talk about this." I hand him the check. "You think I go around telling everyone I'm split at the waist? Don't you know I've sewn my things right there, onto your skin?"

doom and counter-doom

I slam the door.

I know how innocence goes.

I button my coat higher in the wind. Walk quickly to the car. From my pocket, my glove falls in a pool of rain. It turns from raspberry to black.

He was a mistake. I shouldn't have trusted anybody. I unroll a long stream of trash bags across the bedroom floor. Empty my closet, my dresser drawers, throw all my clothes onto the bed.

There must have been a time when I was all one thing.
Black time. Before science and the haircut. A beginning.
Black time. Before black broke into color.

I cram every piece of colored clothing into the plastic bags. Coral dinner jacket, sweaters, camel, light blue, brown. Gardening jeans, green silk pumps, faux alligator slings.

A time when it felt good to wear my red dress. My hair blond and curly. I saw it in the photograph. On Inez' lawn.
I don't need him.
I pull down purses from the top shelf. Eighteen pairs of shoes.
I can get to black time myself.
Already things are calming down.
These empty closets, these empty drawers.

I haul the bags to the front porch. My breathing slows. I rest. All the color gone. The moon shadow from the shingles on the roof. A fishing net dried stiff on rocks.

Slowly, I arrange black items in my closet, dresses, blouses, skirts. Equal space between the hangers. Tissue paper between the sweaters in the drawers. My arms and legs soften, my body fills with air. Muscles, tendons, nerves. My skin lays itself out, wide, across my bones.

"The gals will love me!" Josephine exclaims, energetic in the morning hour. We wedge the bags of clothes between the newspapers stacked in her garage. The Thunderbird surrounded like a boat crowded in a slip.

"Honey, not your Natori!" she pulls my silk robe from a bag. I should have tied it tighter.

"Sweetie, it'd be a crime to cut this into squares. What were you thinking?"

"Don't worry about it Josephine." I twist the bag ends to a knot.

"You're a kookie one," she smiles, and, suddenly exhausted, goes into her house.

8.

Florentine paper, pretty envelope lined in gold.

Dear Daniel,

I'm finally working with someone. But now he's gone. Josephine says you wouldn't recognize me. There are ducks on his pond, and fish. Please send me the photo of Emily you promised. I keep all your cards. Thank you for the gardens. I need beauty now more than ever! These pansies are for you. Touch them—touch my flower pressing hand.

Love,
Barbara

I tear it up.

Dear Daniel

There is no one. I'm sorry.

Barbara

9.

I make lunch, my white foods, Morton Salt Girl, crystals falling from her box.

the roof over us dismantled

This is not peace.
This is not black time. I am that salt she leaves behind.
Barren house. It doesn't help.

I became a proverb to them

The one who knows me is never coming back.

I drive to the beach.

St. John on Patmos, cut off from his peers, in the middle of the Aegean, an island he didn't ask for, didn't choose. Visions rising from his body like my memories. Uninvited, grotesque. War, candlesticks, seven seals. Blood. Fire, devastation.

The pier lights come on. The empty sand, no swimmers, no kids rollerblading on the strand. No dolphin. No birds. Just the sea.

Mother of mercy.
Your blue-black salt.
Take my troubles.
Thigh of ash.
Hide them in your salted seam.

10.

It's dark. I find the flashlight under the seat. From the glove compartment, paper, pen.

I'll write down everything that frightens me. Throw the pages out, over the water like bread. Then I'll be done with this. They'll hit the surface and sink down. I'll imitate the virtues of a fisherman. Faithful how they cast out their nets, hoping to catch what they cannot see.

I lock the car doors.
An hour passes. Two. Three.

The moon claims her place high above the fog.
Behind me, up the hill passes over the Church's center aisle,
Christ's body made of stone.
Wide arms. Body stretched around the planet like a second skin.
My pen does not touch the blank sheet.
Another hour.

Finally the words come. Pages and more pages fill. I can't write fast enough.

doom and counterdoom

I've tapped a poison-stream.

red, hamsters with calico fur, magic shows, plaid, hard suitcases with leather trim, slow movement coupled with anger, gray background on fabric, meat thermometers, ventriloquists and their "dummies," pine needles, Brahms' music heard in a small space, frozen turkeys, turkey basters, the smell of silver polish, total darkness, showers (unless they're public), slapstick comedy, campsites, mountain roads traveled by car in daytime, adult size hairbrushes, flexi-straws, pastel striped tennis shoes, the smell of sage, gooseneck lamps, dental tools laid out on a tray, firecrackers (not public firework displays), my reflection in mirrors or plate glass windows, derivatives of red that go toward yellow rather than toward blue, all camping equipment, animals in cages that are too small, wishing wells, the smell of fresh-cut redwood, toy cook stoves, jack-in-the-box toys, women's wigs, storage areas in basements, any and all costumes, carved pumpkins if the carving is of a face, pink enamel bathroom fixtures, light green 4x4-inch ceramic tile, all board games, slatted decks, roofs that can't be walked on easily such as Spanish tiled or steeply pitched, vises if mounted on a workbench, the squeak of oven doors, the sound of a blender coming to rest, objects near the edge of a table, brown dogs, yellow gingham print bathing suits, the sound of fingernails being clipped in an adjoining room, House of Mirrors at carnivals, veneers on furniture, hard salami thinly sliced if the diameter is small, pendulum-style metronomes when they are clicking, three-minute timers, manual hand-drills, "Yankee" drills, pipe organ music recordings if heard in a residential setting, the smell of turpentine, reel-to-reel tape recorders, Kent cigarettes, Girl Scout badges, pyracantha berries, children being buried in the sand at the beach, people dunking people in swimming pools, water on my face, tongue depressors pushing down the back of my tongue, the heads of dolls with "rooted hair," melon ballers, kites when they are in the air, houses built hanging off cliffs, jigsaw puzzles, dot-to-dot coloring books, all fairy tales . . .

II

I throw the pen out the window. There is too much.
All this and more.

Not natural.
A disgusting thing.

Salt   Ash

Who will sew me back?

I don't go into the house.
Under the branches of my trees, high-ribbed vaulting of night.
Cars and voices die away. The hour darker, more vacant still.

I imagine a cathedral. Chartres, maybe St. Denis, Aucun. Stonecutter's axe buried beside the rampart. Stonecutter's marks, eight
hundred years old, on the walls.

I am an old sacristan. I arrive one morning just before dawn, as
I've done every day for my seventy years of serving. I make my way
down the long nave, stepping across the labyrinth laid in the marble
floor. Past the recumbent statues of the children of the king.

But I stop short. Ahead, the altar appears strangely covered with
a dusting, fine and white. I approach, and smelling, think it salt.
Touch my finger then lick. It is the taste of salt but more delicate.
The salt of tears.

I quickly sweep it into my pockets, return to the small room attached to the cathedral that has been my home. I pour the salt into an empty jar and hide it under my bed. I tell no one, afraid to expose my ignorance. I know of no ritual involving the use of salt except an ancient rite for the healing of the sick. All through morning Mass I wonder, Who is ill? Who is so weak that such a quantity of salt is needed? Never thinking it is the cathedral itself that weeps.

The moon lifts itself high above the spires, bathing the cathedral's slate roof in deep teal blue.

Long gone the sound of marble being cut, the hurried footsteps on scaffolding, the noise of tread wheel, pulleys, hoisting devices. I sit inside the cathedral's vast silence, listening to the sound of longing in the stained glass, wedded to the bands of lead.

I return to my room through the central door where Christ is seated, deeply carved in the tympanium overhead. Stray grains of salt caught in my pocket seams.

On my cot I dream of a boy running out of the cathedral to chase a bird. That night, without pain, I move from sleep into death itself.

In the morning salt is found on every inch of the cathedral's floor, every altar rail, in the crevices of all the faces on the tombs. The capitals, the shoulders of the seated Christ. Like a sheet, like frost. Salt, white, everywhere.

13.

The cold wakes me, moon higher on its course.
Through the windows of the tree, blue light. A requiem.

I dress. Drive to the office.
I don't believe him. He won't be there.

Ash memories.
This is a funeral day.
I should have worn a veil.

The waiting room is empty, just like I thought. Soon his associate
will come out. He'll say he meant to call me, that he's working down
the client list. "There's been a crash," he'll say.
He will be sincere. But useless to me.

"Barbara?"
It isn't the associate. He smiles, which annoys me. He looks the
same, except his shirt.

"You're back."
I trace my loop. I pace.

"I threw out all my clothes. Everything colored."
     I will not ask him about his trip.

"Purses. Sweaters. Twenty garbage bags. Maybe more."
     I will not turn. I will not look at him.
     I want my fists to bleed.
"Barbara . . . ?"

Don't make me look at you.
"Barbara . . . ?"

forgotten sheaf

He takes my fists from the wall.

Tears fall on my arms.

I slide to the floor.

sheaf left for the stranger

"I'm really sorry," I hear him say, he sits near me on the rug.
"Next time I'll give you more warning. There's a lot that we can
do to prepare."

"I didn't want to lose my things."
My fists. The burn.
"I know. I'm really sorry," he says again.
I cry until I'm through.

16.

I finally turn.
"Did you bring back everything I told you?"
"Yes."

"Do you remember what I was doing when my mother came in to
get me, the day she chopped off my hair?"

"You were tearing white paper into snow." He says my words, exactly.

A voice shatters the cedars of Lebanon

"And what did my father say?"
"He said you were going to do something important for science."
"But he put hot dental tools in me instead."
"That's right. He lied."
Tears fall from my lower lids.
"You remembered this on your trip?"

He hesitates. I'm nervous that he hesitates.

"I think," he says, "I will remember it the rest of my life."

17.

The hour comes to a close.
Outside, beyond the glass, the stable deck, the certain rail.

"I made a list of things that frighten me. I was going to give it to the ocean."
"Would you like to show it to me?"
"I stopped before I was finished."

He reads. I can't watch.
"I recognize some of these," he says, his voice unhurried. "They're things we've worked on."
"It's a lot, isn't it?"
"Yes," he says, tenderly. "It's a lot."

Over the water, the eucalyptus tree stretches out its arm.

"Will you work with me for all of it?"
"I'll stay as long as you need, Barbara."

copse of willow   *harps caught in the leaves*

"Is that a promise?"
"That's a promise."

The sun begins to show itself behind the gray.
"I didn't realize you owned any clothes with color," he says.
"You've worn black in here every time."
"Every time?"
"From the first session," he smiles.

It must have been an act of hope. That black time could be
found here.
As if what was left behind could be taken up again.

We stand by the door.
"I went to an art museum. To see the victory of St. Michael over
evil. He just stands there with his foot on the dragon's neck. As if the
battle's already won. As if moral integrity is enough. Do you think
that's possible? I mean, do you think sometimes goodness wins?"

He looks at me, as if considering my case precisely.
"I think it already has."

18.

I return to the waiting room. I don't ring the bell. He startles me, coming in from the hall.

"I didn't mean to interrupt. I didn't mean to see you."

He looks at the white Casablanca lilies in my arms.

"These are for you." Pure white. Fresh, tall, tied with raffia and green string.

horn of salvation

"Thank you for remembering. And thank you for coming back."

He holds the lilies against his chest until the fragrance fills the room.

19.

Josephine flags me down as I turn into the drive.

"The Mormons finally came through! I won the Grand Prize. They're sending me to Hawaii!" Her lips are full, her eyes a dewy shine. "Let's make it a foursome. Dolores Mary and Helene and you. My treat!"

20.

I hear Sister Helene whisper to Dolores Mary through the walls of Josephine's kitchen where I've come to get the coffee. The three of them with maps of Hawaii and their calendars. I bang the sugar bowl against the counter, but still, I hear every word.

"Barbara'll never come."

"Quiet, Helene!"

"She'll never even go barefoot," Sister Helene persists.

"I saw her barefoot just last week," Josephine argues. "In the rain. She loves the damn stuff."

"She's keeping a secret."

"What are you talking about?" Dolores Mary, fair and inquiring, always.

"Maybe that rain washed away the blood," Helene ventures.

"Oh Helene!"

Sister Helene thinks I've received the stigmata? Because she found me covered with camellia blooms? She thinks that was ecstasy? Gauze binding my wounds?

My scars are invisible. There's nothing interesting to see.

Silence around the table when I bring in the tray.

21.

I'll remember this for the rest of my life

It's late. I climb the stairs. Sit with my cello, on the guestroom bed. Spread out clippings from my box. Carefully, I find the small one, just two lines. A quote from a famous ikebanist in Japan who said that the two happiest days of his life were the day his son was born and the day he correctly arranged five chrysanthemums in a dish.

I thread the needle. Sew the ikebanist's words to the young girl in Sarajevo, Ma's playing of Wilde's "Lament," the Morton Salt Girl walking in the rain. Net larger than continents.

To make from many things a single arrangement.

This is salvation.

22.

Tomorrow will be a good day. I'll get right out of bed. I'll assume the posture of an upright mammal. Take my human place among the phyla.

I'll go outside and see what the night has changed. Water my garden. The bottom of my nightgown will get damp and dirty from the hose.

And in every way,
I will be normal.

23.

I turn off the light. St. John on Patmos.
They say he was inspired. I say he wrote his visions down to save himself. Exiled. No one to talk to. No one to listen. His hair in knots, infested with lice. Casting out his net of words. Hoping to catch himself like a fish.

I try to see him.

Perhaps it was like this—

He touches the trunk of a palm, its segmented layers like playing cards, but rough against his hands, and whispers to it, "Wasn't I the one he loved? Wasn't I the one who rested on his breast?" The trunk mute, the fronds silent above.

He pokes a sea anemone with a stick. "You there! Speak up. That last night with the tearing of the bread, didn't he say he loved me?" The anemone closes in, withdrawing its soft, mushy green.

Each night he recites a litany to the fire. "I, John, was there when he raised Jairus' daughter from the dead. I was there on the holy mountain when he became like light. Peter and James were with me. They are my witnesses. They would say, It happened. And I was the one he loved."

When the driftwood turns from red to white he tells himself, "This is corroboration."

He forgets to take shelter from the sun. His eyebrows whiten. His lashes grow thick and interwoven. His skin gathers to itself a calcium casing of sea salts. Sand crabs make their home on the topsides of his feet. His hair grows long, he wraps it around his waist like a belt.

After one hundred days he no longer remembers the house of Jairus. Or Moses and Elijah on the holy mountain, how they stood in the flagrant light. Instead he hears tambourines and the small sound of finger drums in the night. Trumpets. He sees stars falling like candle-sticks. He dreams of locusts shaped like horses, wearing crowns of gold, their tails like scorpions with deadly sting.

He hears strange words, Gog and Magog, in his sleep. Waking he thinks, Now it is happening. I am going mad.

He calls the sand "Whoremonger!" The sea anemone, "Sorcerer!" He curses them all into a lake of fire. He no longer wants someone to say, "It happened, John. Jairus, the holy mountain, leaning on his breast. It is your history. It all belongs to you."

Instead he tells himself, "I am a sea urchin with purple spines. I have no memory, no feelings, no thought at all."

Still the visions come.
An earth scorched by fire. Sea, black as sackcloth. The moon, blood. He curses memory, calls it "Mother of Harlots," "Babylon." He sits as still as stone. Tells himself, "I am no longer a sea urchin with purple spines. I am not here at all."

A silver fish lands on the shore. Large, like none he's seen before. He smells it and thinks, The pelican must have left this for me. Even though he has never seen the pelican. He does not eat the fish. He refuses to believe in miracles.

He feels a pecking on his cheek. With his fingers, he pulls apart his lids. Salt crumbles in his fingertips. On his shoulder, a black crow sits with its narrow yellow beak. He knows it is not an island bird.
He hears voices. Soldiers lift him to their boat. They say, "We have a new Emperor. Your exile is revoked."

In the rocking of the boat, he hears the voice of the one he once loved, saying, "John, I come quickly!" In the sky he finds a woman clothed with the sun.

He sees the distant coastline, white roofs of houses, and thinks, They are taking me to the Holy City. I see its foundation laid with jasper and chalcedony. He calls to the soldiers, "Look! We are going to Paradise."

John's words crossed the Aegean.
New Christians found themselves caught in his net.
So many silver fish, they canonized him.
They didn't call him John the Raving, John the Lunatic.
They named him, The Beloved,
John the Divine.
They gathered his nightmares into a book.
They called it *Revelation*.

In the morning, I put on sunscreen, dress. I finish feeding the azaleas. Coil up the hose. Bob's note tacked above my workbench. Josephine next door, the sound of her television comes through the hedge. Helene and Dolores Mary in their Convent not far away.

And inside my loop, the listening one, the one who returns to me. Bringing all my parts. Remembered. Bringing the sheaves.

I am not on Patmos. I am not alone.
I am the lucky one. I am Fortunatus.

In the privacy of this green, I make a pledge, witnessed by leaves:

That I will vest myself with the crooked staff of a shepherd.
And with my crosier, I will gather even the lowliest memory
that has fallen, lost, into the ditch.
With my staff I will govern my body. I alone will be its curate.
My history will be my new parish.
And I will make inside myself a new city.
A holy place.
A new Jerusalem.

FUNDUS

I

"No one comes here on rainy days but you," Bob says, calling at me from behind the open door of his greenhouse office, sitting on his old wooden chair. He waves me to come in, then draws his hand along the desk's dented metal edge, catalogues for garden ornaments and bulbs, dirt smudged covers, a scattering of dried out ballpoint pens. Dust is on everything, like usual.

It is a comfort to be here and to see him. Dust in the handle of the coffee mug he takes down from the shelf. I sit down on my customary stool.

Rainy days are the best. The nursery is empty, the plants especially clean. The sound of rain is sharp against the greenhouse roof. Fragrance rises from the dusty gravel paths. I'm relieved he doesn't ask me about the holidays, why I wasn't in to buy holly garlands, pinecone studded wreaths, even a single Christmas tree, much less my usual three.

"It had pale pink cup-shaped blossoms. They opened upward," I continue my description of a tree I saw in the neighborhoods around the art museum last week.

"In the shadier gardens, the blossoms were still in bud." Still tight, like a woman's fingers in black gloves.

"Sounds like a Chinese Magnolia. Some folks call it a Tulip Tree." His voice is buoyant again, two years now since his divorce. He holds the coffeepot in the air, hesitating. Through the steamed greenhouse glass, moisture collects in the fuchsia's leaves. Rain hitting the glass roof like thrown coins.

"I've gotta tell you, Barbara, I barely recognized you," he changes the subject. "You look . . . tired or something."

"Thanks a lot!" His long torso bent slightly toward me. "I'm a mess, Bob."

The year he and Annie divorced, his hair turned completely gray, though his eyebrows remained jet black. I came in often, ignoring the larger nurseries with their cheaper prices and truckloads of half-dead plants. Married for thirty years.

"If there's anything I can do to help." He says softly. "I mean it."

He pours more strong coffee into my mug, holding my fingers on the handle, as if, by touch, to pass strength on to me, warmth rising to my face. Over sixty, he moves like a twenty year old. Sure of his step, his body tan from the sun, year round. Always wearing his running shorts, even in the rain. Letting the weather touch him, come what may.

If I stayed in this nursery long enough, I'd wear shorts too. I'd bare my arms, take off my scarf, my coat. I'd let the sun touch me whenever it wanted to.

If I stayed here long enough, I'd be like Bob. Always in his body, in his skin, as if it were an easy thing.

"We're friends, Barbara. You know that, right?"

"I know that, Bob." Tears in my eyes, my wrinkled lids. My arms and legs are useless, like bandaged sticks.

> When Daniel took me to his farm it was early Spring. I was
> strong and pleasure wasn't hard. We sat at the kitchen table
> and I traced the outline of his hand with my forefinger, fruit
> print oilcloth, its background pattern of checks. His fingers,
> white calluses underneath. We both watched this simple tracing,

while the air emptied of speech and sound, except the ticking of
the clock.

Outside, thick damp grass newly relieved of Winter's snow, half
rotten, half full of wanting. I did not know, until then, what a
barn coming out of Winter could smell like. He showed me where
he'd planted thirty bulbs the previous Fall. I thought for sure
I heard tulips underground discuss the time of their appearing.
A blackbird on the wire watched us, his gawking head.

How easily, beside the barn, we leaned into each other, shoes
wedged into the dirt, the field that hadn't seen lovemaking in
many years. Nearby, on the house, straight white clapboard
siding. Inside the barn, a horse that should have been there,
restlessly pawing the ground.

I tasted his skin, the hair on his chest, an unexpected pattern,
six pearl buttons that were too hard to open. My hair was long.
He held it back, kissed my neck, laying down a string of violets,
then harder, lower, sucking, as if for milk. The hair on his head
rough against my breasts. A new perfume lifting between us
from the rubbing.

I filled my mouth, as if in the tropics, fern and banyan tree. He
held my face there. That part of his body, most private, most
familiar. I was fearless then. He put his hand, cold, against my
thigh and I remember thinking, Maybe I'm too warm for him.
My back against the damp grass bed. The clean, uncomplicated
smell. And overhead, the daytime moon.

"Well, show me what you've got" I say, getting off my stool.
"Three specimens. One's real nice. Even you'll like it," he grins. It

feels good to be teased. "Not everyone's as picky as you." He holds the door open for me, the glass dripping with steam. We climb up the bank, steep stairs made of railroad ties. My hair is wet and sticks to my face. Neither of us uses an umbrella.

He's re-arranged the plants in the back lot. Now, bonsaid juniper and cypress are set out on planks. It looks like a lifetime of work. Something I've never seen before. I wonder where he used to store them. Wet rain giving a shine to the matte black pots, rain diamonds in their needled hands.

He rushes me by them. I have seen a private thing.

"Your yard doesn't need more trees if you ask me," he calls over his shoulder, far up ahead, the soft crunch sound of stone under my boots. Piquant fragrance of wet evergreens.

stork abiding in the fir

He's right. Seven tall trees already hold up the sky over my house. Tent over a wound. Soon there'll be no way for sun to get in at all.
"I'm horrible with potted plants Bob, you know that."
"Plant it in the ground then, but keep it small. Bonsai it. You should get into bonsai anyway. It suits you."

He shows me three Chinese Magnolias in fifteen-gallon pots. One is perfect. Equally spaced branches and a fine straight trunk. He carries it down the hill, wet and dripping on his shoulder.

> *"Daddy, over here! We found it!" Cheryl and I scream.*
> *We've found the right Christmas tree. The tallest in the lot.*
> *He doesn't look to see if there's a dent, an opening, a broken*
> *limb.*

"You sure did girls!" he beams. "Way to go!" Wood chips crunch
under our feet. We run between the trees. Lose each other in the
forest of green.
Georgie rides on my father's shoulders.
It is the best part of Christmas. Every year, we please him.
All we have to do is find the tallest tree.
The four of us together in an open, public place.

"Here, read this," Bob hands me a bonsai book. The pages are
water-marked, dried stiff. It is a book for beginners. Clearly, he hasn't
needed to open it in years.

"I'll get this right back to you," I say as he ties down the tree.

"Take your time, Barbara. That's what bonsai's all about."

2.

Bob's book is filled with new words, foreign and promising.
"Singed ends," "jins," "sharis," "the driftwood effect." Nomenclature with Zen roots.

Space. Tranquility. It's just what I want.

Tomorrow, as if in Buddhist robes, I'll sanctify the day. I'll rise
early. I'll move in a slow air of contemplation. I'll meditate on each
aspect of the tree. Measure this against a vision of what, with time, it
will become. With snippers I'll remove what doesn't belong. Then
wrap soft rose-colored wire around the branches that remain.

I'll aim myself toward the future with this tree. I'll be resilient like
Bob. His rows of cypress and juniper, his bare legs.

I'll train my thinking away from my past.

3.

Josephine calls too early. "I'm a hit with the Altar Society gals. Thanks! But Barbara," her tone changes, her voice drops, "for quilts, why did you give me eighteen pairs of shoes?"

I do not know how to answer her. Already my head aches.

4.

I mix organic soil with the sand. Still, my head hurts. Four aspirin and still the pain is sharp and demanding. Something isn't right. Even the sun, good-natured and re-appearing, is drying out the leaves.

> *What if no one came? That student from Cambodia.*
> *What if no one turned on the lights? I was already on the*
> *cold metal floor. Already whimpering.*

I pull a jacket on over my sweatshirt. My arms still cold.

> *Why was his face so calm? His cheekbones? His dull eyes?*

My hands shaking on the handle of the shovel. My boot misses the blade. This is not tranquility.

Luckily, Bob cut the can. It opens like a shell.

> *But that totality of dark. That cold.*

I press harder. My neck, my freezing back.

A man lives in the house he plays with his vipers
he whistles his hounds to come close

"Crawl up there Barbara, a little further"

I pour soil into the hole, set in the tree.
My socks fill with dirt. I can't remember my zip code.
I yank a slip of bark that hangs loose on the trunk.

"Keep going Barbara. Find the shovel."

What year is it? What day of the week?
I cut the branches that grow to the left. Take them all off.
The branches that grow to the right.

My father in his blue canvas shoes

Why is that car driving so slow? What is she looking at?
Nothing stops this cold.
I hack off the top. The crown. Mound of leaves on the walk.
Shrivel in the sun. The heat is killing them. I can't get warm.

A man lives in the house he plays
he grabs for the rod
he looses his hounds
jab your spades deeper
black milk of daybreak
grave in the clouds

The tree isn't a tree at all now. Just a trunk. No branches. No top.
I throw wire around it. Pull hard. Cut off the air.
I'll stop all the fluids.
This cold's going to kill me. I'm dying under here.

"For God's sake Barbara!"
Oh please don't be Josephine.
Yesterday sparrows lived in the hedge,
but today I'm not sure.
"What are you doing?"
I'm probably already dead.

"Give me those shears!"

I'm breaking into enzymes.
"Look at me Barbara!"
I'm disassembling.
Blue canvas shoes
I'm broken into particles.
The soil is taking me in.
"Dammit Barbara . . . Stop!"
"Let me go!"

5.

I hold onto the bathroom counter, the edge, the grout.
She's followed me in.

"What the hell have you done?" She stands at the door. "Where
are all your rugs? The drapes? Where *is* everything?"

Cold tile against my cheek.
Please don't make me look at you.
"Where's that doctor's card? I want his emergency number."
"I'll do it Josephine."
"Look at you!"

I am dissolved. Water carries me away.

"Come here . . . sit down." She sits me on the bathtub edge. She holds me there, cupping my head against her shoulder, hard bone under her blouse.

"This is Josephine Bremen. Of course this is an emergency, young lady! No, I am not a client. Of course, I want him paged. Immediately!"

Her voice is the caw of a crow.

Who will bring me to the strong city?

Her hem flutters against her calf. Fabric against bare skin.
Heat flows out and away from me. I'm hemorrhaging.
I could touch her body. I could touch her life-giving hem.

"The cold is killing me Josephine." She lays me down.
"You've got no color!" She covers me with towels. "He's in session. He'll call within two hours." She puts the phone next to my head.
Perspiration on her forehead, the neck of her dress.
"I'm going to clean up the mess you made of that tree. You rest." My teeth are chattering. "You don't want the neighbors to see that, Barbara."
She stares down at me, exhausted, her body supported by the frame of the door.

Nothing makes me warm. I put on coat, the quilt.
Wrap one of the towels around my head. Crawl into bed.

6.

"Where are you?"
"In bed."
"Can you drive?"
"Yes."
He has an opening at three o'clock.

7.

I make it to the parking lot.
Coat. Quilt. Sweatshirt. Towel. It doesn't matter.
I'm not cold anymore.
I have no temperature.
No pulse.

8.

Far away, two boys play on the bridge. Ducks below.
Nobody breathes.

9.

He opens my car door. He helps me out.
The towel falls off my head. He sets it on the seat.

Shoes move on the wood of the bridge. They are my shoes.
He leads me down a hall.
He sits me on a couch.
His lips open and close.
I do not hear.
I am the girl already dead.

10.

He holds two of his fingers in front of my face.
"Watch me."
He touches fingers to the walls.
He traces a loop around me
like a coffin.

"Show me what happened." He balances a tablet on my lap.
"This is your tablet, Barbara." He opens to a blank sheet.
"These are your crayons." He presses my palm to the box.

"Can you draw a picture of what happened?"

I have no temperature. No pulse.
"Please?"

I take a black crayon.

I touch the sharp point of wax to the white.
I move it one way. I move it back. I move it one way. I move it back.

I move it until all the white is gone. All the light has disappeared.

"Good," a voice says.

He aims my face at his eyes.

"Can you tell me what happened?"
Two blue eyes on either side of a nose.

"Can you tell me about the black?"

"It would make me very happy if you could tell me what happened, Barbara. You've already been very brave, coming here today. Can you tell me what the picture says?"

Water. The drop that hangs falls from the wire.

"My father was in his navy blue canvas shoes. The ones with the rubber soles. He said, 'Go find the candle.' I kept crawling. I thought it was a new game. The space got smaller. It was under the house. A candle was burning in the dirt. The hole was shaped like half a melon. He called up to me. 'Get in.' The dirt was cold against my back. Then he came, crawling on his hands and knees. He scooped dirt onto my legs with his army shovel. Then with his hands. He poured dirt onto my arms and chest. My neck and chin. He patted it down. He put the straws in my mouth. They were green and white flexi-straws. He covered my mouth, my nose. He pressed the dirt on my eyes. I couldn't keep the straws in. I got cold. Then I wasn't cold anymore. I wasn't anything."

"Your father buried you in the dirt under the house?"

"Yes."

I am the dead girl.

I have no pulse.

12.

"Can you look at me?"

a voice shatters the cedars of Lebanon

The tablet is pressed around my face like the bow of a ship.
I bring it down. His face is there, like always.
Two eyes. A nose. A shirt.

I hide myself in the threads of his tie. Under the maple leaf,
there,
in the teal blue.

13.

He leads me over the bridge to my car.

The stillness of the pond is all I want.

It is too much to be a human thing.

14.

"Your father buried you under the house?"

"Yes."

I pull the covers up over my head.

Deepinsnow   Ash   Salt

15.

For two days I do not eat.

I don't get out of bed.

Josephine leaves many messages.

She says this time she's coming over if I don't pick up the phone.

16.

"You scared me the other day."
"What time is it?"
"It's eleven-thirty in the morning. I'm getting you in half an hour."
"Why?"
"I'm taking you out to lunch."
        Oh, please. No.
"I bet you haven't eaten in days. I know you."

I am the broken jar.

"Just get dressed Barbara. There's a whole world you're forgetting about."
"I can't be ready in a half an hour."
"Twelve-thirty then. No more excuses."

I bring my legs over the edge of the bed. Touch my feet to the floor.

Brush my hair, open the box, leaf through the brown ragged clippings until I find the one I want. A flood near Mexico City, walls of mud five feet high moved over the huts. After many days of rescue, a new survivor is found. A young girl, held upright on the shoulders of her grandmother who, though buried, though dead, still stands.

I wonder if Josephine remembers this.

The headline reads, "Buried Girl Lives."

I put on a sweater and skirt. I'll tell her what I'm doing in my sessions, why I drive an hour each way. I'll describe some of what I'm remembering. Then she won't be afraid.
We'll eat in a restaurant, use silverware and cups. We will be civilized. I put on a necklace. I straighten my back. I'll walk upright. I will fit in.

17.

Josephine orders veal, I order vichyssoise. My soup comes, grainy white, topped with fresh-snipped chives. Green and white like flexi-straws.

you won't lie too cramped
Black milk of daybreak

A woman laughs. The man with her takes off his glasses.

your aschenes Haar Shulamith

My stockings have no runs. My earrings. I combed my hair. It's clean. I'm sure of it. That's right. No one is getting hurt.

"You should get away now and then, Barbara . . . "

I am not being buried. She is talking about Hawaii. There is sunlight through the checked curtains on the rod. Josephine lifts a glass of wine.

"I don't want to miss my sessions right now."

I pour salt to cover the white and green.

"What are you doing?" She yanks the shaker from my hand.

Salt piled high on the chives. Salt that saves.

"You're not well, Barbara."

Why is it so cold? I need my coat.

"Why are you staring at my hands?"
"I'm not staring at your hands. Don't be silly! You should see a doctor."
"I am seeing a doctor."
"I mean a real doctor." She signals the waiter to remove my plate.

I miss Daniel. Lying on a beach, sunbathing, that would be
torture for him, just like me. He'd never go on a Hawaiian
vacation. He'd never apologize or explain.

"Smart people like you make everything complicated."
"I'm remembering things that are very important."
"Well, it's ruining you, Barbara. I don't think it's worth it."
She orders me a salad Niçoise. I don't care. I'm not listening.

"When you're my age you'll have a lot more memories, believe me!
You've got to learn to let sleeping dogs lie."

The only person I can talk to sits inside that other room.

"You don't work, you don't go to Mass. Your cello, you're practically a recluse, even your gorgeous hair."

> A hammer comes down on a nutshell. Brittle pieces
> fall away.
> Does the nut meat regret this violence? Does it want
> to go back inside the shell?

"I'm not stopping until I'm finished."
"And how long is that supposed to be?"
"I have no idea."
"And if it kills you?"

> Daniel would tell Josephine to leave me alone. He'd say,
> Keep working Barbara. Get to the bottom of the pit.

"It won't."

"Well," her voice drops, "you're not much use to me this way."

"What do you mean?"

"I've asked Father Dennis to watch the house for the Hawaii trip."

A wet line of pink in her eyes, the yellowing of age.
Almost, tears.

"I can do it Josephine. Really."

"Father likes to get out of that Rectory. The women pick at him like chickens to feed."

The waiter brings coffees. She stirs in cream.

"You should make his acquaintance," she perks up. "He was a musician. Professional. I'm sure I told you."

"You never told me anything, Josephine."

I don't have energy for this.

"He was with the Philharmonic."

Oh God.

> *He shouts play death more sweetly this Death is a master*
> *you'll have a grave then in the clouds*

"Some horn . . . "

"French horn? English horn?"

"Oh, fiddlesticks, Barbara, I don't remember. What's wrong now? You look angry with me."

"I'm not angry."

But live music, so close?

> *you won't lie too cramped*

"He wants some place to practice."

She gulps her coffee. "Are you ready to go?"

18.

I lie down with my cello. The cool spread. The polished, simple lamp. Through the window, the sky dark, the moon at the quarter. My grandmother's room, where, so often, I fell asleep.

> *In the morning, she heated donuts for our breakfast.*
> *The oven held at a soft low heat. And inside, for moisture,*
> *each donut rested on a lettuce leaf.*

19.

A soft rain has changed the garden over night. Through the window, against the green-black of the hedge, thousands of drops are suddenly visible.

It is raining still. Delicate. Gossamer. Silver threads.

As if heaven were saying,

See these threads Barbara? how I bind the earth to myself?

As if heaven were saying,

Open your eyes, Barbara. See what is barely visible.

See these threads and you will see me.

I trace the room. The clipping of the grandmother in Mexico City on my lap. I write in my tablet, using my left hand, like a child. The letters are just right. Awkward and large.

I WAS A BURIED GIRL

I hold it up for him to read.

"Yes," he says, "you were a buried girl."

  A fog horn makes its ugly sound in the dark.
  A necessary sound. Ugly, but wanted.

"Will you say that again?"
"You were a buried girl."

  Free, the fall of kindness from his eyes.
  Falling toward me, a pitcher empties itself.

"I remember this," he says when I hand him the clipping. "It was a long time ago."
"Yes."
"You've kept it a long time."
"Yes."
"You cut it out long before you remembered being buried by your father, then."

  Who will bring me into the strong city?

  My mud upon his shoulders, his chin.
  My mud upon his eyebrows, the top of his hair.

"You are the Mexican grandmother."
He smiles and does not push my words away.

21.

A longing. A gash.

melon shaped hole

I walk across the room. Crouch behind the empty black chair.

there you won't lie too cramped

I close my eyes. Cold leather against my cheek. I press my face
fully into the back of the chair. My arms are cold now, my feet.

"Can you see me?"
I am covered with soil.

Came a word, came,
came through the night

I hear footsteps near.
"I see you, Barbara. I see you there, under the dirt."

I rub my face against the dark. These words are too good to hear.

You, the deeply bowed
I, the transpierced

Finally, I ask it.

"Can you be here with me?"

> There is a pause with no sound in it. Then, a rustling, a jangling of coins. The warmth of a body, near. The sound of breathing close to my ear. I turn and open my eyes.

Soil on his cheekbones. Soil on his lips.

> *Came a word, came,*
> *came through the night*

He is the same. But also a stranger.
"Hello Barbara. It's me with you here under the dirt."

> *If I make my bed in hell,*
> *You are there. If I take the wings of morning,*
> *You are with me.*

Across the back of the black chair, my face powder smeared from crying. A fan of white.
The hour is over. We are by the door.
"Would you write what you said on one of your cards?"

He writes carefully. "Hello Barbara. It's me with you here under the dirt."

22.

I climb the stairs, sit on the bed next to my bound cello. I glue his card onto a sheet. I bind the edges of the Mexico City clipping and sew it to his words. Stitch them to the photo of the bakery girl, the ikebanist's words, Morton Salt Girl, Ma's playing of Wilde's "Lament." The book grows thicker.

I prop the cello up against the headboard as if to see.
As if to teach a broken child how a new world can be made.

23.

I dream. I am a buried girl who now is standing, addressing an audience of adults. They listen. They take notes. I am telling them about the dirt.
I wake. It does not feel like a dream. It feels like revelation.
I go downstairs, sit at my desk, and write every word the young girl said.

24.

"I'd like to give a lecture, if you don't mind," I say after tracing my loop.
"Great," he sits taller in his chair. I stand, as if behind a podium.
"The lecture is titled, 'What Every Buried Child Knows'."

The ducks are on the water. The eucalyptus tree extends its arm.

I will open my dark saying upon the harp

I clear my throat, straighten my papers and begin.

"If someone looks under a house and sees a mound of dirt moving slowly up and down, with two green and white striped straws coming out one end, they might say,

'This is cruelty. That mound breathes so like a human!'

But cruelty is a matter of degree. This is something every buried child knows. When I was under the dirt, my father could not touch me, and afterward there was no blood.

An ordinary person looks through the ripped opening in the foundation of a house, the place where the phone man crawls through to hook up a new line, and says,

'That is dirt in there.' As if dirt were one thing.

But if you are a child, and your father is burying you under the house, you tell yourself,

'Dirt is not one thing, but many.'

The particles come off the pointed end of the Army shovel onto your arms and chest, and you tell yourself,

'Dirt is not one thing but many. Each particle is here with me. Each particle counts.'

And in this way, with the dirt, you outnumber your father.

When he presses the dirt against your legs folded up on your chest, and you feel the cold come in, you tell yourself,

'The dirt is kind. It wants me to be cold. It wants me not to burn.'

When the dirt falls slowly from your father's palms carefully onto your face, and you hear his breathing shorten and accelerate, and his eyes become like glass you know this is the hardest part, because he looks right down at you but doesn't see you there. And because your head is fixed firm, you are forced to watch him become a person you no longer know. And it is impossible to bear. But between you and your father's changing face is the dirt. And you make the dirt speak louder than anything else. And you make it say,

'Watch the way we fall Barbara. We are coming down onto you gently, the way rain falls onto the fuchsia bush, making the leaves dark green with jags of pewter light.'

And you become the fuchsia bush that stands next to the house. How it waits, as if by prior agreement, for the rain's gentle touch.

When you hear the muffled sound of your father crawling away, and you feel the dirt tightening on your face like a mask, as if it were one thing, you still make the dirt say,

'We are not one thing but many, bound together like a mask. Bound together, making a wall between you and your father.'

And you hold onto this as the most important truth around which all other truths must find their place.

When, finally, the cold moves deeply through your body and you can no longer keep the straws between your teeth, and you feel the pull toward sleep, you find yourself able to say,

'Dirt is not one, but many. And the particles are good.'

And in this way you leave behind the world in the condition you expect it to be. Because, even as a child, you refuse to live where cruelty outnumbers kindness. Because even as a child, you demand a moral order. And you create it if it cannot be found."

25.

I fold my papers and look up.
His face slackened by tears.

II.

Into the Straits

DEUS

How is it found? A child runs like a deer toward living water.

How is it found? The thread of uprightness.

Lazarus rising from the tomb, Jairus' daughter,
the recovered wholeness of Mary Magdalen.

How is it found,
    by a buried child?

Blessed art thou,
No-one.

Celan's words. His sea-born salt.

How is it found? The faithful acclamation.

2.

Mrs. Henderson barely fit into the miniature chair at the end of
our low Sunday School table. It disappeared under her print dress,
her wide thighs.

From the louvered window high above, sunlight fell like powder
onto the flannel board she balanced on her knees. Brown hills she'd
crayoned in the background, a tree, white clouds like cotton balls
and a pale blue sky. A landscape that could be anywhere.

We knew the figures well. Joseph and his coat of many colors. Noah and his ark. Shadrach, Meshach and Abednego with their fiery furnace. Figures she kept in her box. Figures from Bible Times, when God spoke and acted directly.

She thumbed through making her selection. Then lifted out David with his slingshot and Goliath, dead, bleeding at the neck. Small tabs of sandpaper glued to their backs.

David slipped and fell to his side. Gently she pressed him back into place. Her short fingers with nails that curled up at the end painted orange frost.

Georgie was in his crib at home. Cheryl in the room next door. Our mother in the sanctuary. I could picture her there, at the piano. Face, torso, all of her body except her freckled legs, hidden behind a spray of gladiolas. The notes of the Doxology coming through the walls.

We left our classroom singing, "Jesus loves me this I know, for the Bible tells me so . . . " and I knew that the words were true even though I didn't live in Bible Times. Because as we walked, Mrs. Henderson touched me the same way she touched David on the flannel board. Gently patting my head, fixing my rhinestone barrette when it slipped down to my ear.

> *psalmhoofed, singing across*
> *open-, open-, open-*
> *leafed Bible mountains*

3.

Cheryl and I attended Vacation Bible School. It was a different Church, a different city, and another new house. Mrs. Henderson was gone.

But Miss Gilchrist had a flannel board of her own. She'd crayoned more palm trees and a darker sky than Mrs. Henderson, but she had the same Noah with the same ark, Daniel in the same lion's den.

We marched along the outdoor corridor singing, "Onward Christian soldiers, marching off to war . . . " And I thought, In the old house my mother found Georgie in the laundry chute. But now we have matching raincoats. Everything here is going to be good.

At the end of the corridor, wide plates of cookies were laid out for us on trays. And under the acacia tree, coffee for the parents, set out in silver urns.

Yea, though I walk through the valley of the shadow of death

psalmhoofed, singing

4.

Georgie's cut the head off his teddy bear
and won't come out of his room

Our Memory Work Chart hung above the blackboard. Rows of stars next to our names. We memorized verses from the Prophets, the Gospels, the Epistles of Paul. This Sunday's assignment was the Books of the Old Testament. I knew all thirty-nine books by heart. It was easy. I made up a song for it in my head. "Genesis, Exodus, Leviticus, Numbers, Deuteronomy . . . "

"Good, Barbara. Pick a star. Lick your finger, dear, and one will come right up." A long trail of stars after my name.

When summer was over, it didn't matter how many stars were

behind your name. We each got a Bible of our own. White for the girls, black for the boys. Inside, I wrote my name, in cursive. Then zipped it closed. Small gold cross on the zipper tab.

> *We, here, we,*
> *glad for the passage*

5.

My father left us for a year. I was in fifth grade. It was another new house. And I could not do long division.

When he was gone, my mother did new things with us. She put her Bible in the living room, a public place. She spoke to me of biblical languages, Greek, Hebrew, Aramaic.

"We'll do memory work at lunch, Barbara," she beamed.

The next day I ran home from school. She had the timer ticking on the counter. "Ten verses in ten minutes!" She sat next to me, not in her usual chair.

"John's is the Fourth Gospel," her voice was energetic, a higher pitch. I brought my arm to the tabletop. Our fingers almost touched.

> *We, here, we,*
> *glad for the passage . . .*
> *when you baked desertbread*

"John didn't start his Gospel with the birth of Jesus," she looked straight at me, as if the rest of the world had disappeared. "He began with the Logos, the Pre-Existent Word." I saw how this notion pleased her. A word. An uttered breath. Clean. No real birth at all. No manger, no cow dung, no straw. Free of longing. Free of skin. Free of loss.

"In the beginning was the Word
and the Word was with God
and the Word was God . . . "

I recited the verses back to her. The Word, above men. Above my
father. Our bodies leaning toward each other. The close tips of our
shoes.

We, here, we,
glad for the passage, before the tent
when you baked desertbread
from co-wandered language

I made a note of it: Closeness that had no pain in it at all.

I took her words and pressed them down, like gold leaf onto
bronze. Smoothed them in place, smoothing the vermeil. Words
above sorrow. Above change. When my father left, he did not say
good-bye. I recited the entire Prologue.

"Which were born, not of blood, nor of the will of the flesh,
nor of the will of man, but of God . . ."

"Good girl!" She hugged me. The buzzer went off. Her hair
smelled of Prell shampoo. I was almost sure of it. I didn't know
until then that her hair had any fragrance at all.

I memorized this: Sliding glass door to the backyard opened
behind her, small lemon tree, sun bright off the yellow fruit.
Between us, a wisp of steam rising from her coffee mug. The
fragrance of her hair.

I ran home the next day and the next.

glad for the passage
when you baked desertbread

And in this way,

from co-wandered language
lemon, shampoo, coffee, touch

I came to know the cool high wind of the Fourth Gospel.

6.

How is it found? The thread of uprightness.
Toward living water a child runs like a deer.

CORPUS

I returned Bob's book, his truck gone. I left it on his desk. Hanging on the back of the door, the jacket Annie gave him for his birthday, its square flap pockets, waterproof, its hood. Never worn, but also never moved from that same hook, after all these months, years.

In the envelope from Daniel, this time two gardens. The script is scratchy, his fountain pen low on ink. Hampton Court looks awful, a frantic maze of geraniums, a nightmare.

Hampton Court

B.

Sorry for the red! This was the only card they had left.
A large white clematis is supposed to cover this room
in July, so don't panic. Pink and cream Helen Traubels,
Speck's Yellow—your colors. For me, not a damn succulent in sight. Hope your therapist's back. Don't kill
yourself doing the work. I'm serious.

D.

The photo of Savill Garden was taken in the Spring. It is very pretty. Beneath cherry trees, daffodils come up through the grass.

B.

Rhododendron in flower here since Christmas! Great
wooded area! Em. says she's got better things to do
than be a tourist in her own country. She wants to visit
the U.S. I'm thinking about it. Had the flu for 5 days.
Wouldn't mind hearing from you.

D.

I unroll the window and stretch my arm out to feel the sun, the
ocean air.

Jerusalem and a lover's thigh, holy book and body, both leafed
open.

Of course there were so few love poems. To be in one's body, one's
skin, and then, to be with an Other, how easy is that?

The poles
are within us,
insurmountable
while waking,
we sleep across, up to the Gate
of Mercy.

I lose you to you, that
is my snow-comfort,
say that Jerusalem is,
say it, as if I were this
your whiteness,
as if you were mine,
as if without us we could be we,

I leaf you open, for ever,
you pray, you lay
us free.

A brown pelican dives for fish, folding back his wings like a paper clip, before the plunge. Lifting himself slowly off the water, with effort, back into the air.

I waited for Daniel in my hotel room, making myself watch the dusk, the slow suggestibility of night. When he knocked, I opened the door slightly and he slid his shoe between the door and jamb, a tasseled loafer, the fine leather thread. My toes on his shoe, bright nail polish against his scuff.

We opened the glass door to the narrow balcony, sheer drapes blew in across the carpeting like sails. How was it he took off my slip? That kiss at the ankle bone while I sat on the edge of the bed?

   I leaf you open

His mouth moved slowly up, the top of his head, brown hair tangled like a nest. We stood then, suddenly, for no reason, as if comparing height. The indentation under his cheekbone, crease of skin along the jaw that was rough against my tongue. He traced my eyebrow with his thumb, as if meaning could be found there.

   . . . this
   your whiteness

Cupping my breasts as if nourishment were there and no other place. I wrapped my legs around his waist, the stripe of darker

hair down the center of his chest, a few strands of gray. I
wanted to count them, to inventory each moment kindness had
broken through.

He reached to turn out the light, his arm over my face, my
round brass travel clock, earrings, a wilted leaf. His chest
muscles tightening and relaxing in a rhythm of their own.
I wanted everything right then, the way a river does not
explain the reason for its downward course.

　　. . . you lay

But he licked instead, the way a cat touches a saucer of sweet
milk. I brushed him with my eyelash, the way the sun warms
petals of a lily, then the stamen. All that could be eaten there
like fruit. Pear-shaped tomatoes, ripe Italian plums. He held
my mouth there. The long expanse of time. The smell of fresh
earth newly plowed.

　　say, that Jerusalem is

Finally he gave me all I wanted. The feathered pillow high
around my ears, the smell of freshly laundered sheets. My energy
gathered low, a rope cinched tight then tighter still. He did not
stop. A balloon set free inside an opera house, rising, sweeping
up, past box seats hanging on the wall, their deeply carved
wood leaves. Past human voices, baritone and bass. High above
the violin and flute. Rising above all these, and then, at once,
released. The high, white, empty bliss.

2.

Near the front door, under the porch light, a spider's web regains its equilibrium after a breeze.

3.

"Last call for Oahu!" Josephine is on the phone as soon as I close my door.

"Not this time, Josephine."

"Come tonight then. I've made apple dumplings. I'm showing Father Dennis around."

Apple dumplings? Josephine? She never bakes. Maybe Dennis won't use her house to practice after all. Maybe he'll fix the broken handle of her wheelbarrow. Or the tool shed door, rusting on its hinge. Maybe he'll clean her pool when the desert winds bring too many leaves, the lantana's many blooms. Maybe he won't bother me at all.

4.

as if without us we could be we,
I leaf you open, for ever

I make dinner, eat outside, watch darkness come. Lights are on at Josephine's. I don't want to hear them. I take a bath, sleep.

The poles
are within us,
insurmountable

I dream.

A man inspects imported cheeses with great care then
throws a block of cheddar in his shopping cart instead.
I follow him. In the elevator he unbuttons my jacket, its
thick pile of tweed. My purse drops to the floor. He presses
my back against the upholstered wall, holds me there with
his legs, my skirt in tight folds around my waist. His hair
against my thigh. I take off my earrings, hold my hair on
my head. He kisses the insides of my arms down to my
breasts. The tight weave of his pants, subtle color between
charcoal and black, a difference he clearly understands.
Why else would I want him? He takes a condom from his
pocket. Why does he carry a condom in his pocket?

It is over quickly. He smoothes the sides of his hair in the
reflection of the door. Steps out on the upper floor. We have
not given our names.

I spray cologne on the carpet, the walls. Button my jacket,
pull down my sleeves.

A tribunal in the lobby finds me guilty. They rope me to a
wooden chair. They hold me over a river. The rushing
stream.

I wake.

5.

The man in the dream had no name. But his tie . . .

That face. That gray hair. Those two eyes . . . like fence posts . . . No!

6.

I find the long blade scissors.

The pond. The ducks. The black chair. There! That grave, that dirt.
How could I ruin that?

I break everything I love.

I grab a handful of my hair. Cut high, right up to the ear.

Grab the other side.

> *your golden hair Margareta*
> *Your ashen hair Shulamith*

I know how to end a thing.

> *A man lives in the house he plays with his vipers*

The back. Cut right to the scalp.

> *Black milk . . . we drink you at night*
> *. . . at midday . . . morning . . . evening*

At last I am hooved. I am stubble shorn.

The marble floor wears my long locks like a crown.

> *Purge me with hyssop*
> *and I shall be clean*

7.

I sweep the hair into a bag and drive to the Church.

> *I lose you to you, that*
> *is my snow-comfort*

There are too many cars. This is no place of peace.

8.

I make myself do it.

> *the poles*
> *insurmountable*

I walk to the very end of the pier.

> *as if I were this*
> *your whiteness*

I open the bag. Let my hair fall onto the waves.

I lose you to you,
that is my snow-comfort

Salt Mother. Easter womb.

purge me with hyssop

Hope of the poor.

Make me innocent. Unborn.

Rub my skin clean. Memory. Purify.

say, that Jerusalem is

Let the sea nets not bring me back to shore.

9.

I dress for my session. I don't look at my hair.

> *Cheryl and I walked to the riverbank. I had scissors in my*
> *pocket, wrapped in a handkerchief, from home. Our first*
> *camping trip since I stopped my father. "Cut it all off," I told*
> *her. Long pieces of my hair left on the granite stones.*
>
> *My neck felt cold, my head light, when we walked back to the*
> *campsite. No one said a word. Georgie stared. My mother lifted*
> *canned stew from a cardboard box. She lit the Coleman stove.*
> *My father moved away, under the shadow of the trees. Like a*
> *dog slinking from a rodent too long dead. And I thought, I am*
> *safe now. I am carrion.*

"I see you cut your hair," he smiles.

I leaf you open

I know how innocence goes.

"It should be August 29th."
"Why's that?"
"The Feast of the Beheading of John the Baptist."
He looks up at my hair.

I leave.

II

A backhoe rips open the parking lot. Bars of broken asphalt slammed into a pile. Rupture everywhere. The violence calms me.

My year hangs between John's Beheading and the Slaughter of the Holy Innocents. Like a hammock, empty and blackened from too much dew.

I know the sound of that beheading feast. Splitting crash of pots thrown against tile. I know this holy one. Father of the tarantula, of dirt packed under the nails. Father of dryness at the roof of the mouth.

I've seen his trace in my garden. Violets with their heads blown flat against brown soil.

12

"I have to cancel my next sessions," I say on the phone. "I don't know how long this will take."

> All the color still in this house. No wonder I had that dream. Gray on the walls, ecru on the ceiling, baseboards, trim. So much pigment I can't think straight. I'm not letting color rob me of one more thing.

"Does John the Baptist have anything to do with you cutting your hair?"

I should live with ravens, locusts, crawling things.

13

Lee's Hardware store is filled with men in paint splattered coveralls. Some of them stare at me. Why? I'm not in my robe. I dressed. I brushed my short hair. On the counter I set down my sandpaper, paint remover, disposable gloves.

The sensuality of olive flesh bitten with one's teeth, pulled from the pit with the tongue. I know why the Baptist fled to the desert. I know how even color can seduce.

> *"Repent! The Kingdom of God is at hand!"*

I'd meet him in his desert. I'd have a pair of robins to his solitary hawk. Robins walking on the sand, leashed to my ankles with gold chains. I'd say, I, too, know how to scour things down. I, too, know what it can cost to finally understand a thing.

I sand the baseboards.

purge me with hyssop

I strip away the paint. I sleep in my sweatshirt on the floor. Order groceries by phone. I work for twelve days. The bathtub fills with worn sandpaper.

I sand everything. Fig flesh. I know when danger comes too close.

14.

At Lee's Hardware Store again, I hesitate before going in. The announcer on the radio describes a shop in New York specializing in fine wrapping papers, some costing ninety dollars per sheet. Papers imported from around the world. Gold leaf papers, handmade silk infused papers, and from Japan a paper pressed with real butterflies.

This is not news. Their wings bent to cover the corner of a box. This is not civilization.

"Sanding a warehouse are you?" Lee jests. There are no painters at this late hour.
"I need more sandpaper. And I always run out of these gloves."

He is kind.

> *. . . as if I were this*
> *your whiteness*

He walks me to the car. The forward slope of his shoulders, his chin held higher as we walk.

What did that mother say? "Give me the Baptist's head on a platter"? Acting as if she hadn't planned it. Leveraging the slow rotation of her daughter's hips. Even the incense was appalled, halting its movement toward the ceiling's coved and musky light.

All cruelty is the same. Only goodness is singular.

15.

Finally it is finished. All the color gone.
I am inside the body of a whale.
Dull, dark. Safe. The ribbed bones, the skeleton.
I've come through the thick skin and the blubber.

16.

I rest.

> *Inez lifts me onto her changing table, even though I'm five years*
> *old. At my back, jars containing cotton balls, swabs, comb and*
> *brush. Across the room, gingham curtains with eyelet trim. The*
> *cotton swab is soft in my ear. She twists it slowly, and when she*

stops I don't sit up. She doesn't take her hand from my cheek. I keep my eyes closed thinking, Inez is cleaning my ears, but she's thinking about the baby that never came.

Walking home through the ivy bank Cheryl whispers, "Inez can't even make a single baby!" But I'm thinking, I have clean ears, and under my t-shirt, Inez rubbed talc onto my skin and I am silver like a fish.

17.

I wash my hair. Put clear polish on my nails. And when I sleep I do not dream.

18.

The pond, the bridge, the ducks. I thought it would be easy.
 But the sky is too open and too blue. I sit lower in the car. Bring my legs up.
 Cut my fingernails to the bone.

19.

"I'm glad you came back," he says. "I wasn't sure you would."

My arms against my chest. Coat over my body.
No lipstick to draw attention to my mouth.

I do not have openings. He will not get in.

"I thought there might be more you could tell me . . . about why you cut your hair."

I have no mouth.

I am a spider. Curled tight.

I'm not going to open my body.

I'm not going to release breath.

"I see you also cut your nails."

I unfold my spider legs. And leave.

20.

In the ivy next to the bridge, the brown duck, the caramel one, stands up, stretches his neck. He settles back into a new position with a wise, recollected gaze.

I press the buzzer. We start again.

21

I feel nauseous.

> *The poles*
> *are within us,*
> *insurmountable*

"You aren't coming inside me."
"No. I'm not," he says.

"I'm not like your father."

> Through a chain-link fence a girl with blond hair squats
> in a school yard filling an empty baby stroller with large
> smooth stones. She is in my imagination. She makes the
> kind of baby that she wants. A baby without openings.

My body stiff. Hooved.

"I had a dream. We had sex in an elevator."
He waits.

"It was my fault."

"So if you cut off your hair you wouldn't have sexual feelings?
You'd be like John the Baptist—beheaded? dead?"

> Isn't this obvious?

"It's normal to have sexual feelings for a therapist, Barbara. Sexual dreams, too."

Is this supposed to comfort me?

"I had sexual feelings for my therapist."

He's talking too much.

"I wanted to be her husband, her brother, her child. Everything!"

He laughs at himself.

purge me with hyssop

"So what happened?"
"We worked through the feelings, that's all."

say that Jerusalem is

"Sexual feelings don't cause bad things to happen."
"You're nuts!"

I stand. He's gone too far.

"How can you be an expert if you don't know the simplest things?"

I open my purse. Find the check. Slam it onto the arm of his chair.

22

In the morning I begin to paint. Walls, molding, the sills, even the switch plates, the shelves inside the closets. Three coats. My arms and fingers ache.

After eighteen days, everything is white.
My body fills with air.

> *My father was away. We'd had our baths earlier than usual. Georgie was quiet in his crib. We went to bed before the sun went down. Sunlight still hot through the waxy pulled down shade.*

> *Cheryl climbed down into my bed. She lay on the edge, on her side, facing the bedroom door. I put my arm around her, my face against her back. We didn't talk. But I knew she was guarding me. Anything could happen when only one parent was home.*

> *The points of Cheryl's long wet hair smelled like bubble bath. I hung onto her like sweet peas on a string. The cool thin sheet across our shoulders like a tent.*

> *I sank into her breathing, the rise and fall of her back. Her steady rhythm telling me, The moon will come out over us. Stars around it like a skirt.*

> *I could hear my mother whistling in the kitchen. It sounded far away. She closed cabinet doors slowly, without the usual bang. A strange mood filled the house. The way a petticoat in a rush of wind is suddenly lifted up.*

Eventually the seam on the shade became a darker line. All color left the room. Still, Cheryl didn't move. Her breathing didn't slow. She stayed awake. Awake and watchful, between me and the door. I drifted like a raft down a stream, until, piece by piece, I fell asleep.

23.

I order sheer drapes, a pair of white silk-covered chairs, an ivory throw for my cold legs, a topiary of small white roses, a bleached pine table, a candle, a shell.

For three days straight, I have no dreams.
For three days straight, I have no thoughts of childhood.

> *we sleep across, up to the Gate*
> *of Mercy*

24.

I trace my loop around the walls. I sit on the chair. We do not speak.

My hair used to be beautiful. I feel this. And weep.

"We're both safe here, Barbara," he says, the hour over.

"Because I cut my hair."
"No. Because of the kind of people we are."

say that Jerusalem is,
say it, as if I were . . .

"I believe you. But I can't feel it."

"That's okay," he opens the door. "You will."

25.

I lift all the empty paint cans to the curb. Father Dennis' car is
parked at Josephine's. In the lamplight, I see his parking permits for
Symphony Hall along the bumper. Some faded, some peeled.
A long row, for many years.

One night with Daniel things went better than I'd planned.

He asked about Halloween and I said, "No, Daniel, don't
come. I've always hated Halloween." Everyone in costumes
and death put at dusk. But he said, "Barbara, no one hates
Halloween." So I agreed. He came for dinner, too.

Onions became transparent and sweet in the olive oil. I added
fresh tomatoes, basil, then the veal. Each time the doorbell rang,
he re-arranged the caramels into a pyramid on the silver dish.
The children didn't make my stomach hurt. I could see that
they were there, behind their costumes. And I made it through.

I felt his tenderness come to me from across the room.
And I felt blameless. Like a woman without catacombs.

26

"Do you have any daughters?" I ask.

On the coffee mug, the photo of two boys with their neatly parted hair. The older has his arm around the younger.

"No." He looks sad.
"Do you wish you did?"
"Sure! Why do you ask?"

say it, as if I were this
your whiteness

"If you had a daughter, would you do to her what my father did to me?"
"Absolutely not."

"What if *I* were your daughter?"

say it, as if I were this
your whiteness

"I would never want to do those things, Barbara."

Sitting on my parents' bed, the spread a deep green ivy print.
My mother gave me her button jar. I set the buttons out in
snakelike rows. Orange, brown, navy blue. My father sat on the
foot of the bed, watching football on his new t.v.
The glittering gold thread running through the speaker cloth.
The movements of the small men. He stood to move the rabbit
ears, sat back down, stood up again. Up, down. Up, down.

Each time he stood, my button lines slid into each other.
Each time he sat back down, I made them straight again.
His white undershirt, the sleeves rolled high, holding a pack
of cigarettes. His back hair slicked with pomade.

So close I almost touched him. So close, my buttons almost slid
right up against his back.

It was an ordered thing. Sunlight watching from the bedroom
walls.

27.

We sit beside each other on the rug, looking out at the pond.
There is a space between us.

In it, all that is not done.

LABORARE

For a moment, he looks past me to something on the deck.

"I'm sorry," he confesses. I turn to see, flying away, an extraordinary bird. Pure white, graceful, with a wingspan of at least four feet. I have never seen such a bird before.

"It's the Great Egret," he says in a wistful tone. "He winters here." The great bird flies over the pond, a slow wafting of wing, and I feel, with an excitement and certainty, the arrival of a teacher.

2.

I buy a brushed stainless steel thermos just like the one I've seen him bring to the office. Fill it with coffee. Take my camera, buy extra rolls of film. So clear, the Egret's white body against the color of the deck. Free and independent. Maybe he will be there. This is Sunday, the offices will be empty. I'll see him up close, without the barrier of the glass.

When I arrive, the Great Egret is on the far side of the pond. His body dazzling white against the ivy bank, even from here, his yellow beak, his long thin black legs.

I set up on the bridge. He begins to climb, moving smoothly and with confidence, absolutely certain when his feet go forward, his body will follow, all of one piece. He does not look back, clearly knowing what is Egret and what is ivy.

I take his picture. A breeze ruffles his neck feathers, rippling his silhouette. Still he stands stark white against the green.

3

He turns and makes his way back to the pond, bringing his foot high above the ivy, spreading it in the air, then placing it back down. Delicacy and sure-footedness combined in one movement. Careful where he puts his feet. Careful in the smallest things.

> *"Do it just right," my mother said, as I stood on the chair next to the ironing board. She showed me how to pull one end of the handkerchief tight, while the iron held down the other end, pulling out the folds.*

> *"That handkerchief could make the difference in the interview, and the interview could mean your Dad gets the job!" I felt important. And she was not angry with me.*

> *I folded the cotton cloth in half, pressed the seam, then folded it again. When I was finished, I held it up in the air.*
> *"Perfect" she came from the kitchen where she was mopping the floor. She lifted me down from the chair.*
> *A clean hot square of perfect white.*

4

His deliberateness soothes me, my body, liquid. I almost lose my camera over the bridge.

Suddenly, he lifts himself into the air.

He does not fly away. He comes toward me, crossing the pond, landing right here, on the railing of the bridge. I stay crouched and still. He looks at me with his small black eye, measuring me for danger.

He's concerned with danger that is here and now. A manageable task.

And he, in doing it, so strangely elegant.

5.

He drops from the rail to the shallow water, and begins hunting with great determination. He spots something beneath the surface, and stops moving his legs, his entire body rigid. Only his eyes move. He studies the pattern of a fish I cannot see.

His long neck begins to jerk vigorously from side to side, as if in anticipation, a movement he cannot control. He stands this way for over fifteen minutes. I time him with my watch. Finally, quickly, he drops his beak into the water and brings it out again.

Nothing moves down his narrow throat. He caught nothing. Again, he stares.

He takes two steps. Freezes again, but for his jerking neck. Ten minutes elapse, then, a second plunge. Again, nothing, not even a small frog.

I watch him for an hour. In that time, he makes only three attempts. And all three are failures. But, mostly, he waits.

I feel discouraged for him, but he doesn't need my sympathy. Clearly, he's made his decision. Without this work, he will not fly.

6.

It is cold and almost dark. Mallards come in pairs from the sky, landing on the water near the Egret. He ignores their calls, their bathing and flirtation. Eventually he flies back across the pond, to the restaurant roof.

He doesn't ask them, Why are my feathers white? Why is my neck so long?

7.

Through the shutters I see Josephine standing on the curb. She's waiting for Father Dennis to arrive with Dolores Mary and Helene. Their flight to Hawaii is in two hours.

She has all her Louis Vuitton. Seven cases plus a hatbox. Wearing her wide-brimmed Guatemala hat with the balled fringe trim. And from under her plaid raincoat, the bold blue and white print of a muumuu, gray socks and pineapple rubber thongs on her feet. She carries the flowers I gave her and the gift to open on the plane. This is the first time I haven't driven her to the airport.

I feel like an invalid watching life through a shade.

Dennis is older than I remember, from that first day when I ran past him out the Rectory door. His body, thick and settled.

Josephine lights a cigarette, annoyed that her suitcases don't fit in his trunk. She hates small cars. As if waiting for a limousine, she looks longingly down the street. Finally she opens her straw purse. Dennis takes her keys and slowly backs out the Thunderbird. Its cavernous trunk takes everyone's luggage in a heartbeat.

8

I hose off stray cut grass from my curb. This is a pretense. My goal is to spy into Dennis' car. On the front seat he has a daily planner, a recent biography of Joan of Arc, a men's fashion magazine, and a museum brochure. So far so good.

But on the dashboard, a slew of cassettes. Music still attached to his life, like a barnacle. He has cassettes everywhere. Berlioz, "Symphonie Fantastique," Bartók, "Concerto for Orchestra," Prokofiev, "Romeo and Juliet," and, worst of all, Brahms. My stomach aches. Yes, it definitely is Brahms. "Variations on a Theme by Haydn." I bring water from the hose to cool my face.

What if he does practice here?

The notes will come through my hedge, then the walls, the windows. I won't be able to stop them. They'll come into my room. Find me, even if I hide in the closet. And what about that Brahms? Another memory will come, then another. I'll have to make an emergency call. He'll ask, "What's so scary about Brahms?" and I'll have to say, "I don't know! It's buried too deep."

Music like this finds all my wounds.

"You have to help me be more like the Great Egret," I say, leaving a message on his phone machine. "His outline is clear. Stark white against the green. Father Dennis might play music next door. I don't have a wall. It will all get in."

9.

How did the Egret get so confident?

Lazarus came out of his tomb. Everyone was amazed that he lived after being dead. But maybe all he wanted was to know his own periphery, his edge. So desperate that he died just so he might feel it.

Maybe when he walked into the light, whitely bound, he finally felt where he stopped and started, what was his, and what belonged to his sisters, his parents, the bush on the hill.

10.

At the store I fill my cart with rolls of paper towels, a few of every brand.

A man buying a magazine looks at me, the cart.

I go back down the aisles, toss in disposable diapers, a few cans of cat food, some motor oil. Now nobody stares.

11.

"I want you to wrap me like a mummy," I say after tracing the room. He glances at the grocery bag.

"Do you have something in mind?"

"I have to feel my boundary. Where my body is and where it ends." I take out two rolls. "I tried all the brands. These are the strongest. They won't tear."

He scratches his chin. Hesitates.

"Won't you feel trapped? Have you thought this through?"

"I wrapped my legs at home. It was fine. I just couldn't do my top."

"I'm concerned you'll feel overpowered. Like this is the burial all over again."

"I practiced at home," I repeat.

Why is he doing this? He asks another question.

"Why are you being so picky?"

"Part of my job is to pace you, so this doesn't backfire."

He'll never be satisfied. A third question. A fourth.

Finally, we begin.

12.

I stand in the middle of the room. He starts wrapping the paper towel around my shoes. My legs, together, my arms, my torso, smooth. He folds the paper in half to wrap it around my neck. There, he stops.

"You're right," I say, "not my face or ears."

> *flexi-straws that failed to let in air, dirt pressed on my eyelids,*
> *the dark, the elevator, the cold*

"I want to see and hear." He winds the paper up, over the top of my head.

"Finished," he says.

And I feel tightly bound.
"This feels really good."

> The rug against the paper-white tips of my shoes.
> The edge of a ball held in a teacher's hand.
> A single finger in a tight white leather glove.
> I am all of these.
> An eel in an ocean of air.

> *"Come on girls! Let's swim like Esther Williams!" Cheryl and
> I stand on the side of the pool. My mother is already halfway
> down the length, swimming sidestroke in long, fierce glides.
> I see her body through the water. Her one-piece bathing suit,
> arms, legs, cap. She seems happy, as if in her natural habitat.
> I see freedom and movement, usually hidden.
> Her outline, clear, against the turquoise water of the pool.*

"Do you want to turn around?" he asks me.

> Maybe the Great Egret is near. Maybe he wants to surprise
> me.
> Slowly, carefully, I inch my feet, so not to lose my balance.
> Eventually I make it all the way around.

"Why didn't you warn me?" I struggle to free my hands.

"How could you do this? What were you thinking?"
> My entire body is there, all at once, reflected in the glass.

"Get me out of this! Help me!"

13

Crying. That's all I do in here.

The pile of wrappings on the rug. A high gathering of white.
Bandages. Rags. Burial clothes.

"I'm sorry, Barbara. I thought you'd like to see yourself in the sliding glass."
"I said I wanted to feel my periphery. Just feel it, that's all!"

"We should have talked more about this. It's my mistake."
"I'm not like Josephine!"
"What do you mean?"

A cheap hand mirror from the drugstore is all I need.
I prop it on the windowsill to do my makeup. Hold it over
my shoulder to check the back of my clothes for lint.

"I never look in full length mirrors, except by mistake."

The Egret is nowhere to be seen.

"The last time I really looked into a mirror I was five."
I can't go back to that room. The tile, the lines of grout.

Your goldenes Haar Margareta
Your aschenes Haar Shulamith

"I just saw the top of my head reflected between the handles above
the sink. My blond hair looked brown like Cheryl's." I am crying
again. "It was filled with dirt."

14.

Now Dennis' car is here again. Maybe he just comes over to read.
Or rest. Or sleep.
Why didn't I plead with Josephine? I just don't want this now.

Scissors to a mesh bag. Apples fall out, bruised, to the floor.
My skin won't hold.

St. Francis always preaching at my door. Can he keep this music
from coming through my hedge? Can he keep my memory free?

Preaching to his birds. What problems do they have to solve?
Being a bird—how hard can that be?

15.

Again, I fill my cart with paper towels. I don't put anything else in.
It does not look normal, and I don't care.

A woman lowers the hand of her child who is pointing at me.

16.

We wrap my body a second time.
Long and strong the rope that holds heavy wet sheets.

17

I face the window and watch as he wraps. My legs are together, arms at my side. When he is done I see the smooth outline of a fish.

"Am I an eel? "

"No. You're a grown woman. You're Barbara wrapped in paper towels."

"Am I connected? Even in the back?"

"Yes."

"You didn't walk around to see."

He circles my body.

"You're all connected. One body."

"If you saw me swimming in a pool, would you be able to tell where my body was, and where the water started? Would you be able to see my edge?"

"Yes."

> *You are still, are still, are still*
> *a dead woman's child . . .*

"Does my body stops where the paper is? Is that your professional opinion? Am I just what's inside the paper? and nothing outside?"

"Your body stops where the paper is. That is your outline. Your periphery."

"Like the Egret?"

"Like the Egret."

"You didn't think about that very long."

"I didn't have to."

> *Cathy brought her Japanese doll in to Mrs. Pinney's class when it was her day to share.*

Mounted in a glass case. Long kimono sleeves dropped green
and still from her white wrists. Her shiny hair coiled at the
back of her long ivory neck. Head tilting to the side, a jeweled
ornament above her ear.

Cathy carried the doll in her case around the room. When she
came by my desk, the doll said, See how no one cuts my hair? My
dress never rips. My face stays powdered white. Look at me,
Barbara, in my windless case. This is happiness. This is safety.
This is how life can be.

18.

At home, I feel along the edge of my body with my hand. Starting
at the top of my head down along my neck, shoulder, my arm, leg,
bottom of one foot then the other, then up the other side. This is the
shell I am in. This is the outer shell.

I rest. The pond, the stillness of the leaves.

19.

Marie turns her shop sign to "Open" and smiles seeing me, the
quiet of morning still on the street. I've come for scented candles to
remind me of the Egret. Gardenia white, or maybe cucumber green.

I prop the photographs of the Egret on the table against the candle.
Light it for Cathy and her Japanese doll, Mrs. Pinney, for all that was
good. All that pointed to another way.

"Wrapped?" Marie had asked, meaning, As usual? The carefully
folded paper, the layering of ribbon, the gentle precision of the bow.

The Gospels record that the disciples found Jesus' grave cloths "folded." Why is that detail preserved? Why doesn't anyone preach on this?
Maybe it means that we can love the things by which we were once bound.

A girl walks out of her coat. She leaves the rest behind.

> *go, your hour*
> *has no sisters, you are—*
> *are at home*

20.

I wake up with a jolt. Turn on the light. I'm cold and sweating. I throw back the sheet.
Check my ankles, my wrists. There are no ropes.

> *your hour*
> *has no sisters, you are—*

Three hours until dawn. I wait. Celan on my lips.

> *count what was bitter and kept you awake*

Finally the sun comes.
The dawn sun, the young one.

21.

He answers my call. I tell him the memory.

It was a Sunday morning. Cheryl was home with me, Georgie in his crib, our mother at Church.

My father stretched us on our backs on the living room floor. He said we were going to be starfish. He tied our ankles and wrists to metal rings in the hardwood floor. He wanted us to be "nice and flat."

When he left, Cheryl and I didn't talk. When we stretched out our fingers to each other, they were almost touching.

Until my father came back, all we did was study the brown and white parts of each others' eyes, the way tears fell onto the wood.

22.

I drive slowly. He has a cancellation.

The sunlight is too brittle. It pulls me back.

My mother standing in the living room, in her pipe organ shoes.
Sun breaking off the walls, the bare, shiny floor.
"Get your father," she said to Cheryl.
"What are these?" Her tone was frosty. She pointed to screw holes in the new wood floor. My wrists burned, and my stomach ached looking at the holes. I didn't know why.

I didn't know why there were holes in the floor.
Cheryl started wheezing and puffed on her inhaler.
"Beats me," my father mumbled, looking down at the floor,
pulling his black oiled hair, his forearm sheltering his face.

23.

The afternoon light casts shadows on his deck.

"My father saw me when he tied us to the floor. It wasn't like the burial. He saw me. He saw Cheryl. He said we were pretty like starfish."

The good thing, the sweetness—

"It wasn't as bad as it seems."

Flesh of a fig, pink and seeded. Sweet flesh
inside an ugly skin.

"I had an outline. It was the outline of a starfish. But that didn't matter. I had an outline. And I was seen."

24.

"Do you think anyone else ever sees your body, whole? Daniel maybe? Josephine?"
"How could they?"

"Daniel, do you think I'm a brain on stilts? A brain with no body?"

"What are you talking about?"

"Sometimes I feel like I'm just a brain. Without a body. Just stilts."

"I like your brain, Barbara. But that's never been the main attraction for me."

"Maybe Daniel did." "Maybe Daniel saw my body, whole."

He hands me the box of Kleenex.

"When he was wiring the echeveria. He saw my long hair."

"You loved him."

"Yes."

25.

In the morning, a postcard.

Dear One,

How's my trouble-maker?
Keep an eye on Fr. D. for me

Love, Josephine

26

I buy butcher paper, spread it on the kitchen floor, outline my shoe. Take off my shoe, outline my foot. Then the other. This is the flesh. This is my body. The invisible wounds.

At the Buster Brown Shoe Store, Cheryl and I are fitted for saddle shoes. This year we choose black and white. I stand on the fluoroscope. The shoe man looks in, says it's a good fit. He sees my toes hidden beneath the leather of my shoes.

On a different section of the paper I outline each hand. My arms. I keep the parts of my body separate. Each holds a memory. Each body part, a box.

They are spread out, random, across the white.

I draw black lines to connect them. My fingers shake. I can barely hold the pen.

I drink another glass of wine.

Poach halibut. Chop fresh dill.

I keep my eye on them. They do not move. They stay on the floor connected by the black lines. I checking as I eat, after the dishes, I check again.

seams, palpable, here
it is split wide open, here
it grew together again

I try to do all my body at once. Lie on my side, reach over myself, outline my head, my chest, my feet.

A long caravan stretches over a course of hills, each camel overloaded.

My body, this caravan, my history carried in parts.

27.

I show him the paper.

"I want you to outline my body. I couldn't do it myself. I want to do it all at once."

"But I notice you're not looking at me."
"Everything bad that happened, to bring it together inside one sheet . . . "
"Like your cello, broken pieces, bound . . . ?"
"Yes."

"Let's wait, Barbara. We're rushing." His voice is gentle. A soft hand gently rocks a cradle.
"I was afraid of dot-to-dot books when I was young. I never connected the last segment, between the last two numbers. Cheryl used to say I was dumb. I'm still afraid of them."
"I remember that from your list."
"It's overwhelming. To link up all the parts with one smooth black line."

28.

For three sessions, we observe the paper I drew at home.
Finally, I'm ready.
We spread a new sheet of paper, books to hold the corners down.
I sit on the white, then I make myself lie back.

"Breathe, Barbara."

He starts at my head. He never reaches over me.

"It would help to keep your eyes open too," he says.

I concentrate on the sound of crayon crinkling the paper. He's almost at my feet.

"Don't go between my legs."

"I won't." He draws around the bottoms of my shoes.

"Do you see lines of blood on my legs like thread?"

"No. I'm not doing science on you."

"Do you see dirt in my hair?"

"No. You're not being buried."

"Do you see me in my shorts and striped tennis shoes?"

"No. You're not lying on the pine needle bed. You're in my office, lying on a strip of paper, on the rug."

> *line of white where two walls join*
> *everything turning blue*

"I'm not going up to the ceiling."

"Good for you. I'm almost done. How're you feeling?"

"Horrible."

"I'm almost done."

29.

When he's finished, I stand, but do not look at it.

"Is it a starfish shape?"

"No."

"Is it repulsive?"

"No. It's not a starfish shape and it's not repulsive."
　　　He's probably lying. When I get home there'll be a message on my phone machine saying he's referred me out.

Our fingers outstretched, almost touching
Cheryl's tears falling to the bare wood floor

"Are you still here?"
"I'm still here. Why don't you open your eyes."
"I need another minute."

I look.
It's huge and ugly.
The shape won't go away.

"Shall I put the paper behind the couch?"
　　　Far behind. I have no air.
"Barbara?"
　　　I can't hear you.
"Shall I put it behind the couch?"

　　　pine needles in my ears

"Barbara, you can open your eyes now. It's gone. It's behind the couch."

　　　I am a blue-headed mallard, through the fountain's broken spray.

"Barbara?"

　　　I'm over the lake.

"We can't know everything ahead of time, Barbara."

I am the mallard. He's far away. He has no wings.

"Barbara, look at me."

I'm above the roof. No one touches me.

"You don't have to see your body all at once, Barbara."

I stop.

"I don't have to see my body all at once, is that what you said?"
I smooth my wings.

"That's right. Can you look at me?"

> Slowly, I'm in the office, on the rug.
> There within reach, he sits. The one who never hurts me.
> I could touch him. If I had hands.

30.

Next week at this time, Josephine will be home. I won't tell her
Dennis never practiced at her house. I won't say I flew over the roof
like a blue-headed mallard, or that I snooped in Father Dennis' car.
I miss her. I'll not say any of these.

Another hotel postcard. A swimming pool lit at night, neon
lights in a lobby, tropical plants, their too large leaves, a bar,
everything I hate. Her shaky script, the smeared ballpoint ink.

Deary,

You should be here getting a tan!

xoxo, Josephine

31.

I call.

"I'm going to look at the paper. I'm going to look at it and stay in the room."

There's late rush hour traffic. By the time I reach his office, only fifteen minutes left in my hour.

I hold the chair. He unrolls a few inches of the paper. I look at the outline of my head for thirteen minutes straight.

"Is it how you imagined it?"
"No! It's too big."

> *She despised my father. Loved him and despised his uselessness.
> Staring at those holes in the floor. He couldn't even do cruelty
> right.*

"Remember to breathe, Barbara."

> *I drove to find her. It was night. I was seventeen.
> High at the back of the church, a single yellow light. Organ
> music coming through the shingled roof, wrapping the branches
> of the trees.*

> *I climbed the dark narrow stairs to the organ loft.*

*Surely goodness and mercy shall follow me all the days of
my life; and I will dwell in the house of the Lord forever*

*My mother's white arms and legs, visible through the screen.
Practicing in her shorts and sleeveless blouse, her gardening
clothes. Heel, toe, heel, toe, the bulky organ shoes gingerly
worked the pedals. Her hands, bright white in the darkness that
surrounded, moving quickly to pull out the stops. One on top of
the other, three registers of keys. Neck extended forward, chin
high, reading the sheet music under the tin lamp's single bulb.*

I cried to see it.

> *. . . in you, from
> birth . . .*

*Released from the dulling, the inconsequential. Great solitary
bird. Returning to its natural habitat.*

> *Deus Gloria
> How forcefully, unbound, it flies out to sea.*

32.

"I'd like to come in everyday just for a minute or two, to look, if
that's possible." He checks, and we arrange fifteen-minute sessions
on five consecutive days.

"I want to warn you," he says on the fifth day, barely opening the
waiting room door. "I have new shoes."
"Okay. Thanks."
I trace my loop. He unrolls the paper.

"What does it mean that you have new shoes?"
"Just that my other ones got old."
"Do you remember everything we did when you were in them?"
"Different shoes don't make me forget, Barbara."
"Is everything else the same? Your socks?"
He lifts his cuff for me to see.
The same socks with the waffle weave.

33.

Five different ties. Five different shirts. Socks. Still, he lays no hand on me.

Even with my whole body right there, on the floor. Even with his new brown shoes.

> A neighbor on the far side of a lake sends food across
> the water.
> In a rowboat, a bundt cake wrapped in a jacquard towel.
> Love coming at me from across the lake. The bundt cake
> still warm.

34.

"I have something for you," he says, the paper stored once again, behind the couch. "It's a gift from your friend."

A pure white feather from the Great Egret.
"He was on our deck this morning. I saw the feather when he flew away."

At home, I find my slim-stitched book, and braid the feather in. Open the upstairs balcony door, and wait for the notes to come.

I vacuum. Dust. Change the sheets. All afternoon, nothing.

Then I hear his car. Then a single light comes on at Josephine's. I hear an oboe. Dennis warming up. Long tones and then a scale.

The notes come through my hedge.
Each note finds itself, becomes a smooth sphere, shaves off its frilly edge, its shadow, its fringe. Each note enters its own separate space.

I uncurl my legs. I am spiderless. Open the window. I have felt this before.

Inez smoothing powder on my skin. Mrs. Henderson fixing my barrette. Sleeping at Daniel's farm.

I am milk fed.
I don't want Dennis to stop.
Even though it's dusk.

35.

Darkness falls through the boughs of the tree like shame. Like humility. Like sisters. He begins to play an excerpt from Mozart's "Concerto for Oboe." The bottom of each note, round and dark as chocolate. The front edge of each note, clean as a knife blade.

I run downstairs, dial the phone, "Listen to this . . ." I hold the receiver to the window.

Lazarus walking, after he was dead. Jairus' daughter rising.
John the Beloved seeing Jesus in the flagrant light.

I carry the cello like a bandaged child out into the darkness. I sit
against the hedge and hold it as if it were the bakery girl, her long,
teenage legs. Together we listen.

He plays freely now, with joy, the notes, a rope. A cable passing
through the hedge.

> *Came a word, came,*
> *came through the night . . .*

>   *. . . it*
> *was hospitable, it*

> *did not cut in*

Eventually, she whispers in my ear.
"I see him!" she says. "He has butterflies in his hair."

36.

The moon moves behind the clouds, and Josephine's house is dark.
But his music is caught, still, in the spaces between the leaves.

There was a painting by Fra Angelico I saw in Italy. "The Annunciation," painted in Cell 3 of San Marco in Florence. The Angel
Gabriel standing on the left, Virgin Mary kneeling to the right. An
otherwise empty room, the empty walls.

Something I've never considered until now, until the Egret, until wrapping myself in white, Lazarus and my outline on the floor, this music coming through my hedge—

I always assumed that Gabriel came to Mary only once. But why? Why have I thought Mary consented that very first time he came through her walls?

I lean deeper into the leaves. Incline myself. The damp, the quiet of this night. Perhaps, instead, it was like this:

Mary's eyes closed, deep in prayer, in meditation. The drape of her dress on the kneeling board. Hands crossed over her breast. Or maybe, just reading. Or maybe even asleep. She did not invite him in.

Of course she was terrified. Of course she jumped back and gripped the wall. Threw books at him. Said "Don't ask such things of me! To carry a child, unwed. To risk death by stoning." And he, the difficult child, the unknown one. "No! Get out!"

Perhaps he left. Came back. The Angel Annunciate.

"Stop bothering me!" she might have said. Thinking, If I even listen to you, I will come undone. His light, his voice. As of another world. A world past sand and crow. Past the laundry drying in the tree.

Why did I think it was an easy thing? A moment of terror and then consent. How could it be? Years, years to do that work.

To look into an unknown world, past lake and market smell, the fish, their hammered heads, the thud, that sound of her father working, her mother, grinding almonds between stone, just so, that flick of water from her fingertip, that bit of oil. The paste. The angel leaving, coming again.

Perhaps he learned to make the sound of knocking, learned to wait until she said, "Come in," before he let go his celestial light. His nimbus brighter than the sun. Perhaps he learned to stay on the far side of the room, hands at his sides. His wing against the wall. They eyed their differences. All that lay between. So that, in time, she came to mark the distance on the floor between where he always stood and where she sat. Forty inches and three quarters. A new, unchanging, sacred space. In time, coming to know the shadow on the floor, cast from his light, to be her own. Many times into her room. Perhaps seventy times seven.

Years, years, trying to see how she was separate from her friends, the water in the well, the raven, her mother's hand, the dust on the stony ledge. Until she knew her own outline, how could she let another in? "Go! Get out of here!" And he, vacating through the wall. His trace, his feather, on the cold clay floor.

She put it in her basket with the others.

The first ones, when Gabriel was young and confident. Proud of his charge. Proud of his vocation. The cobalt blue, the radiating green of the wing. In those days, when his entrance lit up her room.

Now she barely notices when he is there. His gray wings, travel-worn and weary. The fatigue she sees in his eyes. His clumsiness. A jar knocked over by mistake. His wrinkled, callused feet. His tattered nimbus now a simple crown of fish.

Patient, the patient angel. His weathered wing. His mission not accomplished. His old age, his worry. Shame.

Among the angelic choir, silence when he passes by. The Crazy Angel, they call him, The One Who Doesn't Give Up. Gray winged, blue eyed. The gentle one. He waits long. Returning. Leaving again. His life that is no longer remarkable. Frayed. Dull.

Did she have a violation? A memory? A wound? A cave inside big enough to hold the problem child? What wound could this be?

Perhaps only when she remembered it, would there be room.

The day when her work was finished, long, since that first visit when she threw the books, she speaks to him. Knowing to speak louder than before. His diminished hearing, his eyes cloudy, the whites yellowed with age. "I have a ripped apart place," she tells him.

came, a word . . .

. . .

to the eye,
the moist one

"I am ready. I have enough room."

He raises his tired eyes. He spreads his wings, wide, against the wall. His nimbus fills with light.

"Behold," she instructs him. "See before you, the handmaid of the Lord."

37

Come,

music, through brick, where there is no door, through hedge
to my hearing, my seams, gashes, that are open, still. Come
to my eye, the moist one. Gabriel, with cobalt wing, come,
through green and wall and memory,
again and again, come,
until I am Egret-like.
Until I know all my wounds.
Shechinah. Come
to this dwelling place. Frighten me
with your good news.

MEMORIA EXCIDERE

On the way to the airport to pick up Josephine, Dolores Mary and Helene, I pass a man driving with his dog. He makes me uncomfortable, even nauseous. By the time he is out of view, my neck is sweaty and cold, a vision of his life sits in my stomach like a stone.

A man lives in the house he plays with his vipers

And the vision is this: He lives in a garage at the back of a lot behind a house. He eats sausage that he slices tissue-paper thin. He does this so he can slice it many times, liking the sound of metal against something soft. His entire life is composed of precise movements done at close range.

he whistles his hounds to come close

His short-haired dog lives under the car, and is allowed inside only when there is sausage. He peels off the casing one slice at a time, prolonging the act until the dog's mouth drips white with foam.

A mother with small children lives in the house. When the man's slacks are worn thin at the knee, he cuts them off and she hems them for him, making shorts. He doesn't care if, on black slacks, she uses olive green thread. He doesn't expect her to match the fabric, changing the spool. She instinctively feels this and mismatches thread intentionally, so that she can feel safe at the same time she feels kind.

He is not a religious person, but he also does not mind that the garage came with a Catholic calendar tacked to the wall. Above the pages torn off each month is an image of Jesus. His crown of thorns highlighted with florescent paint. When it is dark, the man likes to strike the flame of his lighter and hold it under the painting until the thorns light up, measuring exactly how close he has to bring the flame.

your goldenes Haar Margareta
your aschenes Haar Shulamith

On one single occasion he moved suddenly. A car was coming. The toddler who lives in the front house moved toward the street. The car would not have hit the child but it would have come close. He darted forward, grabbing the child into his arms. He gave the crying child back to its mother, not staying long enough to hear her words of thanks.

He thinks often of that day, deliberately reviewing each part of the scene with curiosity, as if someone else had done it.

he plays with his vipers and daydreams Death is ein Meister

2.

It is a relief to reach the airport, the terminal, the gate. To see the three of them suntanned, weary, their necks piled high with leis.

"I've missed you at Mass," Sister Dolores Mary says softly, squeezing my hand. Helene giggles like a schoolgirl then opens a box of chocolate-covered macadamia nuts and offers them to me, reaching over the seat. Their gaiety percolates the air like finches in a garden.

The car fills with the fragrances of chocolate and plumeria. Josephine sleeps, her head against the window, her eyelids as delicate as lace.

It occurs to me that if I lived in the Convent, surrounded by this air, its solid cheerfulness, its good will, all my bad memories would simply dissolve, unable to withstand this sweet carbonation. I try viewing my childhood in a positive way. I try doing this, in earnest, all the way home.

My father plays bakery with me and Cheryl.
He stops working on the garage, his mouth full of nails, he sets
his hammer on the cement walk next to us.
He admires our cupcakes and cookies.
Taking a handful of mud, he forms something new.
A loaf of bread.
With the back of his fingernail he carefully cuts a ridge
into the sides to indicate crust.

3.

It is too hard, pushing a river with my bare hands.

By the time we reach the Convent, my headache is severe.

"You've got a new hairdo," Dolores Mary says as I pull up to the curb.

"I like it," she adds, "I like short hair." But in the rearview mirror, I see Helene signaling Dolores to change the subject, shaking her head, covering her mouth with her hand.

"So why'd Barbara cut her hair?" my father asked when I was
four. My mother, trimming skin off chicken thighs, slammed the
butcher knife down against the wood.

"So you're a Pixie now," he addressed me, not seeing my mother
glare at his back. "I hear Inez fixed you up for school."

My mother washed her hands, left the kitchen, the screen
door banged. Holding, against her chest, her pipe organ shoes.
The sound of the Studebaker as she pulled away.

4.

Helene wants to show me something in the Convent. "It's a gift
from Monsignor for Dolores Mary's Jubilee!" She leads me to the
dining room, where a large tapestry now hangs on the wall. "Can
you even believe it?" she gasps.

I try to find something truthful to say. It is a very poor machine
reproduction, sterile, the nap not reflecting the work of a hand.

If I forget thee, O Jerusalem

All that was imperfect in the tapestry has been left behind.

"Oops! I almost forgot," Helene fumbles in her bag. "First things
first." She disappears down the hall, carrying a fresh orchid lei.
"This one's for St. Joseph," she calls back, over her shoulder. Dolores
Mary at the table, slumped in a chair. There is an exhausted empty
moment and she does not seem to care.

"Barbara . . . isn't this cute?" Dolores holds up a child size grass
skirt. "Its for Helene's new niece. Our little hula girl."

I want to be like them. But I'm not. Not at all.

If I forget thee, O Jerusalem
let my right hand forget her cunning

In this tapestry I see too clearly what memory has edited
out. This unicorn in his fencing has forgotten the glass of
wine spilled in a French cellar four hundred years ago when
the weaver with sore fingers just tied off her thread. In this
cloth there is no moaning. Sorrow lifted away.

Gone, too, the old monk in the belfry, his clumsy arthritic
hands, pulling the ropes in irregular rhythm. The stumbling
sound of church bells is not woven into these threads.

In the acanthus border, the original weaver must have hidden the fragrance that came through her high window.
From the field beyond the walls, the smell of newly broken
wheat.

"It's beautiful," I say to Dolores Mary, who touches my arm as she
gets up from her chair. The skin of her hand is as soft as moth dust.

5.

"I'm worried about Josephine," she whispers. "She didn't have her
usual 'Get up and go.'"
"I'll keep an eye on her," I say.
My heart sinks.

"You still look tired," Josephine scolds as I carry in her suitcases, line them next to the demilune table cluttered with lipsticks, crumpled store coupons, library books.

"It's that fancy doctor, isn't it? I've read about people like him. Hypnotizing people. Getting them to think things happened that never could."

I don't feel like this battle again.

"Shall I help you?" She looks surprised, not remembering I've done this before, ever since she came back from Turkey and refused to unpack. For weeks she wore a pair of black capris with hot pink trim and her hair turbaned in a hot pink towel.

"Let's have a drink instead." The small menorah in the kitchen stuffed with prescriptions she's never filled. "I'm pooped," she takes a large gulp of her scotch. "That Helene practically wakes up talking." She now keeps her scotch in the refrigerator, the bottles get larger, the brands cheaper, each year.

She props herself on the bed, Pretty Boy, her cockatiel, nuzzling at her neck.

"I saw some pretty little birds in Hawaya" she tells him, but he makes a halting flight to the dresser, barely making it, then stands next to the framed photo of Josephine in her thirties, a Portland socialite, the glistening waves of her marcelled hair.

One by one, I open her suitcases.

"Hang them out to air, Honey, please," she instructs. Dresses piled on the bed, blouses, caftans, swimming suits, skirts.

I haven't seen so much pigment in weeks. Orange next to royal blue. Metallic magenta. Sweatshirts with rhinestones. In an envelope of satin, a black negligee with rabbit fur trim.

"Get any use out of this?" I tease.

"I was with two nuns, Barbara!" she drinks heartily, nearly emptying the glass.

"I missed you," I sit next to her on the bed. Clothes everywhere, hanging from doors, the curtain rod, the light fixture overhead.

> We're in a tent of color and it feels just right. In her world and all she's survived. Her suffering, the white of it, bright colors surrounding the snow.

7.

"I almost forgot!" She jumps up, hands me a small object wrapped in tissue paper patterned like wood grain. "Your souvenir . . . ."

Carefully, slowly, I unwrap the paper, fold the string.

"Am I supposed to like this?" I laugh. "It's hideous!"

A frog playing a cello, the whole thing made of glued seashells.

"I've named him 'Le Saint du Mauvais Gout,'" she says proudly, "'the Patron Saint of Bad Taste!' He's perfect for you."

8.

I trace the walls but his hand is tapping the arm of his chair.

> Maybe I've come at a bad time.
> Maybe I shouldn't be here at all.

"Are you worried about something?"

"No," he looks up, a little surprised.

 His voice is monotone, flat and steel gray. My arms are
 freezing. I should go home. I know this sequence. He pre-
 tends things are normal, then, the next thing I know, he'll
 be pouring dirt on my face.

"I'm going to go now."

"I'm ready to work, Barbara." His voice is rising.

"But you're distracted. Something's wrong and you're not telling
me what it is."

"The work in here's about you, not me."

"But I can't work with you like this. You're not being square with
me."

I drive through the parking lot. The dumpster filled with asphalt
chunks. Torn up. Like us. It makes me cry. Every fucking thing
makes me cry.

I go back.
He lets me in.

"I am worried about something at home," he says as I pace.

"I'm not trying to be nosey. You just can't pretend you're one way
when you're feeling something else. You just can't pretend with me
at all."

"Maybe I was anxious to get into the session to get away from my
worry."

"But that's bad too."

"You're right."

"I never want to do that to a client. It wasn't a conscious decision."

"But that makes it even worse. My father was never conscious . . . "

"Go find the candle Barbara"
"Climb in that hole Barbara"

"When you're not conscious . . . it's the most dangerous of all. That's when the really horrible stuff happens."
"I wasn't as aware as I wish I'd been. I'm sorry."

"If you aren't conscious of your feelings, I can't do *any* work in here."
"I know."

He sits down near me on the rug.

Some precious and failed thing.
Bruised peaches on the ground.
Their broken skins.

9.

Next time I trace my loop, his eyes are red and already he's yawned.
"How are you?"
"Fine," he answers.
My neck tightens. I hold onto my purse.

"But I have a little post-nasal drip. I'm more tired than usual. And I'm hungry. And I'm feeling a bit relieved about the issue at home."

"Thanks for doing that." I sit down, relaxed.
"Anytime," he smiles.

Something comes in my sleep. A reticulation of detail like coral
against a haze of sea.

> *something came to stand*
> *which was with us once already, un-*
> *touched by thoughts*

I sit up. Something after the burial. Hold myself in.

> *he . . . steps out of doors . . .*
> *the stars are all sparkling*

Leaf curled tight against the worm. It comes anyway.

> *My father walks me up from the basement. Dirt in my*
> *underpants, my socks, my shoes. The house is dark and stuffy.*
> *"Go wash up." He points down the hall.*

> *In the bathroom mirror, only the top of my head shows,*
> *reflected back between the faucet and the handles. But*
> *my hair isn't blond, it's dark now like Cheryl's.*

> *I hear him washing in the kitchen sink, the water on full blast.*
> *He sings his Army song, "From the Halls of Montezuma." The*
> *splashing noise and the singing go on and on. I listen. I forget*
> *to wash myself.*

> *I smell his cigarette. He's leaning against the doorjamb.*
> *Arm cocked over his head. Smiling, joking.*
> *"Where've you been, you rascal?"*
> *He's in a clean t-shirt now, sleeves rolled high up on the arm.*

His tears are gone. And the flannel shirt that was against
my cheek.
"Where've you been?" he repeats, louder this time. He's not
joking anymore. The lines of grout around each tile stay
straight and white.

"Answer me!" he yells. The ashes of his cigarette become a
long column of gray. "How d'you get so dirty Barbara?"
His eyes are squinting, as if he's looking at me through
a fog. "Mud pies, right? You were making mud pies again,
right Barbara?"

He hits the jamb. Ashes fall to the floor.
"Answer me!"

His lips are white.

I look one last time at the girl in the mirror.
Her dark hair between the handles of the sink.

I will never look for her again.

"Yes Daddy." I say it. "I was making mud pies."

His jaw falls limp, color returns to his lips. He smiles.
His eyes focus on me. They lose their glaze.
He's not confused anymore.
I have my father back.

"Good for you then!"
He turns. His footsteps, light and carefree, down the hall.

11.

black milk of daybreak we drink it at evening we drink it at midday and morning we drink it at night we drink and we drink we shovel a grave in the air there you won't lie too cramped A man lives in the house he plays with his vipers he writes he writes when it grows dark to Deutschland your gold hair Margareta he writes it and steps out of door and the stars are all sparkling

I will never rise from this bed.

12.

Finally the sun.

*something came to stand
which was with us once already*

13.

"I can't be alone now."
"I have an opening in two hours."

*and they that wasted us
required mirth*

I hold his arm. We cross over the bridge.

"My father forgot that he buried me. As soon as he washed the dirt off his arms. As soon as he switched his shirt."

"I said I was making mud pies. But that wasn't true."

> *he commands us play up for the dance*
> *He shouts play death more sweetly*

I don't want to soften.
"I wasn't making mudpies. I lied. He made me just like himself!"

"He did not make you like himself, Barbara."

He shakes my shoulders. He looks me in the face.

"Listen to me, you said what you had to say to survive."

14.

The hour has no dimension. No clocks move.

"May I borrow the scissors? and some paper?"

He opens the desk drawer.
He hands me a pile of blank white sheets.

I sit on the floor, spread my legs, cut the white sheets into thin strips. Cut the strips again, making square bathroom tiles. Straight, the lines of grout.

"It's a fucking luxury to be so screwed up, you can bury your daughter and not even remember it."

I cut some more.

If I forget thee, O Jerusalem

I cut faster. Then faster still. The cold dirt.
The sun that didn't help.
The hole that no one ever saw.
I don't care about making strips neat anymore.
I run out of paper.
He gets more from his desk.
I cut through. He hands me sheets from the cabinet.
I need more.
He disappears. Returns with more paper from down the hall.
The buzzer goes off. I don't care about his other clients.

If I forget thee, O Jerusalem, let my right hand
forget her cunning

My hand hurts. He gives me more sheets.
The edges blur.
I cut until I cannot see.

O Jerusalem

I cry full out.

Past my hands, the tassels on his shoes, the table leg.
The carpet around me white like snow.

15.

I sit on the lawn, holding my book.

Salt.   Requiem.   Memory.   Wound.

The Morton Salt Girl loses salt from her box. She keeps walking. She does not look back.

16.

I trace my loop.
Outside, past the deck, the Great Egret wades in the water grass.

"I was on the twirl-around slide. My mother returned from her trip, bringing Cheryl and Georgie. I knew it was my job to keep them alive. But by the time they were home, I couldn't remember what the bad thing was. I just knew if I said the secret, they'd all be dead."

"Did your father say something would happen to them if you told?"

"When we walked up the cement pathway from the basement to the house he pointed to the Studebaker. It was new. He said if I told, the car would blow up with my mother and Cheryl and Georgie inside. He said he couldn't help it. It was just the way the new car worked."

"Can you put some language on all this for me? Some psychological terms . . . ?"

Quickly he gets up from his chair, opens books from the shelves.

He speaks softly. He shows me tables of contents, indexes, chapter titles.

abreaction   amnesia   dissociative disorder   multiplicity

"So, they have named it."
"Yes."

> A baby lies hidden in the rushes.
> Her basket is pitch-lined, watertight.
> She is safe. Hidden among the cranes.

By the rivers of Babylon where I lay weeping

With his kindness he holds me.

> A child in the rushes is found by a bather.
> He sees she is safe. Her basket lined
> with memory, like pitch.

something came to stand
which was with us once already

18.

I climb the stairs and go through my CDs
looking for one of the first.
A recording of Gregorian chant.
~~These living monks who let the larger world inside their walls.~~

I open the French doors. Let the music go out.
Their rough sound. Their imperfection.
They throw their voices to heaven
like so many white rags.

ARTES LIBERALES

I haven't seen his stationery in over a year. Crisp, clerical black, the Seminary symbol on the envelope's upper left-hand corner, and under it, his initials penned in ink, as if, otherwise, I wouldn't know the letter was from him.

Father Paul, Chairman of the Department, writes to ask me for a decision. I'm sure that's what this is. But I don't have one. When I left I didn't know days would become weeks and those would turn into months. This tunnel has no numbers marking its walls.

I do not open it. What would I teach? I would cut, by mistake, the Seminarians' zeal, the families pinning hopes onto their shoulders, wanting a son ordained, the prize.

> *There was earth inside them, and*
> *. . . they did not praise God*

I am best here, on my Patmos island. Spider and sea urchin, needle and thread.

All the prophets saw too much. All the prophets were broken-hearted.

2.

I set the unopened envelope under a candlestick. Then on the kitchen table, then in my prayer room, empty, black. Finally, I put it out of the house completely. Tape it behind the plaque on the garden wall. Cherubs harvesting grain, the hopeful plaque, the one for Fall.

3.

The moon is one day past full. Casting shadows around my undraped room. I can't sleep. I put on my robe.

The brick walk is cool under my feet. This garden where my life is written.
A libretto in the leaves.

I reach behind the plaque, open the seal.

> Dear Barbara,
>
> Thought you'd enjoy this. I can't make it. Marquette's invited me for another lecture. Tell me your plans when you know them. The fellas miss you. Rosemary sends greetings. Also Fr. Bernard.
>
> > Pax,
> > Fr. Paul

He's enclosed a holy card with an Ignatian prayer, and, in the same used rubber band, a concert ticket for Anner Bylsma, here, in just three weeks.
I know the auditorium well. Small and intimate, perfect for his Baroque cello, the warmer sound of its gut strings. He'll cradle it in the soles of his shoes, its pear-like body, its wide, arched bow. He'll make the wooden body breathe. Fill the room with sound, rich as honey from a ridged wood spoon.

I sleep well, Father Paul's letter by my bed.

loose spices, the sound of nuts stirred into cookie batter with a wooden spoon, the smell of freesia, all tractors, mother of pearl handles on chased silverware, slim pocket knives, wood cabinetry inside ships when the grain runs horizontally and is well varnished, hat boxes with twisted satin cords, solo English horn playing an exposed part in a symphonic setting, green hospital garb worn outside hospitals, window washers on scaffolding high on office buildings when viewed from an adjacent office building at the same height, escalators in department stores during Christmas, national conventions viewed on t.v., wildlife documentaries, environmental activists who go door to door in winter, gypsum, Florentine paper, simple bold cuff links, men who whistle when they trim trees, clocks that chime in jewelry stores, cafés in art museums that border on gardens, blank sheets of paper stacked on a desk, sharpened pencils in a jar when all the same length, candlelight reflecting off cut crystal vases holding only greens, jacks with a good rubber ball that has no seam, martini glasses with thin rims, wooden clothespins, the smell of vanilla bean cooking in cream, dolphin swimming in the ocean in pods, small black and white televisions, wisteria when bare, fires in fireplaces when seen through mesh screen, homemade dolls, black Smith Corona typewriters, women in heels walking standard poodles on a rainy boulevard, wedding cakes, PowerLock tape measures, wooden stepladders in gardens when stained with paint drips, headless mannequins with muslin-covered torsos when empty, room service, towels in a hotel warmed on a warming bar next to a bath, houses in the framing stage of construction, fresh figs sliced in half with cream, puppies being born, fish tanks with tropical fish when lit at night in a dark room, cement sidewalks with glitter

9

"I think you can go to the concert Barbara. You just need to prepare. Start with something a little easier."

"Easier than a coffee shop in broad daylight?"

"Go somewhere with someone you know. A place you enjoy."

"Are you giving me homework?"

"With some clients, you go around, kick the tires, hoping the car
will start. With you, it's like jumping on a moving train."

I call the Convent hoping to reach Sister Dolores Mary. Sister
Helene answers instead. She says she has never been to an art
museum in Los Angeles. I can't believe it. Not in thirty years.

10

Helene and I are stand in front of George de la Tour's "Magdalen
with the Smoking Flame." Mary Magdalen sits, staring at a candle on
the table surrounded by the symbols of a penitent. Rope belt, skull.

"Ooh," Helene whispers, "the skull! I always dreamed of being a
painter."

"What happened?"

"My parents wanted one of us to enter religious life. Agnes, Joan
and Mary Louise had all married. That left only me."

"Is that why you never go to art museums? The pain . . . ?"

"Oh no," she laughs, her voice, suddenly a high nervous pitch. "I'm
just so busy with the school. I don't regret it at all. Not one bit."

There was earth inside them, and
. . . they did not praise God

II

A gash is covered. Still, the fluid seeps through.

"You never just get to work," my mother said, and I thought, She's
right. I spend most of the time moving objects on my desk, lining my
tooth-marked pencils into a straight row. She knew I had a term paper
due in three weeks.

"Why don't you do it on the Italian Renaissance? You could write to
the museums. The Met. The National Gallery. Get postcards. Prints.
You'd get an A for sure!" I didn't know what she wanted from me
then. It was not about homework. It was never about homework.
I always got straight A's.

Lingering at my bedroom door. Her hip, lazy, against the wall.
Stroking the back of her hair as if it belonged to someone else. My
stomach hurt having her so close, having her be so still. Leaning into
my room in an odd, languid way. She was different since Cheryl left
and my turn was coming. Applications to Stanford, Radcliffe,
Berkeley on my desk.

"Come here," she invited me out to the hallway. I couldn't remember
ever being summoned like that before, as if into pleasantness.

She pulled a small volume from the bookcase in the hall. Emerald green and slim enough to have hidden all this time next to the Encyclopedia Britannica, and not be noticed.

She curled up on the hallway rug, gesturing for me to come down and join her. The pink beige carpet beneath us, sculpted like sea shells. We faced each other, head to head over the book. I saw, for the first time, the gray hairs scattered in her brown.

The book was bound in yellow thread, visible at the ends of the worn spine. A textbook from college, she said, fingering the pages fondly, drawing the book closer to herself, so that it came under her breast. The images on the pages became impossible for me to see.

"Michelangelo," "Raphael," "da Vinci." She relinquished the names one by one as if passing on secrets, precious stones, as if, in doing this, she was feeling her way, reminding herself where she had been, checking her compass, her moorings. As if slowly unwrapping a bandage from her forearm, the long white strip.

I began to see the wound through the layers of gauze. A college class-room, an art history professor, completely unlike my father. Like the men in the Alumni Magazine that came each month. The only mail that was just for her. Hiding it before he came home.

She showed Cheryl and me the photographs. Women faculty, the female College President. Through a library window, younger women, like us, some in pairs, holding hands, clutching books to their sweaters. Mustard-seed necklaces, plaid skirts, penny loafers. One wrote a poem under a tree.

She unwrapped the gauze, and in the red, fresh wound, I heard the last chords of her senior recital. The sound of taffeta when she pushed back the piano bench for the last time in public. "The heart drugs make her crazy," her older brother might have said, pressing the steering wheel home. The only one in the family who could drive. The college just a few miles down the interstate, but her mother unable to attend. The illness in its fourteenth year. Bed-bound and drugged. Her dementia floating on the hat racks like chiffon. Saving all my mother's college letters, tied in purple string. Her final act of order.

"Renaissance means rebirth," my mother's voice flattened. A longing spilling out of her like fluid, her hands spotted and wrinkled on the porcelain page.

Then we did not speak. The silence was long as she drifted further away. Down a stream sorry with minnows.

I could see how she liked to feel it. A fish, caught, wanting to be removed from the water. Wanting to feel the pain. To flap on the hot splintered slats of a boat, beside life preservers, an open tackle box, a net.

"What did you say, Barbara?" she suddenly jumped to her feet. What she meant was, What are you doing here, Barbara? Who said you could look?

Before I got to my feet, she was in the kitchen slamming the dryer door, having pushed the emerald book toward me with her shoe, a useless thing.

She knew I saw the brightness. The notes inside the gash. Fresh. Fresh, the red. The wound that, covered, does not heal.

12.

Time, on its own, heals nothing.

13.

"Let's eat. I'm starved," Helene says, and we walk to the tea room, empty at this early hour. As I unfold my napkin, I catch her glance at my bare palms. I know she wants blood there, a scab, an oozing. I see her disappointment. I'm too ordinary for her world.

"May I ask you something personal, Barbara?"
"Sure."
"Was it something you saw in the Convent yard? A vision? A voice? Is that why you cut your hair?"
"It was nothing like that." She frowns.

"The elevator broke down at work and I was stuck inside, alone, for a very long time. It was very, very dark."
"Oh no," she looks to the tables on either side.

"I panicked."
"Of course you did."
"Then I began to remember horrible things."
"Like what?" her eyes widen.

"I remembered being buried by my father."
Her fork, motionless in the air.

"Jesus, Mary and Joseph," she sighs.

I throw a fish back into the lake.
It swims away from me.
Faster than before.

"Did you know Sister Dolores Mary has to have night lights on in every room of the Convent?" she speaks rapidly, in a hushed voice, her enthusiasm renewed.

"No. I didn't know that."

"She had something like you, only it was her cousin."

"You don't have to tell me the details, Helene."

"He took her into the cellar, after the man delivered coal. He touched her. It was completely dark."

I feel sad and wordless. I want to be alone.

Helene leans further in.

"You won't tell Sister, will you?"

"I won't tell."

"It's a secret. I swore on the Blood of . . . "

"I won't say anything, Helene."

14.

Dolores Mary is nearly seventy years old. For half a century, she's had night lights burning in every room.

15.

Like the host carried in a flat gold pyx.
The pyx wrapped in a linen cloth.
The cloth slipped in the pyx bag.
The pyx bag on a cord, around the priest's neck.

This is the way the Sacred Body enters the world.
Hidden in a pyx.

This is the way pain travels.
Hidden. Covered. Sealed.

16.

A stone covered by a handkerchief gets wet in the rain.
Water seeps through the weave of the finest Irish linen.
The stone, hard and stubborn, keeps its original curve and weight.

Only a lifting of the corporal dries the stone.
Only opening the pyx.

17.

It is a relief to see Daniel's fast dashed handwriting on an envelope when I get home.

This time the postcard is filled with roses. The garden of a Mrs. Close-Smith, boasting old roses, some collected at Malmaison by Empress Josephine.

Dear B.

Caterpillar, mildew, black spot—blooms don't outweigh
the thorns and work if you ask me. Speaking of which
—my boss is an absolute ass. Thinking of taking Emily
to Paris. Cézanne exhibit—best in 50 yrs. they say.
I've been trying to picture you with short hair. Send me
a photo.
I bet you look great.

D.

I definitely do not look great. A sheep rough shorn.
I set the postcard of roses on the mantel with the others.

18.

Josephine says she's invited Father Dennis for dinner to thank him
for caring for her property while she was gone.
"So, Barbara, will you come?"
"Yes," I say, before I realize what I've done.

19.

Josephine answers the door, dressed in a more exotic style than
usual. Her gypsy blouse brought down off each shoulder, through the
sheer cloth, the pleated skin of her upper arms. A cross heavy with

rose quartz hangs between her deeply exposed breasts. On her left hand, a turquoise ring that stretches from knuckle to knuckle. Her multicolored skirt, ruffled and trimmed with orange rickrack.

She's elaborately assembled. Her eyeliner dramatically drawn out toward the temple, her lipstick a fine Kahlo red.

"It's Cinco de Mayo, Barbara," she says, perturbed. "Don't look so confused."

She hands me tortilla chips and salsa. "Could you arrange these for me, and set the platter over there?" She points to a side table over which she's hung the immense framed photograph of Poncho Villa, usually stored in her garage.

Under Pancho Villa, a statue of the Buddha storing rubber bands on the finger of his upturned hand. A book on Chinese erotic art with pages marked, a collection of Navajo pots, travel magazines stacked against the windows.

"Come see this, it's my secret with Sister Helene." She leads me to the spare bedroom, which has been transformed, shows me a new glass beaded lamp in which she's put a soft pink bulb. Scarves are draped over the other lampshades, and the velvet curtains are drawn. On the coffee table is a Ouija board. I haven't seen one in years.

"Do you believe in past lives, Barbara?"

Under the chair, a stack of library books on Edgar Cayce, and some general texts on the occult.

"For me, one life's more than enough."

With Josephine, always something new.

"Please don't suggest Dennis and I play duets together," I say loudly, over the noise of the blender as she prepares the margaritas.

"You haven't practiced in months. I know better. . . . " She dips the rims of the glasses in a saucer of salt.

"My cello's gone, Josephine."

"What?" she hollers.

"I broke it. Last Fall."

The doorbell rings.

Quickly she unties her apron, appliquéd with black sombreros.

"That was a stupid thing to do, Barbara," she calls over her shoulder, walking to the door.

20.

"I saw you my first day here, I think," Father Dennis says, looking at me quizzically, above a broad smile. "But you look different now. I can't tell what it is."

"It's her hair, Father. She cut off all her gorgeous auburn hair."

21.

"I heard your playing the other night," I say.

So short lived, so kingly too

"It was late."

"Yes," he looks directly at me, not apologizing for the late hour, or for his sound, or for anything at all.

"The watery sound . . . is that why you picked the oboe?"

Cranes feed in the reeds.
Freshwater fish.
Safety of a basket, pitch-lined.
In it the child sleeps.

"No," he laughs. "I got handed one in Junior High when the orchestra had too many clarinets."

Josephine brings in the coffee, saucers clattering on the tray.
"I don't think I've ever seen you at Mass, though, is that right?"
"Monsignor leaves a bit to be desired," Josephine chimes in, rescuing me.

> Does he know of Josephine's long-standing feud with Monsignor Kilmartin? That, of her vast estate, she'll leave nothing to this parish? Giving it all to The Propagation of the Faith? Has he noticed how she conducts her battle with him every day at the 5 o'clock, refusing the reforms of Vatican II, insisting that he place the host directly on her tongue, and in that small act, asserting her age and wealth over his meager stability?

But Dennis stares at me instead, waiting for an answer. I take Celan to heart.

> *Speak—*
> *But don't split off No from Yes.*
> *Give your say this meaning too:*
> *Give it the shadow*

"If the Church fails to address pain," I look up from the table, "then it is useless to me."

"You attend another Parish then?" he persists, after the coffee is poured and the cake is sliced. His curiosity seems genuine. The way a toy horn sitting on a tabletop is not hard to understand. Bored, Josephine stares out the window.

"These days I don't go to Church at all."

> The silence complicates itself. A zookeeper opens an aviary door. Birds fly in every direction. Even the tropical birds, nesting, vivid orange against the green.

"You probably know more about this than I do," he smiles, "but I like this story."

Josephine revives, sitting taller in her chair, chest out, eyes opened extra wide, affecting the eagerness of a child. Dennis begins.

"The founder of Hassidic Judaism asked a tailor why he had stayed home on Yom Kippur. The tailor had said to God, 'I have committed sins, but only a few minor offenses. But You! Look what You have done! Abandoned Your people. So, let's just call it even.'

"To which the Rabbi replied, 'Why did you let Him off so easily? With that argument you could have forced Him to redeem all of Israel.'"

"I don't get it," Josephine sulks.

"He was saying," Dennis speaks kindly to her, without condescension, "that God can be found in anger."

> Dennis and I stare at each other.

We are now two people out
from behind walls.

Count the almonds,
count what was bitter and kept you awake

23.

"I brought you something small from the art museum. I went with
Sister Helene."
"Oh?" He unwraps the small gift.

"It's just a paper bookmark."

Monet's water lilies, and on the back, words he said a few
months ago.
"Thank you," he smiles and turns it over to read.

I had asked, "How do you find peace?" And he said
"I find refuge in the present."

"It's not an easy thing getting into the present."
"That's the work you're doing. It's hard."

Only there did you wholly enter the name that is yours
sure-footed, stepped into yourself

This is my goal: that my memories become like Monet's
water lilies. Soft brushstrokes and bold. Ivory, pink, and
a hundred shades of blameless blue.

At home, I open my Van der Weyden book to his triptych, "Crucifixion."

I want to see the young woman on the left-hand panel. Veronica, named for the image on her cloth: "verus" "iconicus," "true" "image." Original icon, face of Jesus on the white, parent to all subsequent icons.

Why did Van der Weyden assume she was grateful for this? Why, always, have I? Not everyone is like Sister Helene, wanting the supernatural.

Perhaps, instead it went like this:

Taking wide strides, she walks through the crowd on her way to the dye shop. Clean white cotton squares in her pockets, she and her mother will select the right color for her special dress. Ochre? Vermilion? They'll dye the corners, make samples, take them home. Four weeks until her boyfriend returns from the Roman Army, conscripted when they were in sweet time.

Through the commotion on the street, she sees another condemned man, another cross. It annoys her. Executions becoming common. But this man staggers. She feels sorry for him. An issue of sweat like blood falls from his face. "Be careful!" her mother cautions, as her daughter moves closer toward him. She does not want to be seen in public so close to a criminal. Her husband, a traitor, buried outside the walls, and, still, the shadow of his shame.

The young woman takes one of the rags, thinking, I have many, and puts it against his face. A soldier whistling, jibing at her beauty. Used to such attention, with her other hand, she obscenely gestures back. "We're late!" her mother scolds, pulling back her daughter's arm.

The dye woman has pigments boiling in pots. One by one, they dip them in, stirring with a stick. But this time the young woman gasps, stuffs the rag quickly into her pocket, excuses herself, runs to the backyard, the dye woman's children playing in the grass. Turning her back on them, she unfolds the cloth, rubs it on a stone. The children watch from a distance, laughing, then return to their game. She folds it away.

The next day, she takes the cloth to her father's grave, lays it open there, flat, hoping the full day sun will bleach out the face. Nothing alters. She wraps it with artichoke and thistle down.

Returning home, she sees her mother in the distance, running out to meet her, waving her arms, calling out her name. There is bad news. Her boyfriend has been killed. His hand returned, cut off at the wrist.

"Come back!" her mother screams. The young woman turns with her bundle, running back through the city gate, running to the death hill. The criminal hanging there. The one she touched.

"It's not your face I want!" she throws the bundle down, artichoke rolling in the sand, she smashes it with her foot. "I don't want your face! I want his!"

Women carry her home. One picks up a rag blown against the stone, falls silent, folds it into her sleeve. The man hanging from the cross, the final one, is dead. In low tones, she speaks solemnly to the young woman's mother. "We must rename this girl," she shows her the cloth. "She must be called Veronica from now on."

They mount the cloth under glass. They set precious stones, candles, oil, flowers, herbs. Pilgrims come. Veronica does not care.

Thinks, This has nothing to do with me. She does not want a miracle. She wants her boyfriend to have found her beautiful in her new bridal dress.

So short lived, so kingly too

25.

Only four days until the concert. I must find the things, delicate and personal, to put against my skin. Textures, scents, fluent combinations.

At the back of my dresser drawer, evening bras and lingerie. Patterns of lace on satin. Black evening hose, silkier, more sheer.

Wrapped in a scarf, my evening purse, soft leather-lined suede. My best earrings, diamond in platinum, pretty against the angle of my newly exposed cheek.

> *"Always buy unlined gloves, and always a half-size smaller than your hand," Josephine coached when I was going with Daniel to New York. "It's the only way a woman from Los Angeles can look intelligent."*
> *Daniel replied, "Barbara always looks intelligent, Josephine."*

I rinse my slip in perfumed water, air it outside on the branch of the juniper tree. Pick my coat up from the cleaners. Iron my grandmother's handkerchief for my purse. My enameled English compact, the matching pillbox. It's been a long time since I've dressed.

A ticket stub from "La Bohème" inside the purse.

> *Daniel in his new suit, his finger stroking my collarbone, my ear.*

Nothing about us was failing. Only for the lovers on the stage.
And they had their music.

26.

"This is what I'm going to wear," I say, showing him the dress. "It has no sleeves."

"I see that."

"All my evening dresses are this way."

"And . . . ?"

"My arms and legs and head will show. Like five starfish points."

"Barbara, no one will see a starfish. You can trust me on this."

"Do you promise?"

"I promise."

I empty the other bag that I've brought. All my solo cello CDs. Fifty-seven in all.

"This is hard."

"Yes," he nods.

Open-, open-, open the pyx.

Only there did you enter the name that is yours,
sure-footed stepped into yourself

the listened for reached you

"Pick one," I say. "They're all the same to me, right now. They're all painful."

"You've mentioned the Bach Suites."

"Good choice," I smile.

He picks a recording by Yo-Yo Ma.
We play the opening of Suite No. 1.
"Let's stop. I'm overwhelmed."

We sit.

27.

"You can always call me."

"And I can always leave."

"That's right," he smiles.

"Remember your friend," he points to the photo I gave him of the Great Egret leaning on his desk against the lamp.

> For an hour he stood, shaking, staring at the fish.
> And caught nothing.
>
> But there he is, strong and upright.
> His wings, his long neck, the slight ruffle of his silhouette against the green.

DELECTATIO

I'm an hour early. The night is dark and cold. The doors of the hall are locked, but inside the lobby lights are on and ushers are busily stacking programs.

Five cello strings coiled in my coat pocket, I feel them through my glove.

In case I forget his emergency number, his card inside my bra.

2.

"When will the hall open?" I ask the guard when he comes down to the outside stairs.

"Fifteen minutes." His Vietnamese accent is thick, looking at his watch. On the street a taxi approaches. I can see only the passenger's white hair, perhaps a grandmother taking herself out for the night. Odd, though, that she sits in the front seat instead of the back.

When the cab stops, the passenger, a very tall man, steps out. He opens the rear door of the cab and lifts a cello case from the back. It is not a grandmother at all. It is Anner Bylsma.

3.

He walks directly up the stairs to the front gate where I'm standing, and gestures to the guard to be let in.

"Fifteen minutes," the guard responds with the same firmness.

"You don't understand," I interrupt. "This is Anner Bylsma!" The guard gives me an indifferent look. Perhaps he doesn't really understand English. Perhaps I spoke too fast.

"Fifteen minutes," he repeats.

"Well, fifteen minutes is not a lifetime, is it?" Mr. Bylsma says to me, smiling at this absurdity, in a jovial way, as if the world must contain such moments. As if the world demands absurdity as part of its beauty.

I feel, at once, completely comfortable. Without veneer.

Without anything to hide.

"You've come for the concert?"

"Yes. I heard you last year at UCLA."

"Oh, good. That's good."

He speaks quickly, words coming straight and fast, like the dash of a mouse across a floor. The guard, looking at his watch, reluctantly opens the gate. But only for Mr. Bylsma. His green uniformed arm held out across me. As if I would storm into a fortress.

"She's with me," Anner Bylsma says to the guard in a decisive tone, propping the gate open wider with his leg, so that I enter in, ahead of him.

"Come along," he walks briskly, full stride, toward the hall. In my high heels, I can barely keep up.

"Do you play the cello?"

"No. I love it though. Especially the Bach Suites."

"Oh? And which is your favorite?"

"The First."

"Of course," he nods, opening the lobby door.

"It's never too late to start," he says half distracted, looking for the green room. "But you don't start with the Bach Suites. Something a little simpler."

He nods for me to go ahead, past the thick curtains, onto the stage. "I'm going to rehearse now." He sets down his case.

"Would you mind . . . Do you think . . . May I watch you rehearse . . . if I sit where you won't have to see me?" He smiles, quickly lifting the cello out of its case, with deep familiarity, a feather lifted from the sand.

"Why wouldn't I want to see you?" With the bow he points to the auditorium, the front center seat, tightening the strings.

Playing a few notes, he calls down to me from the stage.
"How's the sound?"
"Dry."
"Anner, it's fine from here," a voice comes from the back of the dark hall. A man walks briskly toward the stage, apologizes that the lights aren't set. He cocks his head in my direction, as if to ask Anner Bylsma who I am.

"We were stuck at the gate together."
"What gate?" the man wants to know. Bylsma ignores the question and starts to play in, clearly, a random way. He stops as soon as the man has left and, resting the bow on his knee, leans from the chair in my direction.

"You must excuse my friend. He's always a little rude to me when we first meet."

4.

Head forward, long white hair falling over his face, he begins to play, but now in a real and serious manner. Now it is the opening bars of the First Bach Suite. I didn't realize this was on the program for tonight. I open the page to make sure. No. It is not on this program at all. He is playing it for me.

I close my eyes and settle into his journey. I follow his own personal interpretation. Very slight instances of judgment. More vibrato here, less there, minuscule changes. Departing from his own recordings, because it is now, this moment, and this music is entirely new.

As if the music is the body of a woman he knows well, a lover, and yet he shows me that he discovers her again. Almost lost in the looking, almost forgetting her body as a whole. So taken by this exact anklebone, the calf, the knee, the thigh. His ear on the soft plane of her stomach, the valley between hip bones. Just that portion of skin, that tissue, this indentation, under the fingertip, this curve. Then the pale skin of an inner arm. It goes on and on, the notes, one by one, an intimate exploration. And when he is finished, I am out of breath.

> *Only there did you enter the name that is yours,*
> *sure-footed stepped into yourself*
>
> *. . . the listened for reached you.*

"I have to dress now," he says, as the guard comes in to usher me out.

The lobby full of ticket holders, ready to take their seats.

On stage, behind the curtain as I look back, he pulls some white cloth from the cello case. I take it to be a dusting rag. He shakes it out and tosses it over the chair. Then I see in it, the completely crumpled pleats of a tuxedo shirt.

5.

Throughout the performance, I listen for each variation in tempo, in phrasing. Each new, slight choice. Like the Great Egret. Within the disciplined framework. Celan was right.

> *To stand in the shadow*
> *of the scar*
>
> *. . .*
>
> *with all there is room for in that,*
> *even without*
> *language*

6.

During the applause, when the music has stopped, a sequence repeats inside my head:

> *. . . She's with me . . . It's never too late to start . . . You must*
> *excuse my friend . . . Why wouldn't I want to see you? . . .*
> *How is it found? . . . The thread of uprightness? . . . To stand*
> *in the shadow of the scar . . . the name that is yours . . .*

7.

The audience is invited to a reception in the lobby, hosted by the Dutch Embassy. Though I never attend this kind of thing, I find myself

in the restroom, re-doing my lipstick, spraying perfume on my wrists.
I feel like a thoroughbred. Racing ahead. I can jump over trees.

8.

He looks exhilarated and tired, his shirt collar unbuttoned, a glass
of wine in his hand. It is nice to watch him, gracious to each person.
One student asks him why he played differently tonight than on his
recording. His companion, another student, speaks Dutch, and, learning this, Bylsma begins a long story that ends with a joke. Everyone
laughs heartily, the young man explaining in English to his friend.

Three men, all tall and blond and middle-aged, surround Bylsma.
I presume they're from the Embassy. Soon, they are laughing loudly
too, glasses held high in the air.

psalmhoofed, singing across

I'm not sure what to do. But then, in the middle of the laughter,
Bylsma excuses himself, bowing slightly, and walks across the room
to me.

"May I get you a glass of wine?"

open-, open-, open-

He lives in a world much larger world than mine. A world with a
great amount of light. I want to step in, my shoe on the threshold.

Only there did you enter the name that is yours

"I'm sorry, but I can't stay." I regret the words as soon as they come out.

"Well . . . "
He looks very closely at me.

"But thank you," he draws nearer, bending his head toward me, "for the wonderful concert. And for letting me hear you rehearse."
He puts his hand on my shoulder.
"I feel very indebted," I say into his ear. "I wish there were some way I could repay you."

He steps back, dropping his arms to his sides, in surprise.
"You've already repaid me!" he smiles broadly. "You came!"

9.

I sleep without undressing. My makeup, even my shoes.
The pleasure of this evening in the fabric of my clothes.

psalm-hoofed, singing

Should I have asked him for his autograph?
Yes. I'll never see him again.
No. Our contact was too personal.
Yes. Then I could see how he shapes his letters,
the spaces in between.
No. It was already more personal than that.
Deus Gloria!
No. Definitely No.

LATERE

Josephine pours me tea with her rice paper hands, careful to put a silver spoon in the cup first, to conduct the heat. I don't use a silver spoon at my house when I serve tea, and my cups don't break. Different houses have their own rules. Private and hidden, in the upholstery, the drapes.

All of the scarves on her lampshades are gone and she's returned the Edgar Cayce books to the library. Her restlessness feels fundamental, a kind of description of the basic human predicament.

"Did you go to your doctor's appointment?" I ask.

"No," she pops a cookie into her mouth. "I didn't know what to wear."

It's the end of May and we're having our annual Mother's Day lunch. Always a few weeks after the holiday, after, in our own ways, we've each made it through. For each of us, it is a weakening.

"At least in Canada they don't have the damn thing," she said years ago when we first began our tradition, and I thought she was wrong about Canada. I thought they observed the same holiday. But it didn't matter. What was true then and still is: Josephine's had three divorces, no children, and repairs, with tape, the tattered pro-choice sticker on the bumper of her Thunderbird.

"I picked up some nice crab salad," she invited me yesterday.

"He was wonderful," I say of Anner Bylsma, taking my seat at her large dining room table, crocheted place mats she's starched stiff on her drying rack. A large centerpiece of plastic flowers in a footed sterling silver tureen. "His playing, I mean."

"And how old is he? You should have had a drink with him.

Driven him to the airport. He doesn't travel with a driver? You said he arrived in that taxi . . . ."

Maybe she's right. He could practice in my garden when he comes to L.A.

"Where's he tonight? You should go to the concert. He'd remember you. You're memorable Barbara."

"I'm sure he's married, Josephine."

"What if he is married?"

"Josephine."

"Don't be so old-fashioned. Here, let's look," she leaves the table and pulls the newspaper from under the upholstered ottoman in the living room, its long black silk fringe. "Oh, did you see this?" she smoothes the front page next to my plate. "Here's one woman who should've been sterilized, if you ask me!"

The headline reads, "Mother Throws Two Sons Over Bridge. Jumps in Herself."

I skim the first lines, not wanting any of it. Despite my trying, details come through my net. Infant and toddler thrown into the Los Angeles River. Broad daylight. Witnesses. Infant died in the water. The three-year-old and the mother saved by a rescue team in a boat.

Josephine butters her roll.

"Why did you show me this?"

> *I'm in first grade. Mrs. Pinney is asking me about my drawing and I can't answer her.*

The fatty smell of mayonnaise, crab, the ticking of the clock. I'm losing hold.

"I thought by now you'd be reading the papers again. You used to be such a fanatic. Cutting out all those stories. Why are you looking at me like that?"

"I'm not reading the papers. Maybe I never will."

"It's just an awful story for God's sake. Besides," her tone is defiant now, "Helene said you thought your father buried you. Nothing about your mother, though. I mean, of course I asked a few questions. When we did the Ouija board . . . "

Oh great.

". . . besides this was all over the t.v."

"I don't watch television."

"Okay, okay, have a fit. So I forgot about you and television. God knows . . . "

"Where is the toddler?"

"Hospitalized, I imagine. They showed the mother in handcuffs. She'll never get near him again. He'll be fine."

"He won't be fine, Josephine."

Where is my purse, my damn Kleenex?

Josephine hands me her napkin. I wipe my eyes.

"Rescues don't work, Josephine. They never do. No one ever sees anything."

"He's alive, Barbara. You're forgetting that." She comes to my side of the table, sets the newspaper on the floor. "Honey, you're a mess," her voice softens. "Now remember, too, he'll get more attention over this than a lot of kids do."

"The kid's fucked up for life, Josephine."

"Well, I'm more worried about you right now. You don't make sense anymore. Your hair. You don't eat. You give me eighteen pairs of shoes. How can the Altar Society make quilts from shoes? And then all those empty paint cans on the curb awhile back and no painter's truck. I didn't see a painter's truck . . . ."

"His baby brother died right there in the river. To see your baby brother and not be able to help . . . "

"Your brother's a grown man, Barbara." Her voice is stern.

> *Joseph was sold for a servant . . .*
> *his feet*
> *laid in iron*

She strokes my hair, lifting the stubby bangs off my forehead.

"Now listen . . . You're just overdoing it . . . The night Henry passed, he looked just like a baby, all that silver hair gone with the chemo. I just lay next to him, right in that hospital bed. I lay there until all those signals on the machines just finally stopped."

> Tenderness.
> Dew in the crook of a camellia leaf.

"There was nothing I could do, is what I'm getting at. You've got to accept certain things, Barbara. You always take the hard way. You probably always will."

"It isn't the death, Josephine. It's the cruelty."

"What's the difference?"

"The difference is everything to me."

> *That swift. Three robberies in a single moment.*
> *Georgie, the water, the green shower tile.*

> *The three of us in the basement's stall shower.*
> *My face tight against my father's back.*
> *Georgie crying, on the other side.*
> *I can only see his thin legs between my father's.*
> *Hear him coughing, spitting, crying, coughing again.*

Three robberies bound like a sheaf.
And the water coming down.
Unable to make us clean.

We clear the dishes. Pretty Boy is singing in his cage.
"I love you Josephine."
"I know Sweetie." We hug at the door.

2.

Grain left on the field. Who picks it up?
Where is Boaz? Where is Ruth?
Where is the *songfast pennant?*

3.

"I'm glad you called," he says.
"A mother threw her boys over the bridge."
"I know."
"One died already."
"Yes."
"The toddler probably tried to save his brother."
"Yes. He probably did."

I am eaten by black birds. Crows.
They eat me and my kernelled corn.

Everything needs redemption.

4.

I don't want another moon. Moonlight failed me that night we climbed up from the basement shower. My father, Georgie, then me on the narrow outdoor stairs.

> *Blue light from the moon touched my father's hair.*
> *Rolled edge of my nightgown against the round ends*
> *of my shoes.*
> *Brown leather a lighter color at the scuff marks.*
> *I memorized it: shoes, scuff marks, rolled blue nylon edge.*
> *And thought, Stupid moonlight, going on my father's hair as if*
> *he deserves it. Too afraid to come into the shower. Too afraid to*
> *help Georgie. Staying out here with these birds and trees.*
> *Stupid moonlight. Can't even see that I'm a dead girl. Can't*
> *even see that the only thing working about me is my shoes.*
> *Stupid moonlight. More stupid than me.*
> *I don't even know how to read yet, like Cheryl, but I know this:*
> *My father shouldn't have moonlight on his hair as if he were*
> *good like Georgie.*

5.

I bring Anner Bylsma's concert program with me to bed. I do not sleep.

There should be drapes between me and this moon.

The toddler in his hospital bed, unable to sleep. Afraid his mother will find him. Afraid of the green hospital drapes. Afraid of the sandwich on the lunch tray, the cartoon drawn there by a nurse. Perhaps his mind searches. Determined to find that single lost and drifting piece. An automatic, frantic flipping file.

The rough side of the rescue boat, the smell of gasoline, the scream from the bridge, mother in the air, her dangling legs, the swollen back of his baby brother, bobbing, moving further away.

Flipping through the memory file. It is none of these.

And then he fastens onto it. That good memory of sense. When the rescuer held him close to her life preserver. And in her chrome sunglasses, he saw himself reflected back. There. That exact piece. The fragrance of the rescuer's perfume.

Perhaps he will search the rest of his life for that scent. Twenty years from today, he'll be in a crowded department store. A woman will pass him and he will set down the shirt he was holding, and follow her. By the time he is riding up the escalator, he will be weeping, and will not know why.

6.

"I'd like to sit in silence for the boy and his dead brother, if you don't mind."
"I don't mind," he says.

A mallard sleeps on the deck, his body pressed against the glass. Rescues don't work. This is all I'm thinking.

> *Mrs. Pinney leans over me during art time.*
> *Her short curly gray hair, her glasses on a beaded chain.*

"Is this your house?" Her voice is soft like the smell of warm bread at the bakery. "I notice that you always draw the same picture."

I am ashamed. She's right. Every day I draw two straight sides, a pointed roof, a window with criss-crossed curtains trimmed with ball fringe.

There is nothing about this house that is like ours.
That is why I like it.
I color in the hanging balls perfectly.
A different color everyday.
The only part of the drawing that changes.

Across the table, Bonnie's drawing is very complicated.
Her whole paper is full. I see it upside down. A dog, a cat, a girl. So many things that could get hurt.
I don't know how she does it. She is very brave.
She draws a sun across the corner of her picture.

I take a yellow crayon from my box. I make a sun.
I want to be Bonnie.

"What's this?" Mrs. Pinney touches her finger to my drawing.
She must have noticed my sun in the corner.
But instead, she points to the sky outside the house.
I don't want to look at her.
"That's stuffing," I say. "From Georgie's teddy bear."

7.

Joseph was sold for a servant . . .
his feet
laid in iron

"Mrs. Pinney invited herself to our house for lunch," I begin, glad to have been silent together. A marking in time.

"Your first grade teacher? Where Cathy brought in the Japanese doll?"

"Yes. In the house after Inez. She was my favorite teacher."

I tell him the story of that day.

I wore my Sunday School dress to school. Pale green chiffon with a black velvet tie at the waist. The night before, my mother made foods we never ate. Creamy and sweet foods. "Company Chicken," and for dessert, "Pears Supreme." I rode home in Mrs. Pinney's car. A two-tone '56 Ford, chartreuse and black. The lunch was not my idea. I thought, She'll see we don't have curtains with balled fringe. She'll see how our house hangs off the cliff. Then she'll know I draw the curtains because I want someone to look in.

Her key chain read, "I Like Ike." She said she had a son, Roy, and that this was his car. He was in the Army. When she said this, there was sadness in her face, something I never saw in school. And I thought, She'll see Georgie's bedroom door. She'll see how he never comes out.

I kept my hand on the seat between us, hoping she'd touch it by mistake.

When we reached the house, she said it was very pretty and big. I rang the bell. We waited. She stood right beside me, our shoes almost touching on the mat. Her two patent leather heels, skin puffing over the curve at the toe, and my brown shoes with their scuffs. Four shoes in a single row.

> *feet with fetters*
> *laid in iron*

My mother bowed deeply when she opened the door and I thought, She's imitating Van Cliburn bowing last night on t.v. Her mouth was smiling, but her eyes were hard and I thought, Mrs. Pinney is seeing how my mother's face divides at the middle. Mrs. Pinney probably has a stomach ache now just like me. The house smelled like Lemon Pledge. We walked up the stairs.

"Oh, what a view!" Mrs. Pinney looked far, past the houses lower on the hill, past the city buildings, out across the bay. She's looking for Roy, I thought. My mother set the kitchen timer ticking.

Mrs. Pinney liked the food. She finished her chicken and salad, but spilled a pickled beet on the tablecloth. She kept talking to my mother, but at the same time, she poured salt onto the wound and the crystals lifted up the red.

"Barbara's said you're a musician . . . "
That's when everything changed.

I stared at the wooden bird plaques flying across the wall. I wanted to fly away with them. It was over now.

My mother started asking questions one after another, not waiting for an answer. Mrs. Pinney repositioned her weight, crossing and re-crossing her legs. The smell of perspiration from her arms became stronger than the Lemon Pledge or the Pears Supreme. "Will you be transferred to the new school? What does your husband do? Oh, you're divorced? How sad. Who takes care of the children?"

The timer rang. My mother stood. Her food untouched, cut in cubes and spread around the rim of her plate.

Mrs. Pinney's hand shook on the handrail as we walked down the stairs. My mother stayed at the landing, not coming to the door. I drew my hand along the wall, the texture of the stucco, the isolated nubs. She'll save my punishment for the right moment, I thought, just like Georgie saves pennies in his log cabin bank.

Mrs. Pinney surprised me. She turned and looked up at my mother. Her voice was deep and strong. "Mrs. Harris," she held the door knob steadying herself, "I'm going to be keeping a very watchful eye on this wonderful daughter of yours. You can count on it." She opened the door.

We didn't speak much driving back to school. When we arrived, she thanked me again, and said she had to go to the teacher's room.

At the drinking fountain I held my face in the stream of water a long time. I stayed until the cold hurt. Until the cold made a wall between Mrs. Pinney and my mother. When the second bell rang I pulled away. Water fell off my bangs, my cheeks and chin. The top of my dress stuck, transparent, to my chest.

At my waist, on the black velvet tie, three drops of water perched like birds.

8.

"Did anything more come from Mrs. Pinney's visit?" he asks.

Rescues don't work.

"Every year after that, my mother made a habit of inviting our teachers home for lunch. She loved it."

The mallard stands, shakes his feathers, flies away.
Cruelty everywhere.
Even the ducks know this.

"You accomplished something remarkable getting your teacher there, Barbara. It was almost unheard of in those days."

The pond, its still surface,
the darkness that it holds.

"She came because she loved me."

No one ever saw a thing.

9.

—"Barbara, I think you should open your eyes now."

Mrs. Pinney couldn't even save us.
She didn't save Georgie. Or Cheryl.
And she didn't save me.

"That's enough now Barbara."

Rescues never work. Even with someone good.

"Barbara—!"

Someone is gripping my wrists.

> *feet with fetters . . .*
> *laid in iron*

I open my eyes.
My knuckles red with blood.

10.

Let's say the boy thrown from the bridge receives a birthday card
from his imprisoned mother.
Let's say he is sixteen.
He holds the card a moment before throwing it away.
He thinks, My brother would be thirteen by now.
He feels how deeply he wants to kill his mother.
Not because she threw him over the bridge.
But because he cannot remember a time when he felt innocent.

11.

"I never drew the house with criss-crossed curtains after that."
He looks at me, sadly.

"I never drew anything at all."

12.

A mourning dove flies into my yard carrying a small twig
in its beak.
She comes close to me, as if to all I'm remembering.
Time collapsing into itself like wooden nesting dolls.
She comes into my garden from that desk at school
where crayons sprawled across the empty white.

13.

A faded business card falls from my Van der Weyden book.
It reads Old World Art Books, and on the back is written, "Let me
know how you like this one. Mr. J."

> *"Anything beautiful," I instructed him on that first phone call,*
> *"published before 1924 that is."*
> *Before the birth of my parents.*

> *What I meant was, Art without my parents in it.*

> *I mailed my babysitting money to him, taping the coins to a*
> *blank sheet, folding bills with sharp creases to make them flat.*
> *Ten days after sending the first envelope, the Michelangelo book*
> *arrived. Published in 1910.*
> *In the months that followed, Cimabue, Giotto, Raphael, names*

I knew from doing my report. Each night I locked my bedroom
window, placed my desk chair against the door.

Each book was a world for me. I went into the images
the way a person enters a room.

I went into them and did not kill my mother or my father.

I open to Van der Weyden's triptych again.

"I never heard of her," my mother said when I asked about
Veronica. "Probably some saint the Catholics made up."
Every night I blew off the page to remove anyone else's touch.
I followed the logic of her story as if it were my own.
The other figures in the triptych were all sorrowing.
Mary Magdalen, the Virgin, Christ Crucified, the two donors,
four lamenting cherubim, St. John.
Veronica was the only one with a souvenir.
Not a miracle, I thought, to put oneself into an object.
Jesus thrusting himself into her cloth.
A simple and necessary act when things move too quickly
toward destruction.

14.

I stacked the art books under the baby lamp given to me by
Inez. I saved it through four different moves, remembering
the day she gave it to me. The day she emptied her baby room.
Filled the living room with a sea of cardboard boxes.
The Goodwill truck came down the street.
She sent everything away.

15.

*I kept the art books under her lamp, in an open obvious place,
so that no one would calculate their value to me.*

*At night, the barricaded bedroom door, Veronica's image
under my chin.
I slid deeper into her image, into that distant place
when I was low and small and pure-hearted.*

16.

I tell him the rest of the story.

"When Mrs. Pinney noticed that I wouldn't draw, she asked if I
wanted to color a paper napkin instead. Each day I found a napkin
hidden in my desk. I colored the raised patterns perfectly. Greek key.
Flowers. Wreaths. I liked making visible the patterns that lay hidden
in the white."

"Children can be very resourceful," he says. "Sometimes they
rescue themselves."

17.

Sometimes to color a napkin is to redeem the world.

18

The surviving boy, the toddler, how will he find the thread of uprightness?

> *Inez came to visit us in the new house.*
> *"She has a baby by adoption," my mother explained.*
>
> *"Here, Barbara, hold Baby Elizabeth," Inez said to me.*
> *I did not want to hold her. I was not prepared. I thought,*
> *Inez doesn't know I put Georgie down the clothes chute.*
> *She doesn't know that I'm bad for babies.*
>
> *She sat down on the couch next to me.*
> *Together we held Baby Elizabeth. Nothing went wrong.*
> *"You're going to be a wonderful mother someday Barbara."*
> *I looked at her. She was prettier than I'd remembered.*
> *Her blond hair swept back, gold earrings, the pure pearl*
> *buttons of her suit.*

How will he find it, the thread of uprightness?

I bring other art books into the office. We look at Van der Weyden's "Crucifixion," then Fra Angelico's "Annunciation."

> *. . . the angel's wing,*
>   *heavy with*
> *what's invisible*

Michelangelo's madonnas: the Medici Madonna, Madonna Pitti, Palestrina Pieta, the Madonna of Bruges. Jesus as a toddler, resting his elbow on a book on his mother's lap. In another, as an infant turning to her to suck. Cut into marble. Preserved. These rare moments when the covenant between parent and child isn't broken.

20.

Children must have seen themselves in him when he passed. They waved their palms. They shouted,

> *Blessed is he who comes,*
> *so rich in love and mercy*

21.

Last, I show him the pages of my stitched book.

"These are like ligaments to the world outside my hedge."

> The girl in the Sarajevo bakery, Wilde's "Lament in Rondo Form," the Morton Salt Girl, the ikebanist, the feather, the photo of me and Cheryl on Inez' lawn.

There are many others now. It is not slim anymore. The most recent addition, a paper napkin I colored last night. On it, in crayon, Mrs. Pinney's name.

"This will take the rest of the hour," I warn him. "I am very slow."

He smiles as if to say, This is not a problem.

I take out the photocopy I made of the Madonna Pitti. Carefully I bind the edges to the newspaper clipping of the boys thrown over the bridge.

"It's lovely," he says. I sew them into the book.
New canon. New scripture. New sacred text.

> *To stand in the shadow*
> *of the scar*
>
> *. . .*
>
> *with all there is room for in that,*
> *even without language*

22.

A man outside the market is selling summer lilies in tall frosty cans. I choose the best stems for Josephine.

"You have to baby them, you know," he advises. "Sometimes they come in so tight, so green. But then they get whiter. You just have to wait."

Above him the market advertises a sale on Chilean sea bass.

At the back of the store, on the table behind glass, the butcher lays down a very large fish, an opened palm resting on the fish's side.

"Is that the sea bass?"

"Yes," he nods.

There is no blood. None on his apron, the table, his hands.

He makes the first long cut, cleanly, from the head down to the tail, swift and elegant. He rolls the silver body a bit more to the side and slides his hand under its head, lifting the full length of silver blue. He treats the fish with a practical reverence. Seeing him do this, my shoulders relax and I breathe easily.

Gingerly he lifts flesh off bone, directly touching its unnamed wounds. Fine creature, up from the dark, its whole life under the surface, unseen. Its stately body, the only evidence of a complete and hidden life.

It is beautiful to see how he knows her.
I watch and I do not cry.

REQUIESCERE

I.

From the garden I hear the voice of someone crying on my
phone machine. It sounds like Sister Helene. I run inside.

"You've got to do something, Barbara," her voice thick as
clotted cream.

"Do you want me to come to the Convent?"

"No, I'll come there," her words halting, torn.

She collapses onto my shoulder, her head heavy like a horse, long
hair coming from her veil.

"Baby Heloise died in her crib last night."

"Let's go inside." I sit her down on a kitchen chair.

"Everything was fine. She had her checkup, she had her
vaccines . . ." she sobs, lunging forward, her head almost hitting the
table. "You've got to do something," she pulls my sleeve. "Don't
keep your secret anymore."

"What do you mean?"

"That day in the Convent yard." Her lips are quivering. "You
were having a vision. I saw you. Covered with the Precious Blood.
I didn't tell. I kept your secret. But then you cut off your hair . . . ."

I turn away but she pulls me back.

"Dolores Mary said it was nothing. But she wasn't there. She
didn't see your eyes."

Out the kitchen window the bird feeder is empty of seed.

"I know you're hiding special powers."

I want to be tender.

"There's nothing I can do about Heloise's death, Helene. I'm really
so sorry."

A sparrow lights on the feeder bar looking in vain for food.

Her skin is flushed and blotchy, tears gathered under her chin.

"Monsignor's doing the memorial service," she gulps air between her words. "I made him promise."

"Good. That's good. He'll do a nice job."

She pulls away from me, suddenly alert.

"Do you remember the Christmas you played for Midnight Mass?"

"Yes."

"Would you play something for Heloise?"

"I don't have my cello anymore, Helene." She bursts into tears again.

"I didn't believe Josephine last Fall when she told me."

"Told you what?"

"She said she heard a crash. She thought you broke your cello. She told me and Sister Dolores Mary. Even Monsignor. She asked him to help."

There is no privacy. Even here, inside my hedge.

When I told Josephine, she acted surprised, but she already knew.

"Couldn't you rent one?" Helene wipes her nose.

"I'll come to the funeral, Helene, but I'm not going to play. I haven't practiced in months. I'd sound horrible, really. How about asking Father Dennis? He's a gifted player. Maybe he wouldn't mind."

She pushes herself away from the table, stands, tosses back her hair.

"Not everyone's as lucky as you, Barbara. Maybe you should think about that sometime. Your life's so easy. You had a boyfriend and a real job. You got to learn the cello. Then you just throw it all away."

2.

The same neighborhood cat trespasses through my yard each
Spring. He slows to smell the newly hatched eggs, acting as if he isn't
after them. I would shoot him if I could.

> *God said: Take your son Isaac . . . you shall offer him up*
> *as a holocaust*

Death is everywhere and always.

3.

"Those poor parents," Josephine calls. In the background the blare
of a quiz show on her t.v. "I met them once. I'm telling you, that
mother's a real beauty."

I am too weary.

"Are you going to the service?" I ask.

"Is the Pope Catholic?" I hate it when she takes a sarcastic tone. I
know what comes. "You don't even sound sad, Barbara, if I may say
so. You fell apart over those boys on the bridge you don't even know,
and now with this . . . "

"I don't know this family either, Josephine."

> Cruelty is worse than death. A double death.
> This friendship feels over.
> Death is everywhere and always.

> Slice of melon cast from a car,
> dried rind on a desert road.

4.

When will she feel it? This young and beautiful mother.
When will it hit? The core of listlessness.

She will be called into school. Her older son, if she has one, will be
misbehaving. For his sake, she will pretend to care, managing a look
of astonishment in the principal's office. She will not remove her sunglasses. Wearing them always, even in rain.

At the grocery store, she'll pull down the baby seat in the shopping
cart, pleased that she's learned to put eggs there instead. Still, she will
cry at the perishability of mango, papaya, grape. She will avoid the
produce section completely, buying only frozen foods. Then she will
change markets altogether. Even so, most days she'll return from the
market empty handed. The family driving for dinner at still another
restaurant.

Feeling herself drift, she will refuse to wear shoes. Barefoot, she
will try to anchor herself, imagining herself drifting with a multitude
of other invisible women, menopausal, childless. Wanting to tell
someone, anyone, "My Heloise died for no reason. She died before
she bled."

5.

Crystals fall from the salt box.

The flow of salt that never stops.

6.

I dream.

The space inside the elevator enlarges with details of a
death. Newspapers spread out on a highway. Ice plant on
the banks is splashed with blood, speckling the lavender
star-shaped blooms.

A woman screams in Spanish. My daughter is lifted into
an ambulance. Cars don't clear away fast enough.
My daughter dies outside the hospital. Concealed under
crucifixes and a violet rise of incense.

7.

Take your son . . . whom you love . . . and offer him up
as a holocaust

Last year outside this bathroom window, a hummingbird built a
nest no larger than a walnut, the first one I'd ever seen. Each day I
took pictures, squatting on the marble counter.
   She laid two eggs and eventually they both hatched. The small
birds' opened beaks, their bodies pink as erasers.
   One day, she fought off five sparrows in mid-air. I wanted to inter-
vene, but resisted. She fought them all off at once. They flew away.

The next day the nest was empty. Ripped apart on the northeast
side.

8.

I draw a bath. Rub pumice against my feet, body grains on my
arms and legs. The rough sponge. Over and over. I scrub.
Death is everywhere. I can't scrape it off.

I am the resurrection and the life, says the Lord

The last thing I want is to hear these pious words. Celan was right.

Hurricanes . . .

particle flurries, the rest,
you
know, we've
read it in the book, was
opinion

9.

Why did I tell Helene I'd attend?
I need his poem if I'm going to go inside those walls. Already I feel
a tightening of the noose.
"Engführung," the straits, the narrowing, the dread. I need Celan's
words tattooed on my arm.

Taken off to the
terrain
with the unerring track
. . .
Grass, written asunder.

I tape together thin strips of paper to make one long narrow piece.
I copy the poem and roll it tightly. It's the size of a spool of thread.
I put it in my purse.

Read no more—look!
Look no more—go!

IO.

The Church bells offer their dirge. Josephine and I climb the stairs.
My mouth is dry, my hair too short.

Empty clay pots all stacked neatly against the wall. This gardener I
never see, whose soil is perfectly mulched, whose shrubs are without
dead leaf.

"Engführung" in my purse.

visible, once
again: the
grooves, the
choirs, back then, the
Psalms. Ho, ho-
sanna.

And these words . . . shall be in thine heart . . . And thou shalt
bind them for a sign upon thine hand, and they shall be as
frontlets between thine eyes. And thou shalt write them . . .

. . . your hour
has no sisters . . .

Josephine leans on my arm.

II

We dip our fingers in the font and sign ourselves with a cross.

frontlets between thine eyes

"What did Monsignor want?" Josephine asks as we pull down the kneeler.

"He said he thought I'd left his world."

. . . back then, the
Psalms. Ho, ho-

"You try to like everyone," she scoffs.

visible, once
again: the
grooves

"I do not like Monsignor, Josephine."

12.

"The grace and peace of God our Father and the Lord Jesus Christ be with you," Monsignor intones with his loud, customary tone. He calls the congregation to a celebration of life. Who is he kidding?

The statues ignore him. They remember the old days when they were shrouded in black.

Sutures, palpable, here
it gapes wide asunder, here
it grew back together—who
covered it up?

Heloise's mother smiles forcefully, an inch of slip showing below the hem of her dress.

—who
covered it up?

Some woman I don't know turns and waves at me discreetly.
Too much is going on.

"Stand up, Barbara," Josephine whispers. We begin.

"I confess to almighty God, and to you my brothers and sisters."

Ashes, Ashes . . .
Night-and-Night

13.

Only the altar is a relief.
Draped in fine linen. The slender flax plant, blue flowers, narrow leaves, fibers that can be spun into thread.
I put Heloise there, between the fibers along with the dead infant and the toddler who survived.
Living threads holding the dead.
Every Mass is a Feast of the Slaughter of the Innocents.
Life and death together on the marble slab.

14.

Marie showed me her new boxed cards from the National Gallery of Art. Among them, a reproduction of "Rest on the Flight into Egypt" by Gerard David.

Mary rests on a flat rock, holding up a bunch of grapes, the infant Jesus on her lap. A dainty wicker basket at her feet, its latch, handle, lid. The donkey rests contentedly while Joseph hits fruit from a tree. Mary with her strange and necessary child, everything about him a problem to be solved. Joseph, guided by nothing but the film of his dreams.

The trees lean over the family as if weeping. The sky looks the other way. The stubborn mountain, remembering the others, wants the travelers to move on. Even the delicate ferns harden against the dirt.

Escaping the slaughter of his peers, wrapped in gauzy white, the lucky child reaches for a grape. In the middle of slaughter, rest. In the middle of disaster, food.

> *Find*
> *that eye, the moist one.*

His potted English ivy plant had been dead for several weeks. He did not dispose of it but kept it in full view, outside on the deck. "When are you going to do something with that plant?" I asked, finally, after I traced the room. He glanced at the deck and then turned to me. "I am doing something with it," he said.

Sometimes salvation enters the world
wearing destruction like a coat.

15.

"Prove it!" Daniel challenged me, when I said I'd memorized
all of Celan's Bremen speech. He didn't know me as a child.
He didn't see all the gold stars on all my Bible Memory Charts.
I recited the speech verbatim. He followed with the text.

I am the resurrection and the life says the Lord.

Celan's Bremen speech and "Engführung" in my head like a round:

> *In this language I have sought, during those years . . . to sketch*
> *out reality for myself.*

> *But it had to pass through its own answerlessness, pass through*
> *frightful muting, pass through the thousand darknesses of*
> *deathbringing speech.*

Voices to my left and right, one voice, speaking in unison.
I close my eyes.

"We believe in one God the Father, the Almighty, maker of heaven
and earth of all that is seen and unseen . . . "

I reach over to Josephine. "Don't leave me."
She pats my hand.
Lifeboat tied to the side of a ship.

I crawl into their language, all around me, one voice.
Crawl into the lifeboat, curl under the wood slatted seat.

Poems . . . are making toward something . . .

Toward what?
Toward something standing open, occupiable,
perhaps toward an addressable Thou . . .

16.

"You'll like this," Josephine hands me Heloise's holy card. All of
the dates of her short life occurred within one year. Birth. Baptism.
Death.

On the other side a picture of Jesus the Good Shepherd carrying a
sheep. Carrying the young one, the lost one, the favored.

Rest in Peace Heloise.

I will look after my sheep, says the Lord, and I will raise up one
shepherd who will pasture them

17.

"Mrs. Pinney, Barbara's in your purse!" Clarisse called out in
a loud voice. I closed the gold clasp quickly. In line for recess,
Clarisse in front of me, Cathy behind. My chest against the
wooden edge of Mrs. Pinney's desk. Her purse sitting there, on
the corner.

Both lines fell silent, the girls' and the boys'. Mrs. Pinney leaned against the door, her face high above the others, her eyes puzzled, looking down at me. I wanted to say, I don't know why I did it. I don't remember ever deciding.

Cathy adjusted the Snow White clip on the side of her hair. Joseph held the rubber ball. There was a long space of time in which nothing happened. Mrs. Pinney walked toward me, her body sideways to fit between the rows. Over my head, she reached for her purse, squeezing my shoulder with her other hand.

"Barbara would never go into my purse," she said, looking, one by one, at each face as she walked back to the door. Things became settled and smooth. Her wide arms crossed on her chest, her purse over one arm, she waited, as if to make sure no one disagreed. Her gray eyes on me saying, I know you meant no harm.

On the floor, two rows of shoes all faced forward now away from me. Two rows of scuffed heels, and at the end, the toes of Mrs. Pinney's patent leather shoes.

I ran for the grass. I didn't stop to play dodgeball, four square, tetherball. I ran to the chain link fence. Through it, a row of new empty houses, a single tree planted in each yard. I sat facing the corner of the fence, my shoes against the wire. Inside her purse was perfect. Dark glasses in a gold woven case. The "I Like Ike" key chain. Crumpled Kleenex, I wanted to go into it, to close the purse. I wanted Mrs. Pinney to take me home.

In the brown dirt between my legs, I made two grooves next to each other, one that was Mrs. Pinney and one that was me. I made them close, the way, sometimes, two birds fly off a telephone

343

wire at the same time. I ran my fingers in the grooves over and
over, feeling how she'd convinced everyone I wasn't bad.

The sounds of the playground were far away. I was separate
from all of it. Cathy, Joseph, and all my friends. It didn't
matter. My fingers holding the two grooves together in the dirt.

18.

The bread is blessed. The wine.
Today the cup is cobalt blue.

"Take this, all of you, and eat it: this is my body which will be
given up for you."

Reachable, near and not lost, there remained amid the losses
this one thing: language . . .

I am the resurrection and the life says the Lord.

. . . and these words . . . shall be in thine heart

. . . but it had to pass through . . . the thousand darknesses

The law of the Lord is perfect,
refreshing the soul;

It passed through and gave back no words . . .
yet it passed through this happening . . .

The command of the Lord is clear,
enlightening the eye.

In this language I have sought, during those years
and the years since then, to write poems: so as to speak,
to orient myself, to find out where I was and where
I was meant to go, to sketch out reality for myself.

19.

We form two lines and process down the center aisle.

Poems in this sense too are under way: . . . Toward what?
. . . perhaps toward an addressable Thou . . .

"The Body of Christ," Monsignor Kilmartin puts the host in my
upturned palm. Blond, pale, round, like the cheek of a sleeping child.
This is the Body broken.

"Amen." I raise it to my lips.

20.

"The Mass is ended, go in peace."

So
temples still stand. A
star
may still have light.
Nothing,
nothing is lost.

Ho-
sanna

"Thanks be to God."

21.

I set the table. Cook my fish.

Taped to the cabinet above the stove a card Daniel sent many years ago from Rome. It smells of garlic when I take it down. An image of Mary, solemn and luminous, holding her infant son. I check again the painting's date, fourteenth century, Italy, which means it was done during the Great Plague. The plague that took, from Europe, one person in three.

I set it on the table, next to Heloise's holy card and my small white printed spool.

How did this painter create something this fine in the middle of death?

How did he remember something that he could no longer see?

Perhaps Celan will tell me. I am in that Bremen audience. I'm on my folding chair. This unknown painter,

> *who . . . shelterless . . . goes with his very being . . .*
> *stricken by and seeking reality*

Perhaps it was something like this:

He gets up from his bed, leaving the familiar muslin weave of his sheet. Goes to the window reluctantly, wakened by the noise of another funeral procession. Everyone wailing, holding cloths to their faces. He looks down at the priest's weary eyes and notes the cut pattern of sunlight on the lace of his chasuble.

Next door a woman with delicate hands tips a cistern out into the street. The stench of the bile and blood rise through the air. The priest recites his delicate Psalms. Again, today, he thinks, the mix of stench and melody.

In the alley two boys shake sticks at a rat they've cornered. Laughing, one throws a stone. No one knows then that the rat carries the plague.

The painter wants to go back to bed. He squeezes lemon into water, drinks. He wants to paint the Blessed Virgin with Christ Child. But he can't remember a day without wailing. Not sure he can remember what normal skin looks like. He stares at his canvas, the pencilled lines, his experiments in color. Around him, and close, so many bodies swelled up and blackened, tumors the size of grapefruits, rank expulsions of puss.

It is everywhere. And it is not what he wants.

He examines his brushes, upright and clean in the jar, pulls bristles between his forefinger and thumb, thinks of his three sisters he buried last year, his brother who ran screaming past the orchard to the Carmelite monastery on the hill.

His mother sits in the kitchen below. He knows what she's doing. Staring at the wall, tearing rags. At dusk he will find her slumped over and silent, rags piled around her like a nest. He will burn the rags, and the next day she'll do the same. This is not the mother he wants to paint. He wants Mary enthroned by the moon, her cape studded with stars.

He waits for memory to bridge the gap, touching the corner of his canvas like a prayer. Instead, he hears more commotion. A woman yanks the curtain down from its rod. Her red hair is uncombed and wild, her lips purple and swollen. She throws the curtain from her window, down into the street. Everywhere helplessness. Everywhere laceration.

Some cry out, "God is punishing us!" The tanner predicts the end of the world, runs through the streets, waving his knife. Every week a new soothsayer, a new jumble of language, beads.

> *Reachable, near and not lost, there remained amid the losses this one thing:*

Surrounded by bloated and black festering bodies,

> *. . . through its own answerlessness*
> *. . . through the thousand darknesses*

this painter somehow remembers tenderness, the beauty of healthy skin.

22.

I type up the Bremen speech and take it to my session. I show him "Engführung" written on the paper spool.
"What's the English translation?" he wants to know.
"Stretto." The straits. The narrow place.

Holy card. Poem. Card from Daniel. A structure, a net.

"People find Celan cryptic, dark." He looks up from the things I've laid out in a row. "But I think he's the most hopeful poet of the Twentieth Century."

"How is that?"

"I've decided hope isn't a matter of disposition. Now I measure it by what a person dares to hope against."

"The Holocaust, you mean."

"Of course."

"Then you are also a hopeful person?"

"My history is not the Holocaust. They can't be compared."

He waits.

"Okay. Yes. I, Barbara Harris, am a hopeful person."

23.

"I'd like you to have this."

I hand him the card smelling of garlic.

"Look at the skin," I say.

"And her sad eyes," he adds.

He props the card on the top shelf, above works of Carl Rogers, Milton Erikson, Fritz Pearls. So many spines, so many briny chapters.

Even from this distance, the lush gold leaf shines out. The faces, lucid. Above books piled high like bones, he's set my card, alongside feathers and a gathered stone.

MUSICA

There is a sequence that moves over pain.
One memory leading to another.
A single row of wheat falls under the thresher,
then the next.

2.

"I'm going behind the chair," I say, trying to touch this forward rolling thing, to touch what already feels good. I press my face deep in the leather. The answer is here, in the cool leather, the dirt against my face.

"Can you ask me some questions?"

"Sure." I don't see, but I hear his voice.

"Is there something more about the burial?"

> I grab the chair by its wooden frame. Pull my torso into it.
> The cold against my chest. It comes. It doesn't hurt.
> I feel my way toward it.

> It is the smell of my father's flannel shirt.
> The press of flannel against my cheek.
> It all comes out.

"I was cold a long time. Then the straws failed. I was without pain or sensation. I don't know how long it lasted. I heard a faint sound, far off. It woke me. I felt a focus of my attention onto it. It was someone calling out my name in broken pieces.

> 'Bar . . . ba . . . ra . . . Bar . . . ba . . . ra'.

And in between the syllables, weeping. It was my father's voice. Calling for me to come back."

I press deeper into the dirt, to find this piece, to get it all.

"I felt scraping. I became more alert. I felt his arms over my chest, the weight of them, pulling off the dirt. Pulling with his forearms."

"He lifted me out. He carried me, my head against his chest. My right cheek was against his shirt. I felt tears on my face. Warm. Sticking like mud. I kept my eyes closed so he wouldn't stop. I didn't want the sound of his crying to end."

3.

At home I unwrap the fragments of my broken bow.
Horses bred just for their manes.
The ebony tip, the dot of inlaid pearl.
Bow that makes the cello weep.

I play Samuel Barber's "Adagio for Strings," turning the volume up, play it a second time. There is a piece of this memory,

Reachable, near and not lost

I start it again. Listen a third time. There is some thing I need to find. Some shred.

there remained amid the losses
this one thing

Finally, I listen outside, dig my hands into the dirt. I play it once more. Then I find this: That my father's voice, waking me, bringing me back, became, for me, the root of all music. There, in his weeping, in his calling out my name.

I gave this weeping sound not to him, but to music itself.

As if music rescued me. Pulling away the dirt. Lifting me out with arms under my legs, my neck. To a place where I would not be afraid. Nothing harmful to my right or left. A meadow, yellow and sun-ripped green. Fear, like slices of metal in my palm, delicately removed. Music putting everything back where it belonged. Feathers from masks given back to the birds.

I turn the volume up so the music fills my garden, reaches out through the hedge.

In this . . . I have sought . . . to orient myself, to find out
where I was and where I was meant to go,
to sketch out reality for myself . . .

Music, great excavating lover. I have no logic, no reason
why you came to me through soil, through
my father's voice, halting and broken.

This garden, my abbey. These birds, its bells.
Dirt smudged on my gardening shirt,
my pectoral cross.

5.

"I must have always looked for the sound of my father weeping," I
tell him, "not just in music but in the sudden way the branches of a
tree move, natural yet unexpected."

The tears that came down and fastened themselves
on my cheek.
Messengers from some place deep inside him
that I could not reach.
Telling me that under all this, there was something good.

Inside my loop we play the "Adagio for Strings."

"Hear how the music comes from a labyrinth?" I ask. "The cadence,
the rush of energy lit by sound. How the music goes into the darkness, making light rise up? Do you hear it?"

I'm not seated anymore but moving around the room, swaying my
arms. I'm not embarrassed for him to see me this way.

"Do you hear it?" I ask again. "Do you see?"
He nods several times, smiling.
"Yes," he nods. "I am seeing something entirely new."

6

Music, strings adagioed and fair,
angels with continents at their polished feet.
Invisible one who waited all these years, who came
with capes of tasseled gold, not bound
by parent, rope or limb.
One who found me where I lay hidden,
folded like a cloth.

We stand by the door, the hour already over.
"Your face is radiant," I tell him.
"I'm very happy for you, Barbara."

7.

Bylsma, Ma, Casals, Starker, Fournier, Rostropovitch, Du Pré.
For hours, I lie in the backyard and listen.

Long brown table of the earth, in which all seeds lie buried.
Soil that holds magenta for the primrose bloom and green
for the daylily's leaf.

8.

The air is cold. I go inside, turn the music off.
Dark, the thick silence of night.

I know what the earth can hold. Forced against its will.
Forced to swallow. But I also know this:
Music is the respiration of the earth.
The way it purifies itself.

The earth exhales music because
it wants to be holy.

there remained amid the losses this one thing

Music, I see your gown holding fallen birds,
all that is unborn and wanting.
You come with armies of ships, oars churning
the frozen sea.
You broke through what was compacted
around my neck, my feet.
You showed me what I couldn't see.
That justice is your shawl, mercy your cuffs.
You came to me through soil.
Voice larger than my father's.
Voice I chose to believe, that said,

This will never happen to you again.

III.

Solstice

ARS MAGICA

I

"It could happen any day now," my father said, cutting his pork chop. "George, go get the globe."

He held the globe in his hand, his other fanned out over the top.

"The fallout will drift everywhere," he demonstrated. Telling us this as if it were the first time. As if he hadn't announced it the night before and the night before that.

"It'll kill all the plants and animals. The water will be poisoned. The air too. Only people in bomb shelters will survive."

My mother rose from the table.

"What are we supposed to do?" Cheryl asked.

He set down the globe, took out his mechanical pencil, slowly unswirling the slim piece of gray lead, and drew a triangle on his napkin, holding it up for us to see. It was the same picture as last night.

"Look for buildings with this sign on it. It means there's a bomb shelter under the building and anyone can go in."

Cheryl and I watched for buildings marked with the triangle sign, but only saw them when we were downtown, in the car.

"There aren't any close enough to walk to," Cheryl told him.

"Then you'll just have to run for it," he said.

> *O daughter of Babylon, who art to be destroyed . . .*
> *Happy shall he be, that taketh and dasheth thy little ones*
> *against the stones*

Huddled under our desks at school, heads down, arms over our necks, we thought, The Russians can't get us here. The fallout won't get under our desks.

Curled like pill bugs, violet black, the sequenced shell pulling tight around the squirming fringe of legs.

Cheryl and I asked our father to build us a bomb shelter.

"I've got something better," he set out graph paper, its even grid of quarter-inch squares. His penciled floor plan, the extreme slant of his letters, labeling each room. "It's a playhouse," he smiled.

The playhouse had two rooms and was big enough to walk in. The space in the wall for a door was left bare. And the windows were not fitted with glass.

We played doctor. Store. Bank. But we never played house.

I didn't bother sneaking cans of food down to it from the kitchen. The fallout will come in, I thought. It won't protect me or my dolls.

2.

"Cathy Hansen's going to have a bomb shelter in her backyard," I pleaded.

"Mr. Hansen must not be as smart as your Dad, then," my mother said, but it was not about being smart. When he went into the living room, she reached across the table to clear the butter dish and whispered, "Barbara, Christ is going to come before any silly old bomb."

She crouched on the floor beside my bed. Newspaper in one hand, Bible in the other. "All this 'Cold War' hoopla is just another sign. Christ is coming any day now, Barbara."

What she meant was, You know the Bible, Barbara. That makes you smarter than your Father and his scientist friends.

Her sleeveless blouse, her bare shoulder next to my mattress edge.
"We'll join Christ in the clouds, lifted right from our cars, our
houses . . . " Her voice was breathy.
"It's the Rapture of Believers!" But I thought,
Daddy is not a 'believer.' The logic was clear.
He would be caught in the flames.

I saw how this pleased her.
A kind of odor, fetid, an excitement seeped through her skin,
her bare white feet. A leaking. And I wanted to be at school.

3.

My father brought a small metal object home from the lab. Thin
like a flashlight and small enough to fit in one hand.

"It's an atom smasher," he said. "The smallest one in the world."
Georgie looked away.

"It's also called a 'nuclear accelerator' George." My mother did
not look, banging the ice tray against the counter, dropping cubes in
our glasses of milk.

"The first atom smasher was bigger than this house," my father
continued. Georgie stared at his napkin. Cheryl moved closer and
touched the atom smasher with her hand.

I did not want to touch anything at the same time as my father.

"Can I take it to school?" she asked.

"Sure," he put it in her palm, softly curving her fingers over it.

He spent more time with Cheryl after that, calling her "the
smart one."

"You can help me stop the Russians, Cheryl," he said, and bought
her a science kit with test tubes and small metal utensils. He taught

her how to make slides, to use the microscope, how to manage the burner's flame.

The kit opened outward, with two folding doors. Inside the metal racks held jars of brightly colored powders—yellow, turquoise, orange. I liked the rattling sound the jars made when she opened the doors. I wanted to be her assistant.

"You can't even read," she said, not looking up from the instruction book.

She was right. I could only read at school, with Mrs. Pinney. I was in the highest group. The Bluebirds. But at home, my arms felt cold and weak and the words blurred on the page.

I thought, If the bomb comes, I want to be at school with Mrs. Pinney. Crouched under my desk.

Cheryl called her bedroom a laboratory.

"Maybe fairies could stop the bomb," I offered.

"You're stupid, Barbara. Fairy magic can't stop anything."

She measured out blue powder, scraping it with the tiny spatula into a glass tube. She looked like she could stop the Russians. So I didn't interrupt her anymore, thinking, If she makes a bomb to stop the Russians, Mrs. Pinney won't get hurt.

4.

The next time my father went to Los Alamos, it was Valentine's Day. He brought home a nightgown for my mother. Layers of white chiffon covered with small pink hearts and thin spaghetti straps. She pretended to like it, but gave it to me the next day, for dress-up. It was a perfect fairy dress.

My mother took Georgie downtown to the Buster Brown Shoe Store to buy school shoes. It was a Saturday. I was sitting on my bedroom floor in my new fairy dress, gluing gold glitter onto the star end of my new fairy wand.

I felt my father in the room, behind me. I did not look up.

"Come here, Barbara. If you're going to wear Mom's nightgown, let's see if you can do what mommies do."

I followed him down the hall, holding up the chiffon, taking my wand with me, the dripping glue.

"Get Cheryl," he said, pointing to her room.

"You're the smart one, Cheryl, you first. Barbara, pay attention."

He pointed to their bed. The high windows with no curtains. The house hanging off the hill. The bright day sun cut wedges of light onto the wall.

I pressed my back against the cold Formica of the new dresser my mother just bought. The "modern" one with no handles, "no frou-frou to dust." Nothing to grab on to, nothing to hold.

Cheryl screamed.

He put his hand over her mouth.

> Up and down . . . his white back . . . up and down . . . like a whale.

I closed my eyes. I tried fairy magic. Fairy numbers. Fairy words. Nothing stopped him.

> *O daughter of Babylon, who art to be destroyed . . .*
> *Happy shall he be, that taketh and dasheth thy little ones*
> *against the stones*

5

When he left the room, Cheryl's head faced toward the bedroom door. Her mouth was frozen open. I climbed onto the bed. She didn't move. She did not blink her eyes.

I lay beside her. I wanted to be with her. Dead.

O daughter of Babylon

"Use this to clean her up Barbara," my father handed me a warm washcloth and turned to leave the room.

"What're you staring at? You think you're next?" He laughed. He straightened his belt. "I can only do one at a time!"

I wiped the sticky fluid from Cheryl's leg. Her skin was cold. Her hair matted like the coat of a dead dog. The only thing that moved were two fingers. They flicked and twitched and would not stop.

> *Dies irae*
> Day of wrath
> *Dies illa*
> O day of mourning!

Cheryl stopped trying to make the bomb to stop the Russians. I found her science kit thrown against the gardening shed. Yellow, green, copper powders spilled out of their jars. Broken pieces of glass in the dirt, reflecting the bright sun.

I put on my toy high heels and stomped up and down the hall outside her room.

But she did not come out.

I slid paper pictures under her door. She slid them back again.

7.

Shame can build a house.

> Day of wrath.
> O day of mourning!

The foxgloves against my fence fall over in the breeze.
I should have staked them.

> *A word—you know:*
> *a corpse.*

> *Let us wash it,*
> *let us comb it . . .*

8.

At the drugstore I buy a sheet of poster board, gold glitter, glue. Sit
on my kitchen floor and pull my pants' legs up, to feel the warm
wood against my thighs.

I draw the star. My hand shakes. I'm not careful enough with the
glue. It smears onto the floor.

Cheryl's hair matted like a dead dog
She did not flinch. Only her two fingers,
twitching, twitching.

It's a mess. It's too hard.
I throw it all in a paper bag.

9.

"I tried to make a fairy wand."

A tank rolls through the village. It is peace time.
Still it smashes the flowers.

I show him the contents of the bag.
"I'm going to drive to the Poor Clares and see if they will take this
away from me."

we hung our harps among the willows

I cry again. Again.

10.

Finally the valley, strawberry rows, lettuce, grapes on stakes.
Clean scent of lemon from the hills.

"Here," I held out the chiffon nightgown.

My mother scoured the grout between the kitchen tiles
and did not look up.

Cheryl on the bed,
her mouth frozen open
on the chenille's soft white grooves

"Here, I don't want this," I said as loudly as I could
without yelling. The steady scratch sound of bristle a
gainst grout. The cleansers' tart smell.

"It's time for you girls to set the table." But it was not time.
The sun was still high and had not dropped behind the barren
distant hills.

II.

At dinner Cheryl sat with arms and legs like wood. Bright, the yellow corn piled next to the mashed potatoes on her plate. The potatoes held deep brown gravy like a moat. Finally she picked up her fork.

fingers twitching, twitching

She brought the tines of the fork to touch a single kernel of corn. Slowly she pushed the kernel into the mashed potatoes, burying it there. Then she moved another. One by one she hid each kernel in the mound of white.

The moat stood this way, the same as before. And the gravy, undisturbed.

Voices traveled unheeded, out to the dry hills.
The daughters of Babylon weeping. Their cries, like gold,
woven into the brown blades.

12.

Cheryl stood and asked to be excused. My father gave permission
with the waving of his hand.
Her chair lay empty.
Ice cubes melted in her glass of milk, slowly bluing the rim.

13.

My fairy wand was in my bedroom, stuck to the inside of the
wastebasket. It's dripping glue, dried.
"Georgie, you can have my fairy wand." He looked up, smiled.
"But don't try to stop anything with it."
My father pushed away his empty plate, folded his napkin,
straightened his silverware into parallel lines.

Shame can build a house.

14.

When I cleared the table, Cheryl's plate looked like my mother's.
Food untouched. This time, my mother did not call her back to clean

her plate. And I thought, Cheryl is the same as my mother now. Cheryl is seven. She is a grown-up.

That night Cheryl and I took our baths together in the tub. We did not speak. The only noise was the lather from the soap bar against the sponge. She kept her legs together.

She told me to get out first. Still, I saw her cry when she stepped out of the tub. I saw the blue-black bruises when she dried off on the mat.

I could hear Georgie walking the hall in his new school shoes, and the sound of the fairy wand he dragged against the wall.

15.

Irrigation sprinklers water the dark fields.

> *. . . you know:*
> *a corpse*
>
> *Come let us wash it*

16.

The nuns are not in chapel. Streetlights come on. The fading pink of air. The wall. The Monastery garden. Agapanthus along the walk. Their pure white, their blue.

17.

The foyer remarkable as always, in its plainness.

"Excuse me,"
"Yes." A body answers. Breath.

Through metal, a word.

18.

I hold up my paper bag, as if for her to see.
"Will you take this from me? Inside there's a small jar of gold glitter and a star I've cut from poster board. Something a child might use to make a fairy wand."
"Yes . . ." she begins.
I do not want to cry here. Not here. This delicacy. This uprightness.

". . . of course we will take it from you. And we will pray for all that pertains to the jar of gold glitter and the star cut out of poster board that is like a fairy wand a child might use. And we will pray for you and for whatever has caused the suffering in your voice."

"I lost Cheryl. My fairy magic didn't work."

I am sobbing and cannot refrain.

"We will pray for you and for Cheryl. And for all those involved in your loss. God bless you."

I set the bag into the turn, and slowly spin it in toward her. It comes back, a holy card, its gold-feckled edge. Small, dainty, bright against the darkness of the turn.

It is too good. I do not pick it up.

> *a corpse . . .*
> *. . . let us turn*
> *its eye heavenward*

19.

Perhaps—

a statue is set in a grotto on the side of a hill.
It is of Mary standing on the crescent of a moon.

Pilgrims no longer come to her,
leaving their wild flowers picked from the field.

The edges of her plaster toes crumble in the rain.
A private disintegration, witnessed only by ferns.

LIBERTAS

How is it that the arms, hanging like planks of wood against a torso, are set free? Cheryl slowly taking up her fork, touching the tines against that first kernel of corn.

2.

St. Dunstan was a Benedictine anchorite.

Perhaps—
On the Feast of Corpus Christi they sealed him in. The Abbot requiring Dunstan to wait until the anniversary of the fourteenth year of his profession.

It was not an entirely new idea. The Abbot had heard about other monks with the same request. They had discussed it at the gathering of Abbots, remembering to each other the deserts of Nitria. St. Simeon and the stylites were recalled and there was much nodding of heads.

It was not that it was a new idea, but that it was Dunstan who had come to him with the request. Dunstan who would not extend arm from torso, his body as if made from wood, arms rigid at his sides, except in the playing of the harp.

Brother mason, under obedience, assisted in the construction of the cell. He had tried to like Dunstan, but had failed in love, and felt this failure with each laying on of mortar to stone, ashamed for the coldness of his heart.

He built the cell as instructed: Five feet long, two and a half feet wide, adjoining the wall of the Abbey Church. A tomb, Brother mason thought. But Dunstan thought, far from the Refectory. Far from the mice.

It was after the Corpus Christi Mass that the Brothers, headed by the Abbot, processed again into the Abbey Church, followed by men and women from the village, curious, and children with candles in their hands. Not knowing what other texts to use, they sealed Dunstan in with the words used for burial.

The cell five feet long and two and a half feet wide was tall enough for Dunstan to stand. Three stout iron bars divided the light that came in from the nave. Far from the mice, but close to everything I love, Dunstan told himself. His hands pulled on the robe at his sides. Waiting for the noise to die away. Waiting for the emptiness.

And yet part of himself, buried in the cloth, part of himself wanted the mouse to come. He knew it would not be the same creature, of course. Perhaps a ruffled back, a shorter tail. But he knew it was a necessity. It was the reason he wanted everything else stripped away: the commerce of the Brothers in choir, his own bodily movement down the halls, legs taking their full stride. Not like his rigid arms. Stripped away, too, the breathing of Brothers across the Refectory table. The array of musculature on faces seen over porridge and cheese. The melody of sandal against wood.

So there was some pleasure in the terror when he woke that first night hearing scratching. Moonlight caught a tail between the iron bars, then gone. Dunstan shaking.

His hands wet and useless. As before. As then. That morning when his brother, newly swaddled, lay sleeping. Gauze nibbled away at the toe. And Dunstan was too afraid to move, to reach into his brother's bed. Fur. Blood on the teeth. The whiskers Dunstan still sees moving, in his sleep.

Brother cook brought to Dunstan's cell a second forty-day loaf and, returning, reported to the Abbot that, perhaps, Dunstan was not eating. The Abbot sent word back through the cook, that moderation in terms of the body, even for an anchorite, was still advised. So Dunstan asked that two loaves, in that case, be brought. He did not say, One loaf for my forty days and one loaf for my teacher. Whose ear and length of tail I am coming to know. Whose fur, since Advent, has come to rest against these bars.

It was further to be noted, Brother cook reported to the Abbot, that Dunstan had reached out to receive the loaves. His hands, to the wrists, came out through the bars. For this, the Abbot offered, privately, prayers of thanksgiving.

Upon returning to the kitchen, through the wheat fields that lay on the hill, warmth of the sun through the grain like threads through a fan, Brother cook wept for the sight of Dunstan's hands, to the wrist, freed from his sides. It is a miracle, he thought. In that tomb, Brother Dunstan is working out his salvation.

The sound of the harp could be heard at all hours of the day and night. The mouse having grown, by the Feast of the Nativity, too fat to enter through the bars, lay resting against the iron that divided the light coming from the nave.

For five loaves now, Dunstan told himself, I have broken off bread and reached out my arms, and laid crumbs on the ledge. I have used each arm, each hand. The tail of his companion falling, from his fat body, into the cell, onto Dunstan's side of the stone wall. Dunstan coming to see in it a kind of beauty.

His brother, without the single toe on his left foot, having grown, having married, and bearing to the world three handsome sons. His fields famous for the sweetness of the corn. Having professed, since childhood, to carry no bitterness against Dunstan, though Dunstan could not believe it. The tale of his cowardice more vivid than the sweetness of his brother's corn.

Rumor spread, and was discussed at the gathering of Abbots who prepared the case for Rome, that a woman had brought her daughter to Dunstan's cell, and by the laying on of hands, the girl's blindness had been cured. Dunstan found sleeping the sleep of death the next morning. Inside the cell, the harp, resting in the corner, and on the ledge, a rodent, letting himself be viewed by day, as if in vigil.

Upon investigation, the story of the blind girl was found to be a hoax. But the Benedictine Brothers recorded what, to them, was the truer miracle. The extension of limb from torso.

They preserved it for themselves by burying the miracle in words that could have been written of any tenth century Benedictine monk:

"St. Dunstan occupied a cell of five by two and a half feet.
He remained there until his death, occupying himself with prayer, manual labor, and the playing of the harp."

IGNOMINIA

I

Josephine calls, inviting me to her yearly Fourth of July barbecue.
"Will you bring your potato salad? I love the capers."
"Sure, I'd love to come," I lie.

I hang crepe paper streamers for her in the trees.
"Tell me how I look Barbara," she comes out, carrying lemonade.
"I'm in my Gucci."
Last year she wore a Statue of Liberty headdress made of crimped
tin foil. Now, on top of her pantsuit, she's flung a fake boa dyed red,
white and blue, and has pinned matching feathers in trios behind
each ear.
I photograph her, throughout the yard, in different poses, which is
our custom. Leaning against the patio door, boa held above her head.
Sprawled on her lawn, legs scissored, boa draped on her raised knee.
Bending over her lush tomato vine, showing her teeth in a mock bite.
She will enlarge the prints and check them for signs of aging, then
she'll frame the best ones and scatter them throughout the house
until next year.

2.

Hanging streamers in her trees, I glean the fields of memory.
In the fields of my father I glean, looking for signs
among the sheaves.

Rite of Reconciliation of Individual Penitents

The penitent should prepare for the celebration of the sacrament by
. . . silent reflection
The penitent . . . is invited
to have trust in God

3·

Once after I traced the room I asked, "Do you think contrition is possible without memory?" and he said "No."

> *My father slammed his fist against the bathroom door jamb,*
> *cigarette ashes falling to the floor*

"But there is always memory at some level," he added.

4·

"I'm not coming to the party this year, Josephine," I fold the ladder. "I'm sorry."

"But Father Dennis will be disappointed," she puts down her glass. "Dolores. Helene . . . ."

"I'm just not up to it. Not this year."

She taps the pocket of her slacks, feeling for cigarettes.

"Are you sure? You're looking so much better now," she cocks her head. "Your hair's longer and it's not falling out . . . ."

"What do you mean my hair's not falling out?"

"Used to be, whenever you'd leave, I'd find handfuls of it on my sofa, the chaise, everywhere." She stands, looks up into the tree.

"One of these decades, I'm going to have my old Barbara back."

When she is in the kitchen and out of view, I feel my hair. It is thick again. And when I gently pull on it, it almost reaches my chin.

5.

A turning. I want to see a turning, no matter how slight.

> *It was in the harvest time of wheat and barley that Ruth the Moabite came to the fields of Boaz. She worked in the fields until evening. She counted what she had gleaned. It was an e-phah of barley.*

In the last house, through the full succession of homes, nothing changed. Cheryl and I shaved our legs. We teased our hair. We wore Erase lipstick, black eyeliner and angel blouses.

But he never stopped himself. I left my hair on the river stones.

6.

The noise from Josephine's party swells. Her dark and throaty laugh floating up to me, above the crowd. Fireworks sound in the distance. A siren. I sit upstairs on the bed.

In the harvest of wheat and barley, I find only this: That my father wept when he dug me out of the dirt. He wept and called out my name, Barbara.

I hold him to this, his tears. And I can say his weeping was the most true thing about him.

Still, even if I do this, it is not enough.

7.

In my clippings I find the photograph of a shirt now in the
Hiroshima Peace Memorial Museum. It belonged to a young boy,
Akio Tsukuda. The identification patch is still sewn on the upper
chest. He was engaged in fire prevention work 800 meters from the
hypocenter. On August 6, 1945, he was thirteen years old. His body
was never found. His father found just his shirt, hanging in a tree.

I thread my needle.

> *"You just got rich and didn't want to see the family anymore,"*
> *Cheryl said. There was nothing more I could do.*

I bind the edges of the frail photograph, strengthening it. On the
back I write, "Cheryl wanted to be a scientist. Her two fingers,
twitching, twitching." I write it like a death date. Cheryl who
stopped laughing when she was seven years old.

I sew the photograph into my book.

8.

The night comes creeping in.
Gray
and graying still.

The Poor Clares will sing tonight for the brokenness of the world.

The phone ringing, now? past midnight?

"Why aren't you at Josephine's? Isn't she having her party?"

"Daniel?"

"No, it's fucking Ben Franklin. Why don't you ever answer your phone? It's dead over here." He's drunk.

"I wish you were here . . . "

We rented horses. Riding in the tall grasses around the farm. A wild poppy blown against the stone. Hawks circling in the air like placards.

"Tell me about Cézanne."

"Unbelievable. I thought about you a lot. Especially the still lifes. I sent you the catalogue. You should get it in a few weeks."

They say it rarely happens. Lovers becoming friends.
Passion inside friendship like nutmeat in a shell.

"How hard would it be for you to get to Philadelphia?"

"Hard." Impossible is what I should have said.

Our feet shall stand within thy gates
O Jerusalem

Daniel traveled to India to find God. I can hear him telling me this. We were sitting on the sand. He showed me photos of coconut groves in Kerala. A nut vendor outside with baskets of saffron, cassia, cloves. But it was when he got sick that something happened.

He was staying with an Indian family. From his sick bed,
through the window he watched the oldest daughter rub mud
and dung onto the patio wall while the younger sisters made a
mandala for the Feast of Onan. Flowers he'd never seen before:
scarlet java, yellow champa, ganda, blue aparajita. Petals
arranged in a complex pattern on the ground.

The mother bathed his face with a cool sponge, the thin bracelets
on her arms made a tender gilded sound, and in that moment,
in the fragrance of curry and coriander, when she fed him
broth, he felt himself change. Oil tracing the grooves of his
cracked lips.

"You go halfway around the world to find God, and you're
converted by the damnedest thing," he laughed.

10.

"Daniel thinks I should go to a Cézanne exhibit when it comes to
Philadelphia," I say after tracing the room.

He waits.

From behind the couch I take the rolled papers, the outlines of my
body. Red gashes across the legs.

"Tell me the truth," I ask him, "can this person travel?"

"How much time do we have to prepare?"

"A few months."

"Definitely," he says.

"Journeys can be a good thing, right? I mean, sometimes?"

"Of course. We often don't know what we're looking for until we
find it."

I tell him about my first journey. It was in the house before Inez.

*Doreen lived upstairs. I was a toddler, without language.
It was night. My father ran upstairs to Doreen's carrying
Georgie on his hip. He ran back down for me, his shoes
banging on the wood, the end of his belt flapping loose
against his gathered pants. His white t-shirt, a moving patch
of light. He carried me on my side, my back against his waist.
Doreen's vine moved quickly past my eyes, moonlight on the
petals like sugar.*

*Cheryl and I stood on Doreen's porch, holding her legs. She had
Georgie in a blanket against her chest. We watched the street
below, the flashing light of the ambulance cut a ribbon of red
across the faces of the dark apartments. They lifted my mother
into the back, my father threw down his cigarette, an orange
flicker in the dark quadrant of grass. He finally climbed in.
They drove away.*

I did not miss them.

*Inside Doreen's apartment, Cheryl fell asleep sucking her
thumb. Georgie lay on the seat of Doreen's deep blue brocade
chair. The living room was dark except the light from her
television.*

*She held me on her lap and, keeping her arms around me,
opened a white milk-glass pedestaled jar, lifting its lid. I
smelled the chocolate candies arranged in brown pleated paper
cups. She gave me a piece. It slowly cracked open between my
finger and thumb. I lay back onto Doreen. Chocolate melted in
my mouth and I fell asleep.*

"What happened after Doreen's?" he wonders.
"A dulling."

> The dulling a child knows who leans his ear against the
> cool side of a washing machine to hear the agitation
> and the spin.

II.

Josephine looks tired and hungover, sitting under the trees. I pull
the crêpe paper streamers down, their colors running from the dew.

She's dressed in her black satin kimono day robe and matching
slippers. In one hand she has a long, empty, mother of pearl cigarette
holder, and in the other, a bag of pattypan squash she's picked for
me. She leans her weight into the ladder to steady it for my protection. This is not necessary. I climb ladders twice this height at home.
But that is the luxury of it, the kindness almost too sweet to bear.

"Daniel called. He wants me to go to Philadelphia to see an art
exhibit."

"And?" Her face suddenly livens, the way a clam opens its ugly
outer shell revealing the soft pink cinside.

She holds the bag of squash up to block the sun.

> *Our feet shall stand within thy gates*
> *O Jerusalem*

"If I go, will you help me? It's not until Fall."

She snaps the heels of her satin slippers together, almost losing her
balance.

"Mrs. Josephine Bremen at your service!" She salutes me.
Bright yellow squash tumbling out of her bag.

INFIRMA

1

"Barbara!" a man's voice calls from the street. I'm on my tallest ladder, trimming the obelisk's ragged tip. It's Father Dennis calling out. "Josephine's collapsed."

"Did you call 911?" We run into her house. She's propped herself against the living room chair.

"What are you two staring at?" She fumbles with the low neckline of her blouse, the turquoise pendant.

"You look fine," I say. "How do you feel?" She checks her earrings. I wipe the smear of lipstick from her chin.

"I'm glad you were here when it happened," I say to Dennis as two paramedics lift Josephine into the back of the van. They are young, and she is smiling.

"I'll come as soon as I lock up the house," I tell her, my heart sinking.

I am losing Josephine.

I don't want to plough another field.

Helene, Dolores Mary and I sit at the foot of the hospital bed watching Josephine sleep.

"The doctor said it's nothing serious," Dolores offers. "Just exhaustion."

"She kinda overdid it at the party!" Helene giggles.

But the party was weeks ago.

"We missed you on the Fourth," Dolores Mary taps my hand then whispers, "Don't go in too deep, Barbara."

"I've turned St. Joseph to face the corner," Helene explains, "until he makes Josephine better!"

The shade pulled against the daylight. Through it, the bare arms of a tree.

"How are plans coming for your Jubilee?"

"Sister Bernadette's been diagnosed with breast cancer," Dolores Mary's voice is subdued. "It'll be a tragedy if I'm the only one left."

"You're the best of the bunch anyway," Josephine chimes in, raising her head, fully alert, apparently listening the whole time.

I cover Pretty Boy in his cage, bring in Josephine's mail, turn the lights on for night.

> *In the Tenebrae, the Crucifixion*
> *is commemorated*
> *by the extinguishing of candles.*

Outside the leaves move, then cease.

3.

"I was wondering if you'd help me in the garden," Father Dennis leaves a message on my phone machine. It's early. Only Josephine calls at this hour. "I want Josephine's yard to look good Thursday when she comes home. What do you think?"

Gloves, sunscreen, trowel, rake. Above the gardening shelf, tacked
to a stud, bright spot in the dark garage, the photograph Daniel
finally sent of Emily. She's standing in front of the tall boxwood
hedge at Hidcote Manor. Those hedges trimmed into open arched
rooms. Her knobby knees, pamphlets in her hand, her dress a dazzling white against the green. "Here she is!" Daniel wrote on the
back, his large, sloppy scrawl.

Did he take her to the garden's cottage for tea? Scones and jam
cakes piled high on heavy silver plate, the teapot's short, straight
spout? Later, at home, did he show her a manuscript unlocked from
the case and say, "Go ahead, touch it"? Gold bound. Hand-painted
margins. Perhaps a harvesting of grapes, the slaughter of an ox. Pelican and mackerel. Vermilion ink. The vibrant blue of woad.

Did he think, Touch this, Emily. Touch what will outlast me.

Dennis is in the backyard when I arrive, sweeping the ledge with
his arm, a thick blanket of leaves descending.
   The birch trees now bare. The top of the gate, dry leaves, more
between the pots.
   We rake. Scooping, sweeping, hefting the bags. Leaves everywhere,
like coins.

A ruby throated hummingbird hesitates at a fuchsia bloom, busily
inspecting something I cannot see.

"Do you know how to do these?" Dennis holds up a bag of bulbs in a brown mesh sack.

"Dutch bulbs, daffodils. She'll love them."

In her dark work shed, the tulip trowel next to a purple gingham apron with white piping at the neck.

Compass me with songs of deliverance

We plant the bulbs on each side of the walk. Not in straight lines, but in natural drifts.

Who will lead me to the strong city?

I expose an earthworm by mistake, ripping off his darkness, his small protection. He squirms until I cover him again.

I hope I'm not like him. Loving my share of darkness, my own peculiar pain.

Decollo!
Decollo!

I carried my doll, her body and her separated head, in a grocery bag. My father drove me to the "Doll Hospital," narrow pathway, a small white house. The grandmother led us through to her workroom in the back. A sunny glass-enclosed porch. Window panes painted glossy white, the sunlight broken into squares. She stepped behind the Dutch door that divided the porch from the house. We lay my Susie doll on the flat wood shelf there, on her back. She examined her like a real doctor, lifting her arms, her legs. A dish of lemon drops. The smell of pipe tobacco coming from the other room. "What's wrong with your dolly?" she asked. "Her head came off her body," I said.

On the wall, shelves with doll parts in glass jars. Arms and legs. Pink skinned, white, dark brown. On the top shelf a row of doll heads, in diminishing sizes, facing to the left. An ironing board, a rack filled with stiff pressed dresses. The smell of starch, the tinge, that fragrance just before the scorch.

A week later, my father took me back. Susie's head was re-attached. The dirt between her fingers washed away. Her hair smelled of shampoo, the lace collar was mended on her dress. Tissue paper wrapped around her body like a blanket. A wide pink satin bow tied at her waist.

We walked along the narrow path to the car. With every step, his pant leg brushed against my shoulder. Susie rested against my chest. A row of hollyhocks, pink and white, stood beside the fence, the sunlight felt gentle, and time felt long.

6.

I screw the nozzle onto the hose. It feels good to be concerned with operable things. Dennis sweeps. Our backs are to each other. Silence, except the scraping of the tools.

7.

The sun is behind the wall. The leaves are bagged. The furniture wiped clean.

Josephine's garden, like a farmer's, full of vegetables. So unlike mine, my yard with nothing edible, no plant that has to work.

Dennis and I rest on the lanai.

"Shall I play something?" he asks as I set down the iced tea.

His oboe on the table, the already opened velvet-ined case.
Delicate, the red highlights streaking the ebony's black. Cane dust
in the zippered case, his reed carving tools. The near black of
grenadilla ebony. The rubbed-soft surface of the silver keys.

"How about a little Haydn?" I nod, he starts, hesitates, starts
again.

> I want to touch this sound.
> Canto. Foundation stone.
> I press the notes flat between my shoes and the brick,
> as if to preserve them there. Violets between waxed sheets.

> *Count me . . . count me among the almonds*

I keep my eyes open this time while he plays and nothing changes,
nothing hurts. And there is no heat. His sound, a moat. Outside, far
away, he puts my mother. Unable to find me. Unable to lift me up.

> A bruised girl steps out of all that went before.
> She steps out all at once, as if out of a stream.
> I lay my head against the chair. Closure.
> Dusk and the licking of an envelope.
> Cracked bells in a clay tower calling
> the Angelus for the end of day.

> *. . . finds its way through, a heartstream,*

you know its name, . . .
you feel round its shape, with your hand:

Alba.

The first time I read Celan I thought, We are touching. But only at the fingertips.

almonding, almonding

Through a *speech-grille* we touch,

sanctus   sanctus   sanctus

8.

He drops the weighted end of the swab into a section of oboe, and pulls the rag through.

"Have time for more?" he wonders.

"Of course!"

He plays an excerpt this time, from a larger piece. My stomach tightens.

"That was Brahms wasn't it?" My mouth is dry.

"Yes, from 'A German Requiem.'"

"But it was beautiful!"

"Of course!" he smiles. "The 'Requiem' is one of my favorite pieces of music."

My neck tightens like a rope.

"I have it on CD. We could listen to it together sometime."

He doesn't understand. I can't listen to Brahms like that! in a closed space, a house, a room. There would be no air.

But maybe. Maybe if I could listen with him, through him, like Celan translating Mandelstam:

> *you undo the arm from his shoulder, the right one, the left,*
> *you fasten your own in their place*

9.

"We should do this again," he says. The breeze is colder now. "It was fun." We walk to the gate.

Perhaps I could say "Don't you see . . . I still have dirt on my lips," and he seeing it, would not flinch.

10.

What is being built here? in this music?

this exchange? this conversation?

A garth.

A garth in which my intellect can fly.

FRACTIO

Marie arranges her Thanksgiving merchandise just like she did last
year: notecards, tall bronze candles, place cards, thank you notes,
ribboned bunches of pale dried wheat. This place where kindness
fastens around me like a suit.

I buy polished gourds.

It doesn't help. This holiday, an affliction.

> *"Sometimes things go better than we expect," he smiled,*
> *after I described Josephine coming home, all that did not*
> *go wrong. Her long rest, but no more. I didn't lose her.*
> *We were watching carp swim near the deck.*

I unwrap the gourds and layer them in a crystal bowl. I make
myself remember the particulars of Josephine's return. How I
wrapped a new nightgown and slippers with pompoms, bought her
waterless shampoo, prepared for a second stage of convalescence,
prepared the care for her at home. But she was on the phone when
I arrived, ordering the removal of the hospital bed and shower chair
that very day, canceling the nurse. She looked great. While Sister
Helene praised St. Joseph for the complete, if not speedy, recovery,
Josephine looked at the ceiling, lit another cigarette.

We laughed at the contents of her refrigerator, filled with foods
from the Altar Society: tuna noodle casserole, ham and scalloped
potatoes, Chinese chicken salad, cucumbers in sour cream, a crumb
coffee cake. On the counter, chocolates from Monsignor and Father
Dennis. Sister Dolores Mary smiled when she joked that no one
thought to replenish the bar.

She surveyed the colors in her manicure caddy and soon the room
again smelled of nail polish remover, Chanel No. 5 and cigarette
smoke lingering in the drapes and the silk pillows of the Turkish bed

she uses as a couch. "I should get a little sick more often," she smiled. "Everything looks great!"

2.

The next morning, she walked to the Altar Society meeting in her running shoes and gardening hat, holding the rim down against the breeze.

Still, nothing fixes it.

Still, Thanksgiving.

Last year I just slept through.

The sky is tender gray and reluctant. Yet, even under its watchfulness, I can't steady my legs.

> *Every Thanksgiving I ended up in the bathroom, curled on the*
> *mat. Shaking, perspiring.*
> *Fifty relatives in the other room.*
> *My face pressed to the cool porcelain of the tub.*

In the market, cranberry sauce cans in pyramids. Roasting pans. Trussing kits on paper cards. Stuffing mixes blocking the aisles. Turkeys everywhere piled like dead children.

The memory is in the patterns. Caught there. A code. Paired diamonds on linoleum, red crescent on enamel, brown splotches burnt on glass.

3.

"I can't stay with you in that shirt," I say, even though I traced the room. "I'm sorry."

> That exact pale gray background.
> Thin red and black lines.

"I've worn this shirt before."
"No! You never have. I'm absolutely sure."

> Registered in the patterns like a code.

"Barbara . . . "

> I'm getting out of here.

"Barbara, hold on. Let's try this."

He takes an ivory sweater from the cabinet. Puts it over his head. Cable knit starts to cover his torso. He pulls it down. Ivory over the plaid. Like a cleansing.

"Can you pull it over your collar? Your cuffs?"
He tucks every aspect of the shirt under the white.

Everything becomes still. My back. The bookshelves.

I rest between the fibers of the sweater.
A basilica of breath.

"What happened Barbara?"

"I was in my playpen holding the wood bars."

It falls out. Stones.
I hear them drop.

"Pans were everywhere. My mother was on the other side of the
kitchen in her plaid dress. Blue veins on the backs of her legs. I was
trying to stand. Holding the bars of my playpen. Wood bars against
my cheeks. I wobbled. I cried out.

The plaid spun. A wooden spoon under my stomach pressing up. She
carried me across the floor. The pattern moved beneath me. Overlapping red and black diamonds on the linoleum.

A red crescent shape on the top of the stove. Red stain on the white
enamel between the burners. Cranberries in a pot. She lowered me
down. Squeak sound of the oven door. Flat and open under me, the
glass window. Pattern of brown splotches on the glass like mums.
My hands hot. My toes. I screamed. The roof of my mouth burned.
Lips. Tongue. Then nothing. The last pattern, rows of bumps on the
turkey's skin."

4.

There is no time.
He holds me up.
There are people in the waiting room.
We go the other way.

5.

"I can't do this weekend."

"Call me. As often as you need."

"It's a holiday."

"I know. Here, let me write it down for you." He takes a business card from his wallet and prints the letters clearly.

> "Call me, Barbara, as often as you want,
> It's okay. Even though it's a holiday."

I put the card in the secret compartment of my wallet with the pressed elm leaf from Daniel's farm.

> *You were my death:*

> *while everything slipped from me*

6.

I do not drive. I do not move. Sunlight leaves its trail across the pond. Mallards sleep in the dark ivy bank.

> *My forehead stung when I woke up. Everything was far away. My mother's footsteps were quick and light on the linoleum. I did not lift my head from the plastic playpen pad. Through the bars I watched the plaid hem of her dress.*

> *The air was too full of smells. She turned the radio louder. Music all around me. Running on the walls like horses. She*

came across the room. I closed my eyes. I pulled away. I heard her near, bent over the bars. "It's Brahms. He's my favorite."

She walked away. I tracked the sound of her footsteps even above the sound of the horses.

He comes out of the office, wearing a yellow rain jacket. "Call me when you get home."

> I am a fish
> caught in a weir. He, the one
> who wove the sticks,
> who set them in the stream.

7.

The UPS man has left a package on my door. It is from Paris. I don't care. Thick as telephone book. I put it in the garage under Emily's photograph. I don't want one more meaningful thing.

8.

Dolores Mary calls to wish me happy Thanksgiving. Helene, Father Paul and Daniel have sent cards. Josephine says she'll come by later, when she's home from the shelter, to bring me Thanksgiving dinner.

> At the center of the planet, a body stands.
> Arms outstretched, holding tight

the continents swirling on the surface.
Hideous and beautiful. All at the same time.

I crawl into bed.
Glad for the covers. For impersonal things.

9.

I imagine living alone, perhaps in a tree.

I do not come down. I run the branches like a monkey. I keep a jar
of water, for the visitor who never comes.

When I come out from my mask of leaves, it is the Sabbath. Someone has tied food for me in a scarf. Palm cake. Coconut butter.
Grilled fish. Dried peas. Skewered bits of lamb. I bury the sweet
things high up in the trunk. Eat the dried fish. It lasts forty days.

I remember when they pillaged my house. How they found a bolt
of red silk hidden under my bed. I am Zaccheus.

I cheated them.

And yet, on the Sabbath, someone brings me food. I weep.

10.

Outside, my pine. The crow cawing in triplets.

When she lowered Georgie into the hot water
to make him scream
I said "Mommy, you have pretty hair."

In his crib Georgie finally fell asleep. Piano chords shook
the floorboards.

I went down to the backyard with my dancing doll.
We slept under the swing.
Her arms and legs were blue cotton with white polka dots.
Her face was plastic, red lips, a painted smile.

11.

The light turns everything blue.
The sun absconding.
Sorrow in the gashes of the tree.
Contrition running down the bark
stripping away the leaves.

12.

It was the Faculty Christmas Party. I said to Daniel,
"I don't understand. I'm reading Celan and can't get enough
of him." He filled a napkin with cayenne scented cheese sticks
and joked, "You don't understand that? You?" And then I
remembered my childhood.

Private, the grotto, where the world destroys itself.
Private, the same grotto, where the world, in increments,
saves itself.

There was a knocking at the screen door. My mother turned the radio down. Through the playpen bars, I watched the movement of green silk against smooth brown calves. Doreen came downstairs to borrow ice. My mother slammed the ice tray against the counter, the crank-grind sound of the handle, the ice cubes falling into a paper bag. Doreen leaned down over me. "Got yourself a little sunburn?" Her cool hand on my cheek. Her long fingernail softly marking patterns in my hair. My mother watched Doreen climb the stairs. Standing at the screen door, hands behind her back, twisting the apron string into a knot.

I find the four volumes of my Psalter. That close, death and infancy. That close, the final breaking.

> Mother of mercy.
> Flesh. Tabernacle. Thigh.
> Lap of deliverance.
> Corpse on your knees.
> *Tantum ergo Sacramentum*
> Slit.
> Blood.
> Water.
> Salt.

13.

It must be that infants possess a grammar for order.
Doreen's hand over the playpen bars, cool against my cheek.
A bolt of cloth tossed from a balcony. Green canopy of silk.

It must be that infants come equipped with a code.
Locked in the chromosomes.

Ready to register the difference between touch and burn.
Ready to record the marks of a predator.
Timeless. Infallible.
With a hunger for the good. Ready to record, also,
the marks of grace.

14.

"I'll be right over, Missy," Josephine calls. It's close to midnight.

Fifteen minutes pass. A half an hour. A blackbird, then two, on the wire.

"Here," she hands me a foil-covered plate. Under her bathrobe, a pistachio shirtwaist dress, the rusted metal rivets in the matching fabric belt.

"I re-heated it," she says, meaning, I'm sorry that I took so long. Not believing in microwaves, their unpredictable new heat.

I know what lies beneath the foil, red Jell-O melting into meat.

while everything slipped from me

"Thank you Josephine."

15.

Tomorrow all the neighbors will hang their holiday lights and wreaths. Fall colors will be pushed aside. Oak leaf, moth brown, the gray green of sage.

Christmas will come from the sky. Foil gold, trumpet-sound crimson, cloister blue. Assertive and clear. Pure like a chant.

Five years from now, maybe ten, maybe two, I'll be like them. I'll cook my first turkey, tolerating the open oven door's dry heat. I'll invite guests. We'll eat by candlelight.

But the next day, before hanging my wreath,

If I forget thee, O Jerusalem

I'll dig a hole in the backyard, lay the bony carcass down, like a foundling. I'll bury the bones under my pine tree where I've buried fallen finches.

16.

Standing in my playpen outside on the grass, I could see Doreen coming home. Her tall body bent to the side, pulling her shopping cart. Her polka dot dress, scooped neck, patch pockets on her wide thighs. Hat tilted forward, sunlight bouncing from the rhinestone butterfly pinned to the brim.

"Sugar!" she called to me, taking off her gloves. "Special Delivery!" she smiled, lifting me high into the air. Her breath warm and woodsy, the evergreen scent of her pomade.

"I can't sing much," she said, "but I can hum . . . ." She swayed, rocking me back and forth. My head against her chest. Her voice, softer than the sound of cars and buses on the street.

I dropped into the deep sound of her voice sliding over the notes. Her chest rising and falling under me. Three strings of yellowed pearls up, around her neck. Behind her head a palm tree, its long fingered fronds separating the sunlight into a crown.

POETA

1.

How is it that a poet's words reach into the life
of an other?

black milk
smokemouth

His field of compounds taller than the grasses.

2.

A balustrade explodes, plaster and stone fly into the courtyard
below. Celan feels the earth tremble. He covers his ears. He comes
upon the balustrade, picking shards up from the ground, putting
them into his leather apron.

He will not attempt to recreate the house or the balustrade. As if
nothing happened.

He puts the pieces together. Not erasing the veins, the separations.
The seams that do not align. This is how he covers his head. This is
the prayer shawl.

For your sake happened what happened

He tells himself, I will not describe the bombing of the balustrade.
I will be the balustrade, bombed.

Fear does what it can. Floor. Window. Gash.
Cement through which sunlight comes.
Fear does what it can. It is accurate. It looks
upon the dead and commits what it sees
to memory.

4

Celan comes,

> *telling me what I already know*

> *White it is white, a water—*
> *stream finds its way through, a heartstream,*
> *. . .*
> *you know its name, . . .*

> *Alba.*

I wanted to fall down into the traffic below. But then I thought of
my students. Newspaper photographs. Shame.
The security guard watched me too carefully.
I buttoned my coat.

Celan did not write about the slam of water against his face.
(This came as an insight of not inconsiderable significance.)
I reconsidered, thinking, What if he revised on the way down?
I took my hand from the rail and went back inside.

> *Alba*

5.

A child locked in a closet for three days sits at a neighbor's kitchen table. He sees the word

icesorrowpen

and laughs
because he understands it,
completely.

Scholars gather yearly in Paris to unravel the cryptic poems of Paul Celan. The boy at the table knows it is a simple matter:

Celan forced the German language to remember, he would tell them.

He broke its bones.

6.

I sit in a therapist's office bounded by my touch on all four walls. Remembering and dismembering

scale and fist

the aggressive act.

> *You were my death;*
> *you I could hold*
> *while everything slipped from me*

7

Plagiarism charge that would not go away. Of course Celan
jumped into the Seine.
His blistered arms.
Running into the wood. Carrying the child: Speech.
Running from the language house, burning. Smoldering village.

Of course he jumped into the Seine. To be told, The child is not
safe in your hands.

> *Through*
> *the sluice I had to go,*
> *to salvage the word back into*
> *and out of and across the saltflood:*

8

Jesus grilled fish for his disciples.

> *in bright blood:*
> *the brightword*

But they did not recognize him.

> *Still . . .*
> *unbinded:*
> *. . . that light*

How do words of one reach into the life of an other?

Yizkor

9.

After a reading in Tel Aviv, people who knew Celan's parents came up to him. A woman gave him the kind of cake his mother used to bake. At this, according to his biographer, Celan wept.

> *There stood*
> *a splinter of fig on your lip,*
> *There stood*
> *Jerusalem around us*

10.

In Rama, Rachel weeps for her children because they are not.

Lord have mercy

Divine dwelling place.

Shechinah

Sister Helene called to tell me Heloise's mother is pregnant again. "Your prayers are the best Barbara, I mean it!" I slammed the phone.

423

Of course Celan jumped into the Seine.
Rachel weeping is the divine dwelling place. And no other.

Shechinah

11.

Translation. Transfusion. Child carried across
the *saltflood.*

Yizkor

12.

"Todesfuge," in some German schools, was taught this way:
Shulamith and Margareta "once again extend their hands to
each other . . . in reconciliation."

Of course Celan jumped.

You, clamped in your depth

In the bathroom mirror my hair, between the faucet handles
reflected back, was no longer blond but dark like Cheryl's.

Aschenes. Aschenes.

Some, I suppose, would call this reconciliation.

13.

Deep
in the time-crevasse,

. . .

a breathcrystal,

What waited for me? Unannullable.
That one thing.

  . . . witness.

14.

Buried high in the trunk of the tree, the sweet things.

  Yizkor

15.

The day after Thanksgiving, last year, I walked through the
shopping mall. Waited on a chair outside the dressing room,
handing bras of different sizes in to my daughter.

  Ho, Ho

Holiday Sale. She was not my daughter.
There was no dressing room.
There was no one.

Ho, Ho
Hosanna

Something snapped off.

16.

If it hadn't been for Nelly Sachs, then what?

 deer running toward living water

Touch! Touch!

 . . . name-awake, hand-awake

In their tunnel of letters,

 Almonding
 Almonding

another gate.

17.

She checked herself into a psychiatric hospital. Her head filled with images from Hieronymus Bosch. Having heard the news, she died the day Celan was buried. Her head, laurel wreathed.

> *The floating word*
> *is dusk's*

Crowned, their friendship, a sweet bay.

18.

The field that lies fallow in the seventh year feels joy.

> *glad for the crossing*

Sabbath joy: silence.

Word made flesh.

> *Sunlight reflected off the lemon bush. On the table near me, my*
> *mother's hand, leafing open the Bible, its pages thin as moth's*
> *wing.*

Corridor of memory.

Celan with flour on his hands. Rolling out the dough.

You said,

> *no one*
> *witnesses for the*
> *witness*

This is not true.

> *Shulamith   Margareta*
>
> *Aschenes   Ashenes*

You combed my hair clean.

A fisherman found Celan's body seven miles downstream.
Folded like a cloth.

> *as if I*
> *were this,*
> *your whiteness*

Rachel's tears wet my palm.

In your apron soaked with the Seine, You
baked *desert-bread*. Lamb shank and bitter herb.

In language *co-wandered* you said, Barbara

> *climb out of yourself*
> *for ever*

PICTURA

I bring Daniel's package in from the garage, sit with it in the black prayer room, cut the tape. It's the catalogue from the Cézanne exhibit, a thick hardbound book.

Randomly, I open to a painting titled "Apples." Seven apples, four and three. Their shadows, holes from their stems.

It is just seven pieces of fruit. But they are everything. I can feel Cézanne's pleasure moving down, falling, into the fruit, without measure.

Unbound, even to the core.

Daniel was right. Even the crawling things under the dirt

feel this imperative

to silence.

The thickness of the book, and this, only one painting! How can a single person inhabit so rich a world? And all this brought together now in Philadelphia?

I don't know what to do.

I sweep the driveway. Hose out my trash cans. The shovels. The rakes. Look at "Apples" again. Sit outside with it.

The sky is overcast. Even the fog hovers below the branches of the pine, wanting a look.

In bed, I open to a second page, the full body of a single figure, "The Harlequin." The bedroom falls away. Into oblivion. Into nothing I want.

Even the "Apples" are gone now.

This is entirely new. This territory with its conflict and strife. The Harlequin addresses me and I'm forced to speak back.

> Baton in your hand. Your feet secure on the ground.
> But—the slant of your back.
> The diagonal of your body—
> > receding! Moving away from even these,
> the bright diamonds. Recoiling from the leotard's
> reds and blues.
> Upward, upward and back—but
> > to what? what refuge?
> Into your cap!
> > Crescent shaped.
> > like a cave
> > a moon—
> > Without pigment.
>
> Safety!
>
> Your face, the only skin that shows.
> And it, almost without feature.
> Here, but disappearing. I watch
> you move away from touch.
>
> The text says, "Cézanne used his son to pose."

Of course.
Childhood.

That nausea of touch. I understand it
precisely.

I see you, Harlequin. I see you and step back.

*Through the sliding glass door, I saw my mother watering
ground cover underneath the wooden swing. I had never seen
her gardening before. Like music, she kept it to herself.*

*I stood near the drape, careful to chew quietly, careful not to
bang my spoon against my cereal bowl. She must have forgotten
I had cheerleading practice before school. Everyone else still
sleeping.*

*The fan-shaped nozzle broke the water into an arc, the way a
grandmother's hair spreads across a pillowcase and, as she
sleeps, moves slightly with each breath.*

*Her back, like a rag doll. Her hand loose at her side, fingers
heavy and limp. Her legs bare below olive green checked shorts.
She touched the back of her thigh to brush away an insect and
for a moment I wanted to be there, on that exact patch of skin,
touched in that absent-minded way.*

*Grateful for the glass, I inclined toward her and could not stop.
I felt empty and drawn in to that sleeveless arm, that limp drop
of her hand.*

435

I see you Harlequin, pull into yourself, away from skin, toward skeleton.

Guarded by your straight back, the sureness of your feet.

> *The woman on the Mission balcony looked up at the sky,*
> *imploring it. Casting her prayer upward and away.*
> *The work of disappearing.*

Fig flesh.
Softness that cuts.
I understand you Harlequin.
I close the book and weep.

3.

Through all the rooms of the house, I make myself touch the blank windowpanes. Make coffee. Pace. I can't resist. I open to another page.

It is a letter from Henri Matisse to the curator of the Musée de la Ville de Paris. Matisse was donating a Cézanne painting, "Three Bathers."

> I have owned it for thirty-seven years . . . it has
> provided me with moral support in critical moments
> . . . I have drawn from it my faith and my
> perseverance . . .

From the index I find all the paintings dealing with this Bathers theme.

I move through the Bathers canvases in chronological order. Over and over again, a certain group of elements. Nude bathers on a river's edge.

This is not like the apples. Not like the Harlequin who appears once and flees, from his suit into the safety of his cap.

I slow down. Go through them again. I see a profound evolution. A stripping away.

The earlier canvases are small and detailed. But in the end, the "Large Bathers" of 1906 are much larger than life. And in this increased space, increased dimension, instead of more detail, there is much less.

A dropping away of finger, leaf, cloth. Other basic elements stay the same. Nudity, water, tree.

Viewed over time, things become raw, increasingly stark, bare. The standing woman on the left becomes more distorted, until eventually she has no face at all.

In the three final largest paintings, the flying white of pure canvas, with no paint at all. Shining. Shining through.

Pure white. A final reduction.

I go through the sequence again. The stripping, the push toward clarity, but with greater and greater discomfort. Increasing starkness, increasing tension.

This is not a movement toward peace.

Nudity. Nudity, proximity, water, tree. Grating energy. Something that in the end, cannot be resolved.

I close the book. To my surprise,
I've passed through dusk completely.

4.

This is not about bathing. This is about memory. I'm sure of it.
Something behind the work. Something lodged
at the beginning of memory itself.

Pleasure.

5.

To find it. That lost thing. That particular experience against
which all the rest has been endured. That experience about which
one is certain. More certain than anything that follows. Anything
that might contradict.
   To retrieve it. To put it, once again, before one's eyes.

6.

All art is this. All art is memory.

7.

I see Cézanne at his dinner table.
Perhaps—
   it is the accidental brush of the maid's arm against his.

He flies into a rage. Yet, under his black coat and shirt, suspenders, tie, in that same body that does not want accidental touch, he carries a picture, as if a hidden slide, a specific and unchanging composition: Adults grouped on the side of a stream, having shed their clothes, relaxing.

He holds this imaginary slide up to the light, in private, in the studio, or in private on the hill. Even here, at the dinner table, he feels the blue of that afternoon, when he saw them there, highlights in the stream. The stillness of it. Safety. Pleasure. Arrested there!

The maid serving soup spills a drop next to his plate. He clenches his jaw, thinking, Soon I will be away from all this. He taps his fingernail against the glisten of cherrywood, noticing a drop of water further down the table near the tureen—its handles, angry gray fish heads. The highlight holds him. The white. He thinks of the bathers, the small group, how they were proximate, skin not far from skin, and still, no violation.

He studies the fish heads and thinks how he wants to capture their moderateness, this scene he sees even when he despairs. He wants to capture feeling that does not produce sudden action. The good of it. Something not quite tenderness.

The next day, he stretches a canvas above his head. Hammers it to wood. Sketches in the figures larger than life. Shrinks himself in this way, in comparison to them. He notices how this helps. He more easily goes back to that afternoon when he was young. When he watched them. The stream water splashed the brown wool of his cuffed shorts.

He remembers how he went back to the stream the following day, pestering his nurse. But they were gone, the whole group of them.

"They were gypsies!" his nurse scoffed, tugging his arm. He turned and looked back at the water, his hands blocking the sun. He made a square with fingers and thumb and framed that portion of bank, of stream. Trudging up through the thicket he thought of the woman who had been on the left. Her straight stiff back, long hair, her full lunge toward the stream, her enormous thigh, bare as fresh cream.

"I saw ghosts and then they left," he wants to say to his father that evening, to shock him, to get a laugh, but instead he says, "I played at the river with my boats," as if he were just a nursery child.

From his bedroom window he sees, as proof of yesterday, his wool cuffed shorts spread out to dry on the arms of the lilac bush.

His wife at the other end of the table, his son. He compliments the maid, despite her poor serving, and pushes back his chair. He watches as she clears the plates, considers how he loathes her back, her crossed white apron straps, her thin striped blouse. Wonders why touch can't be like then. When he saw those other adults bathing by the stream. He wonders, in himself, what went wrong.

During dessert he thinks, Painting is archaeology, a sifting through, with soft brush, removing grains of sand until the hard small shard is found that can be held. Held!

He orders more brushes and works on the large canvas, turning it to the wall, turning it back again. Disgusted with himself, he thinks, This does not look like nudity. He feels how reluctant he is to let the figures touch. It is no secret. In the studio, on the hill, he knows how he fails them. Fails himself, then, his small bare feet on the wet stones, his nurse calling after him, "Plus tard! Plus tard!"

An archaeologist re-constructs the history of a village covered with ash, from a bracelet, a jawbone, a tooth. Filling out the soft fleshy parts. Cézanne knows this. He reads about ancient discoveries, Egyptians, Sumerians. Cheek, thigh, the softness, the nausea. When he brings the figures on his canvas close, the hair on his forearms stands on end, bristling, every single time. He cannot make it go away, year after year.

Reliquary. Memory. Brush that opens the hinge. And no peace.

8.

I pour a glass of wine, scramble egg whites, stir in zucchini. My arms are cold. My neck aches. Cézanne is speaking to me, saying,

> Come see my Bathers, Barbara.
> See how I failed them.
> See me fight.
> Be brave, Barbara. Come close.
> See me remembering.
> See my Bathers and you will see me.

CREDO

"Why are you grinning like that?"

"I noticed something remarkable just now," he says. "When you came in you didn't trace the room."

He can't be right. This whole time? Sitting here with him, this whole session?

Door, wall, bookshelf, glass door, wall again.

But he is right. I didn't touch the walls at all.

"What do you think it means?" he asks.

Outside, the deck retains its usual shape. Boards and nails. Thin spaces in between.

"It means you're finally as safe as your watch," I say.

"Which one'll it be today, Barbara?" my father asked,
thumbing through his ties. I moved closer in to him.
"Hmmm . . ." I touched each one. I made my selection.
"That one, are you sure?" It was our joke. Because I
was always sure.
I was more sure of his tie than of any other thing.

2

Think of it:

earth, suffered up
again into life.

from the unburiable

I sit at the beach, Celan's words at my side. I write out
what it means for a man to be as safe as his watch.
I write it exactly.

"I have another lecture," I say, and he straightens his back.
"The title is, 'How A Buried Child Organizes The World,' or
'Why Art Is a Necessity.'"

I stand and read this:

"When I was buried by my father, nothing worked in its normal
way. He'd said we were going to play a new game but it was not a
game. The Army shovel he ordinarily used to cover our campfires
was used to dig the hole and then to put dirt over me.

He stared down at me in the hole, but his eyes did not see. My
shoes and socks did not keep the dirt from between my toes. My
arms and legs did not stay warm. Nothing worked right except the
dirt. The dirt just fell, as always. Letting itself be moved. First it fell

from the end of the shovel onto my legs, then it fell from his cupped hands onto my neck and I thought, It's behaving the same way it does in the sunlight, on the cement walk, when Cheryl and I play bakery, fashioning our cookies and small loaves of bread.

After my father put in the flexi-straws, and before the cold moved inward from my skin to the deep center of my body, in that space of time before the cold itself disappeared and I was no longer a thinking person at all, I thought, The dirt is the most moral thing because it is faithful to itself. Faithful to its own immobility.

I felt this with great conviction. And I believe I lingered on this, fastening onto it the way a leaf, having fallen from a tree by the wind before its time and still green, lands on a wire, and wilting there, lets out the remainder of its fluids, but meanwhile holds fast, folding itself over the wire, perhaps even loving it, as the only remaining verity.

After, when we walked along the side of the house up to the kitchen door and I noticed the strip of dirt next to the cement walk had not changed but still lay there as immobile as ever, I found proof in this, that the dirt was superior to my father. And I felt a kind of relief. Because I had found a principle around which to organize the flurry of my world. And I came to treasure the dirt, on my shoe or under my fingernail, as an artifact of this primal reckoning.

And later, in Sunday School, when I heard the Bible story of creation, I recognized myself not in Eve but in Adam because he named and categorized all the things of his world. And I began to categorize according to the stillness of dirt.

So that a wooden box that houses a clock was viewed as safer and more moral than the pendulum moving inside it. And the giant redwood tree in the campsite where I was always afraid was seen as much less frightening than the new eucalyptus tree planted in the sidewalk by the city which grew too fast, and by the end of summer was taller than our house.

I came to see the safest thing about a man was his watch, but I knew the watch was even safer when displayed in a jeweler's window and not attached to a man at all.

I knew the stories on the flannel board were true, not only from the kindness of my teachers, but also because the cut-out figures did not move. I knew the world of Bible Times was superior to my own because God acted in their lives in a miraculous way. And this made sense since the figures did not move themselves, but were immobile and moral like the particles of dirt.

And when human beings were described primarily as sinners, this also made sense because, compared to watches or trees or clock cases or even cats and dogs, I knew humans to be capable of the greatest variety of movement and capable of making other things move for their own harmful purposes. So I knew humans were, by far, the most dangerous objects of all.

Later, as a teenager, when I was lucky enough to discover art, I moved more deeply into the implications of this learning.

When I saw that an artist had taken a lemon and frozen its stillness in a frame, I was glad because I knew the lemon had been rescued, its morality preserved. I knew that the lemon could no longer be taken up into the palm of a mother who, humming to herself, squeezes it into the eye of a quivering child.

I came to see art as a necessity because in this way it preserves the moral order by preserving stillness.

The artist, in doing his work, redeems not only lemons but also himself. Even if he is a horrible person, I considered this to be self-evident. Because what he releases into the world lasts forever. It outlasts his own cruelty.

And for this reason, when he dies, I knew the soil would welcome him, and as he decomposes, he would re-enter its innocence, particle by particle."

4.

I look up.

> *earth, suffered up*
> *again into life*

5.

A winter sky gathers over the pond. Ducks sleep, heads tucked under their wings. I show him the Cézanne book. He follows the marked pages, through all the Bathers canvases one by one, covering the entire thirty years.
"It looks like if he could get the Bathers right, all his suffering would end," he muses.

"Can we go out onto the deck?" I ask.

He opens the sliding glass door.

Despite the weak sun, there is a shadow on the slats. It's the shadow of my body.

I bring out the Cézanne book. It casts a shadow too.

"I would like to see this work. I would like to see it with my own eyes," I tell him.

I say these words here, outside, in public, where even the ducks can hear.

"Congratulations!" He smiles.

Cheryl and I stood looking up at the Golden Gate Bridge,
the sweep of orange cable disappearing in the fog.
A woman next to us told her son, "Every year someone jumps
off and gets killed."
My mother's hands, gripping Georgie's stroller, got white.
She looked at Cheryl and then at me, saying, sternly,
"Last year a girl jumped off and lived."

IV.

Come the Sabbath

MOBILIS

Why is Bob in long pants instead of his usual shorts? He must be going to a funeral. Maybe his son, the older one, who was always so kind to me that Christmas, carrying my three trees.

"You're all dressed up . . . ?" He touches his hair.

"You need to feed your lawn, Barbara. I drove by your place the other day."

He turns. "I've got a date in an hour. I'm nervous as hell." There is a leaf stuck on his shirt, at the shoulder.

"You look great, Bob." Even his fingernails are clean.

"You're looking good again yourself, kid," he smiles. "I like the short hair."

2.

"I can go to Philadelphia, right?" I pace back and forth across his rug. "I mean, if I go to the beach, I don't have to stay in my car the whole time, right?"

"That's right," he says. "You sure don't."

"I can move around. I could have been a move-around girl, then, right?" I slam my purse against the couch.

"Absolutely."

> *"We're here girls." My mother thought our Brownie troop should learn about trees. Our station wagon parked under the tall oaks and pines.*
> *"Barbara, you stay in the car. I can't show favoritism, just because I'm the new leader." I stayed in the car. Watched my*

455

friends scurry under the canopy of branches collecting leaves.
They didn't have to stay in pairs. She didn't care about the
buddy system. She didn't care about any of the Brownie rules.
Her white legs, iridescent in the shade. Veins on the backs like
morning glories.
"More fun than I've had in a long time!" she said, catching my
eye in the car's rearview mirror driving home.
I smiled back at her. Don't feel guilty, my look said.

3.

I get out of the car. Walk down to the sand. Carry my shoes.

Only there did you wholly enter the name that is yours

Air blows against my ankles, my toes, my cheeks.

"I've walked for an hour now," I leave a message, using a pay-phone. "Next, I'm taking off my sweater. If anything goes wrong, I'm going to page you."

It is nearly five o'clock. The sun moves toward the horizon, taking the light with it. I can do nothing about it. Past where I can go.

4.

I make myself watch how dusk actually occurs. This is what I see: The afternoon lays itself back. The afternoon gives itself over to the night.

I put on my sweater. I keep my eyes open. I see this: Dusk is not a girl on a pine needle bed.

5.

I make a chart, a calendar. I put on a gold star for today. A gold star because I went out and came back again. Because I got out of my car and nothing went wrong.

I find a map of Philadelphia.

For three consecutive days I get out of my car. I take off my shoes. I walk barefoot on the sand.

6.

"I am ready to see my shadow on the sand," I say. "It's me, Barbara. I'm at the beach."

So far every time I've looked westward, toward the sun. I didn't want to run the risk of seeing my shadow on the sand. I also didn't want to look and have my shadow not be there.

I take off my shoes. I walk in the same direction. But this time I look back toward the houses, east. Then I look down. It is there. Just like on his deck. Pure black. And connected to my feet. Even when I stretch out my arms. My five projections.

But I am not a starfish. I tilt my head. I am not a potato. I fluff my hair. Nothing falls off.

The sun and the sky and the sand are not lying. I hear what they are telling me: Barbara, you are one piece.

7.

I put another gold star on my chart. I sleep outside under the stars.

The birds wake me with their determined songs. The thin cerulean blue of the predawn air. I re-arrange the blankets and wait for the first copper glint of day.

Even in a sunsuit, even naked in the tub, it is true—I wore an invisible coat. A garment into which adults stitched their precious things: tears, shame, forgetting, even their goodness. As if I, like an immigrant, would take these to a new shore.

Sewn into the hem, a key behind the satin. In the breast pocket, a lock of someone's hair. A pair of ruby earrings stitched under the collar. Cuff links of celadon hidden in a sleeve. A hand-drawn map with names I did not recognize.

A legacy sewn in with coarse thread.

The sun comes over the fence. I take off the blanket, then my nightgown and my robe. I feel the heat on my back, my shoulders, my breasts.

I command the sun to touch me like a bare chested child.

8.

I walk bare shouldered in the sand.

My feet begin to tan, up to the line of my cuff.
Nothing goes wrong.

At home I have a long row of gold and silver stars.

I take it in to my session. We look at the map of Philadelphia.
Around the art museum I draw a circle in ink.

9.

Today the sand is wet and flat and silvery. Footprints left by another person's running shoes. Past the pier, sand dollars by the hundreds, left from the high tide.
I fill my pockets for Josephine.

If I forget thee, O Jerusalem

10.

I come and go, day after day.
I leave my car and come back to it again.
The car remains. Nothing burns. Nothing explodes.
Moving my body is not the same as death.

Now I have two long rows of stars.
I call the airline. I book my flight.

11.

Josephine rests her head on my shoulder.

"I've decided to take that trip," I say, spreading the sand dollars across her lap, the coffee table piled with dusty magazines.

"The art?"

"Cézanne in Philadelphia."

"I'll lend you my fur."

She squeezes my hand, her bony fingers covered with rings.

12.

In his office, we look, again, at the map of the city. I draw a circle around the airport and hotel, then make lines in ink connecting the locations.

"You still think I can do this?"

"Of course," he says.

13.

The sun hangs like a patch of foil against the fog. By the time I get
to the shore, it has disappeared. I walk on the sand. I have no shadow.
My stomach tightens. The bench is empty of visitors. There are no
sand dollars at the waterline.

I make myself note this: that other things have stayed the same.
Sandpipers in black silhouette busy hunting crabs, a fishing boat
with a blinking light. The comfort of random scattered shells.

I try to be tolerant. Perhaps it is understandable. The sun behind
a curtain hastily drawn. Not wanting, always, to be so public.

Even without the shadow, I walk. It's different, but it counts.
At home I put a gold star on my chart.

14.

Saturday the beach is full of motion. Planes take off.
Sailboats, wind surfers, two kayaks in the waves.
Everything that lives, moves.
I roll my pants above the knee.

15.

The sun drops into the ocean like the Easter candle
plunged three times into the baptismal font.
Blessing, in that action, all the waters of the earth:

The great seas holding the whales and sharks,
the freshwater basins with their egrets and their plovers,
the finger streams hidden under prairie grass,
the salty waters around every unborn child.

16.

A young man is finishing an elaborate medieval city made of
sand. He pours wet sand like liquid through his palms fashioning
decorated spires and turrets, making roofs of slate, shingle and
thatch. Not just a castle, but a whole city. Fields laid out in a grid,
straight rows of haystacks, a church, the fortressed wall, clustered
huts.

He works in the dark sand, close to the waves, close to the rising
tide. Why does he build something so elaborate knowing it will soon
wash away? I so want what I am building to be permanent.

It is a wonder. And he, generous. Making visible his own seques-
tered vision. A whole city, innocent. A whole city, without guile.

Our feet shall stand within thy gates, O Jerusalem

When I return only the turrets remain. Inside the wall, a hole is
filling up with water. The rest has washed away and the builder is
also gone.

17.

This is how we discover ourselves. In ruins.
The parts that have survived.

18.

A row of six brown pelicans moves south over the waves.
They follow a leader, flying low, looking for fish.

Here, all of evolution can be seen. Sand, the broken shells,
the fish, the birds.

Myself, too, coming from the water womb. With the mollusks,
the sand crabs, the other crawling things.

Surely the earth is not a passive thing, a mass without intention.
Just so much sediment, a crust, a molten core. Filled with small
betrayals, false deposits, slowly cooling because it has nothing
better to do.

I see the longer line of my lineage. Wider than a certain father,
a certain mother. That the history of my family is this:

That we have come from the water and the mud, raised ourselves
to our amphibian elbows, then to the three-pointed gait.
Finally walking on two feet with our weak but upright backs.
Anchored in our shoes, clutching our paltry inclinations toward
the good.

Surely, we are this, the earth's intention.
The evident groaning of the earth
for its own freedom.

APPETITUS

I.

"I think I should learn to eat colored food again. Especially for my trip."

His tie, his shoes, the pressed cuff of his slacks.

"Are you sure? There isn't much time. You're doing a lot of new things already."

"I saw a family at the beach yesterday. They were having a picnic. They had all kinds of foods. All different colors. It made me sad. I miss it."

"I loved the way they sold mascarpone cheese in Florence. Not in large containers, but in tiny muslin bags, just four ounces at a time. Perfect for a palm."

"And how would you want to start?"

He looks at the bag I've set down on the couch.

I take out my cookbooks, just the Italian ones. We flip through the photographs:

> Easter pizza, rich fruitcake with cocoa and figs.
> Tuscan chestnut cake with pine nuts and rosemary.
> Trout from the River Nera.
> Red mullet, sold already scaled.

nourished by figs

"This doesn't bother me too much."
"You liked eating in Italy then?"
"It was the best."

"Were there any foods you particularly liked as a child?"

"My birthday cake. In fact, I liked the whole day."

> *All thirty-five kids in my class, at my house, at once.*
> *My father with his stop watch, pencil behind his ear,*
> *clipboard in hand. Leading us in game after game.*
> *And inside, my mother finishing my cake. A princess cake,*
> *the real doll in the center, her head and arms coming out*
> *the top, the dome-shaped cake her pink ruffled skirt. Another*
> *year, a train cake. Thirty-five separate cars on a licorice*
> *track. The coal car, my favorite, filled with chocolate chips.*

I return to see the sun. It sets every day, a little earlier.

> *There is a river whose streams will make glad the city of Zion*

I put a star on my chart.

It's not that I didn't notice them. Of course I saw them, first thing. On the end table behind the round rock. Two green apples and a red, in a triangular configuration. Inside my loop.

"I don't have to eat those."
"No," he says. "You don't."

5.

This time I bring a small leather case lined with cobalt blue silk.
Inside, two silver fruit knives, their blades engraved with ivy, their
handles in mother of pearl.

"You go first," I say.
With one of the knives he cuts a single slice from the red apple.
I move back. I watch him chew.

"I'm not going to come in here and eat as if it were a simple thing."

> That day I watched the Egret dive for food, he made only
> three plunges in an hour. Mostly he just stood there, stiff.

I snap the case shut.
"Maybe next time."

> Maybe if the Egret is back, pure white and solitary.

6.

"I can take hard boiled eggs in my suitcase."
"True."
"And jicama sticks and crackers."
"That's right. I'm sure Philadelphia will have everything you need.

We can work on this when you get back."

"You can picture that?"

"Of course."

"I'll come back and you'll be here, and we'll work on this?"

"I'm not going anywhere."

"That's a promise, right?"

"That's a promise, Barbara. You can count on it."

7.

It is raining hard by the time I get home. On the doorstep, sheltered, a tall bunch of China mums. They're from Daniel. No one else would send such pure white. Cut and simply wrapped, with bear grass, lemon leaf, brown paper, twine, just the way I like.

Who will lead me to the strong city?

8.

Some people underestimate how erotic it is to be understood.

9.

In the middle of the night I call London.

"This is Dr. Harris," I tell Daniel's secretary.

"Yes, Dr. Harris," Daniel jokes when he gets on the phone. He's sent the flowers because I'm going to the Cézanne. "Because you said it would be hard," he explains.

"Are you happy?" he wonders.

"I don't know."

10.

I cut off the stems and arrange them in a vase.

Say that Jerusalem is

SALVUS

We look again at the city map of Philadelphia, the airport, hotel, the art museum. We go through the Cézanne "Bathers" and my chart with its many rows of stars.

We have one more month to prepare.

Ruth left the field of her parents to glean in the fields of Boaz

"Do you still have the phone numbers?"
"Yes."
"Josephine's?" he nods. "The Convent? Daniel in London?"
"I still have the sheet."

We sit. We do not eat. It is perfect.

"Black Time comes in increments, doesn't it? Isolated moments, like this, when there is no pain."

"None of us can go back, really," he says. "All we can do is be in the present as fully as possible. That's the goal. At least that's my goal," he corrects, and I see on his desk the book mark with Monet's water lilies.

"Georgie burned his face out of all the family photographs."
He shakes his head.

"I will never have to do that."
Not now. Not after this room where the weaving is done.
A dress that fits my own body. New dress from old rags.

"This is for you," I say. "Haven't you been wondering about it?"
"Well, yes. What's it called?"
"Brunfelsea."

> *Bob said I could bonsai it. We laughed. Remembering*
> *the Chinese Magnolia, he said, "Barbara, even you can't*
> *learn everything from a book."*

"The common name is Yesterday, Today and Tomorrow."
"Well, thank you."

He arranges the objects on the end table to accommodate the plant.
"The blooms will change from purple to lavender and then to white before dying. I thought it was like therapy."

> *We were*
> *hands,*
> *we scooped the darkness empty, we found*
> *the word . . .*

"Like life," he adds, getting up from his chair, repositioning it again. Fussing.
"Thank you very much. I like it," he smiles.

3.

At the beach, for the first time, I have a beach bag and inside it, my stitched book, all my Celan books, and the Cézanne.

I spread out a towel and lay them around me like a family. Take off my shoes. Roll up my pants and sit. Even through the towel, the sand is warm against the backs of my legs.

4.

I noticed, yesterday, a new store next door to Marie's. Without going back to the car, without putting on my sweater, I walk with my beach bag up to the street.

I look like everyone else. I look very normal.

Two elderly women are taking pictures of each other on the sidewalk, with the ocean and the shops behind. One is in an emerald wool suit, the other in a matching suit of cherry red. They look like sisters. Maybe even twins. Their movements are slow and cheerful. They seem to gather up into their delight all the fragments that have been left behind. Birdcage, first born, bakery girl.

I let them carry me.

5.

The new store is like a small closet, a mere six feet wide. The lettering is sleek and perfect on the carefully fitted awning. According to the sign they sell only a single line of purses and women's briefcases from a designer in Brussels.

I open the door and step in.

Each purse is displayed in a glass cubicle of its own, jutting out from the wall. There are very few items in the whole store, ten, maybe fifteen in all. That is the beauty of it. All of the empty space. Each purse surrounded by light.

On the center table a Ming vase with tall twisted reeds.

Deep purple alligator briefcase. Kiwi green evening bag. The colors are unbelievably stunning.

"You like red, yes?" a young Japanese woman says.

Me, like red?

"You've crisscrossed the store," she points. "Red to red to red."

It is the exact color of this red. Not paprika. Not burgundy. A clear nail-polish red with an undertone of elegant blue. Beautiful with black. Supple. Strong. Flawless.

Give me back the joy of my salvation

She takes the red purse out of the case. Leather lining is as soft as talc.

I step back, startled with myself, the way one steps back from a dog at the pound, already knowing it will be the one to be brought home. The purse is obscenely expensive, which adds to its allure. I have never owned an article of clothing in this price range before.

"We have three of these on the West Coast," she offers. "New York received six. Isn't it wonderful? You know, a little spice!"

Even with the clasp open, it sits like a creature.

Capable of standing on its own. On a table, a chair. Or next to me on the plane.

6.

Again, we look at the map. We go over the foods I'm going to take. He shows me that he still has the list of names and phone numbers. We set up a time when I will call him on each of the three days I am gone.

I practice sitting in the plane. I pretend to look out the window. We go through the "Bathers," the flying white.

"I bought a purse," I say, lifting it out of its flannel drawstring cover.

"Very nice," he says, smiling. "Red."

"A bluish red," I correct. "Not paprika."

"Of course. A bluish red. Not paprika. It's beautiful, Barbara."

> *Give me back the joy of my salvation*

RATIO

I.

"Barbara, can you give me a hand?" Josephine calls. "Today's
the Baptists' paper drive and I've got to get these newspapers into
the trunk of the Thunderbird. Father Dennis was going to do it but
I didn't catch him before his retreat."

Columns of papers tied and stacked to the ceiling of her garage.
It will take many trips. I tidy the remaining piles. Leopard print scarf
around her neck, flying out the window, as she drives away.

2.

There is a headline. I can't help but read it. The conviction of a
man who murders small boys and eats their body parts. I run home.

Turn on the garden hose. Wash my hands. Let it flow over my
head.

Everything that is here, every comfort, feels like danger.

The kitchen counter, the tiles, flowers in the yard.

Purge me with hyssop and I shall be clean

I want to hide in his round rock, his shirt, the pant cuff, the sleeve.

Instead I roll out toward this criminal like a rope uncoiling off a
deck. There is an urgency. And I can't stop.

3.

I know his face.

Through the particles of falling dirt, my father stared down
but didn't see me. There was just the white glare on his face,
a radiated heat, like a film overexposed.

I push away the stranger. But he returns.
I name him for his face. I call him White Man.

Purge me with hyssop

I crawl under the sheets. Still, he is with me.

4.

Perhaps it is a simple red shoe box—

White Man stands on a tiny leather stool made of antler legs.
He reaches for the box high on the bedroom closet shelf. Sets the lid
on the bedspread next to his thigh. He drags his manicured thumb
across the row of small white boxes inside. He doesn't open them
this time but instead returns the shoe box to the shelf, adjusting its
gold tasseled tie. So many baubles in a row, he thinks. Fingernails,
wisps of hair, the parts that don't erode.

I have seen this.

On a tray next to my head, my father straightened dental tools
until their slim silver handles lay in perfect parallel.

Concentrating, his tongue pressed against the outside of his upper lip.

Always, order.

5.

I close the windows in the house to block out the sound. Agapanthus under the jacaranda tree rattle their tall dead blooms. Their wooden heads, their pods, interwoven by the wind. Even in my garden, a mingling of death and appetite.

6.

Perhaps White Man cut things off simply because they protrude—

On my back, in my red dress. How my mother wanted to
cut not just my hair but every appendage. Peeling me
like a potato.
To want the smooth outline of a bean, a pebble, a ball.
Not the complicated moving outline of a girl.

Sometimes a thing must be created because it cannot be found. A pleasing fish. How it must be shorn of fins.

7.

White Man holds a dead boy on his lap.

Just then, just in that moment, he feels himself cohere. He tells himself, Now I am clear and solid, like marble.

He remembers Michelangelo's "Pietà" at the New York World's Fair. Jesus flung across the marble lap of Mary. He stares down at the broken body across his knees and thinks, How innocent, how good. He tells himself, Finally I have a mirror. Finally, I am truly here.

8.

Perhaps White Man lies in prison—

Resting on his cot, he watches the moon. Through the small window it is broken by the iron bars. He notes the parceled silver light. He does not remember the boys' names or their individual faces. Perhaps he thinks, These are the things that mammals do. Death and disassemblage. It is necessary for evolution. One must think in macroscopic terms.

Then he remembers the only thing he liked in high school. Reading *The Old Man and the Sea*. The one assignment he completed. The one thing he understood.

The great old man all alone, hunting his marlin.
How hard it was for him to eat the raw dolphin he'd filleted.
Long red slabs laid across the bow. But he did it to stay awake.
The rope across his back, cutting in, the long night.

Eating the raw flesh to stay alert when things began to drop away.
First the shore, then light and sound, texture, feeling, time.
How he fought off nausea and ate.

White Man consoles himself thinking, Some people like the old
man know it is not about what feels good in the mouth. He tells himself, I had to eat my dolphin. I am the old man in the sea.

9.

Perhaps when he sleeps White Man dreams of himself when he
was young—

Taken to Church. He smells his mother's perfume and perspiration
through her sleeve. The only part of her body that touches him, rubs
his side. He thinks, This is the best thing about her. This sleeve, the
arm inside. In Church, where he has her all to himself. The quivering
of her auburn lips, her blue bruised leg hidden under a graceful drape
of rayon at the ankle.

He hears the priest proclaim, "Take. Eat. This is my body."
He watches the elevation of the chalice, the patin. The priest's solemn
bow, the incense, the folded hands, washing of fingertips.

It could begin here. Through glass bound by strips of lead,
fragments of magenta, cobalt and ochre light. The young boy learns
it is not a foreign thing to eat flesh in broken pieces. In this place of
lace and arm and touch, he forms a sweet configuration:

Love and the taste of severed things.

10.

Perhaps White Man moves more deeply into sleep—

His body presses against the prison wall. A filigree of fissures in the cement, by his elbow, the back of his hand. Buried in the walls of his cell, there is a net he doesn't see. It reaches to the outer walls, the barbed wire, pushing past the roots of trees, the mountains and the sea. The great net holds him.

Fish shorn of fins.
Great net of mercy.

11.

I turn out the light. Always, there are reasons.

ROSA

1.

All through the night I saw faces: Inez, Mrs. Pinney,
Mrs. Henderson, Doreen.
I tuck in my nightgown, tie up my boots.
I saw how they lifted me over the terrors of childhood.
A pergola of kindness, a lattice, their arms.

I mark a circle in the center of the lawn with stakes and string. I'll
plant roses in their honor, a garden within a garden. Small circle set
off in quadrants, with raked pebble paths, contained by trimmed
boxwood, guarded by sheared towers of yew.

Until now I've loved my bog garden. Canopy of canary and stone
pine, jacaranda, liquid amber and pepper trees. The tall hedge. A
place for more reticent, shade-loving plants. I haven't missed the
gladiola, hibiscus, their fiery, hot, unexamined hues.
But now I want roses, their complex beauty. My garden should
have both the snake and the thorn, both the blossom and the frightening thing.

2.

Bob's Nursery sign boasts "260 Different Roses," modern and old
fashioned cultivars. I walk past the ferns, the broken shade.
In the broad sun, bare canes sprout red-tinged green leaves. Flori-
bunda, grandiflora, climbing roses, miniatures, China, hybrid tea.
The selection astounds me. Hours of attention and labor to achieve
such a range.

3.

White information cards are stapled to posts at the head of each row. I'm surprised that they don't mention the thorns. Breeders tell me the color of each rose's blossom but not how easily it will make my forefinger bleed. So many thorns here already, so obvious, yet edited out.

Unlike these breeders I have an opposite bent. I'd catalogue thorns, their size, the date they appear. Maybe I lack a rosarian's temperament. Maybe this idea won't work out at all.

Eugène de Beauharnais, Alexandre Girault, Miss Atwood, Rosette Delizy. All these people leaving their tracks. I don't know what roses would be called if I named them. Maybe Outrage, Bloodstain, Betrayal, Chagrin. Certainly not Sanguine, Bridesmaid, Gloire de Dijon.

Yet over these empty brown canes, something floats like a scarf. A conspiracy of language gently bending my perception in a more hopeful arc.

4.

I can imagine one of these breeders, say, a woman in England. Cotton apron, shears in her belt.

Jotting in a notebook, her small desk in a greenhouse, squares of light broken by the white painted metal bars. Gray-brown hair held by tortoise-shell combs. Her nails, beginning to thicken with more calcium each year.

She licks the end of her pencil to darken the mark, records the day's graft, the time, the conditions. She likes the sound of pencil against paper, the dusty cluttered top of her desk. Her awards in a pile, two honorary degrees. Pursuing her winding road of experimentation. Almost erotic, the forward pull.

She feels herself condensing around this attentiveness. Her handwriting becomes smaller each year. Trial and error. Diversity created one plant at a time. Gradually she lets go of the rest of the world.

5.

"Roses aren't hard, Barbara. They're just picky like you."
I'm tired and discouraged. Mrs. Pinney, Doreen, nowhere here in these countless mute canes.

"Why don't you come back when they're blooming?"
February, April, maybe June. When I can see each of their faces, hear their voices, smell their skin on the leaves.

6.

I rest outside on the newly turned dirt. In my box, my most recent clipping. The ink is still bright, the newsprint still soft.
It is an obituary for a Japanese plastic surgeon who devoted himself to the victims of Hiroshima. In his retirement he grew roses, creating the Hiroshima Rose as a symbol for world peace.

A girl in a bakery makes herself blind. Wilde composes his "Lament" while riding on a train. An artist during the Great Plague tries to remember healthy skin. Cézanne struggles with his "Bathers," the reduction to white.

I bind the edges of the soft clipping and sew it into my book. The bound sheaves. Celan's Bremen speech, a melody in my head.

> *. . . there remained among the losses this one thing*
> *But it had to pass through its own answerlessness . . .*
> *frightful muting . . . the thousand darknesses of*
> *deathbringing speech*
>
> *yet it passed through*
> *. . . I have sought to write poems: . . . to sketch out reality*
> *for myself*
>
> *Poems . . . are under way: they are a making toward something*
>
> *Toward something . . . occupiable*
>
> *. . . perhaps toward an addressable Thou*

BENEDICTUS

I.

I practice calling him from the museum, from my hotel room.
I imagine making coffee, eating my hard boiled eggs and cheese.
I even practice deciding to come home early, staying three hours
instead of two days. Practice thinking this is not failure.

Still, I feel like I'm seeing everything for the last time. The hang
gliders, the pier, the pilings, the pelicans, each individual piece of
sand. This does not lessen. It does not change.

Father Dennis came back from his retreat. Josephine came back
from the hospital. I see this, but cannot feel it, no matter how much
we prepare.

A cricket hiding in the ice plant stops his song when I approach.
As I move past him, he starts singing again. I make myself notice this:
In everything, not only endings but beginnings.

2.

At night, I dream. A boy holds out his finger. A cricket comes to land on his hand.

3.

Josephine invites me for drinks, a small going-away party. Dolores Mary, Helene, Dennis. I have two martinis. No one notices that I don't eat. It is simple.

> *from the purplewood we sang*
> *over, O over*
> *the thorn*

4.

Two more sessions before my trip. I unlock the guest room door. It has been a long time. I lay my cello in the backseat of the car, fasten the belt.

Joseph of Arimathea, carrying the corpse.

5.

I trace my loop around the walls, not because I have to, but for the pleasure of it. He watches. Like always. Witness to all that is carried on, and over, and through.

I lay the white bundle of my cello on the floor.
I untie the two black strings.

Joseph of Arimathea carrying the corpse.
Careful, descending the ladder. Careful
to keep the rope, the nails.

White Symphony. Burial cloth.
White Ode that stretches around the bloody century like a cloth.

I take the box of newspaper clippings and empty them onto the
white. Broken body. Broken language. Broken century.
Broken covenant between parent and child.

All of it the same. Fragile. Transparent. A fluttering of wings.

On top of the pile, the smallest clipping. Just a few lines of text.
A quote from J. Robert Oppenheimer saying that his first
conscious thought, on seeing the bomb he had created explode,
had been Krishna's:

> *I am become death, the shatterer of worlds*

7.

We sit on the floor, facing each other, the cello parts and clippings in between.

"Reachable, near and not lost," I begin, reciting phrases from the Bremen speech, "there remained amid the losses this one thing. . . . Yet passed through . . . "

He listens.
Witness for the witness.

8.

Then we recite the words the way they first came out, lifting each cello piece from the sheet, as we do.

"I was sitting on the floor in my bedroom," I begin, taking the fine tuners.
"You were tearing white paper into snow," he lifts the cello's dark curved neck.

If I forget thee, O Jerusalem

"My mother came into the room," I take the bridge.
"She said, 'Why aren't you dressed?'" he lifts the coiled strings.

We continue this way,   antiphon! antiphon!
piece by piece,
until the whole story is told.

9.

Lord open my lips and my mouth will proclaim your praise

10.

This is our last session before my trip.

"I'd like to take something from the office with me, if you don't mind."

He holds out the small round rock from the corner of the end table, the place where the two grains of wood meet.

"Yes, that's perfect."

It warms quickly in my hand.

> *Read no more—look!*
> *Look no more—Go!*
> *Go, your name*
> *has no sisters, you are—*
> *are at home.*

There is nothing that will make this easy.
Already I miss him.
Already I miss the Great Egret and Josephine.

Who shall lead me to the strong city?

Came, came
Came a word, came,
came through the night
would lighten, would lighten
Find
that eye, the moist one

I walk out under the moon. Tomorrow I leave.
Circle of soil, Ruth gleaning.
A sprinkling of moonlight like platinum beads.
Inez, Mrs. Henderson, Mrs. Pinney, Doreen.
Theirs, the faces of Boaz.
Theirs, the field where I climbed from dirt into air.

The moon crosses the night sky. Shadows lengthen and shorten and lengthen again. By the fluids in my body, the moon draws me close.

> *"It's easy to get to the museum," the concierge reassured me. "Yes the hotel's in a safe part of town. Yes, there's an iron in the room."*

My luggage lined up, just inside the front door.

Three car alarms go off. A motorcycle rips down the street.

> *Once*
> *I heard him,*
> *he was washing the world,*
> *unseen, nightlong,*
> *real.*
>
> *One and Infinite,*
> *annihilated,*
> *ied.*
>
> *Light was. Salvation.*

14.

We are ready for takeoff.

On the seat next to me, the Cézanne.
Round rock in my hand.
On my lap, the slim stitched book.
Next to Cézanne, my new red leather purse.
Carefully hand rolled edges of the strap.
Ruby studded eyes of the serpent head clasp.

I am flying thirty thousand feet above ground.
I am doing all this without a problem.
I am doing it like everyone else on this plane.

My cheek pressed against the smooth cool of the glass.
Outside, the sunset is midway through its course.

A counterpoint of salmoned pinks and blues.
Exuberant and forthright. A testament
before the coming of the night.

NOTES

A.

The names of the four parts of the novel (A Thousand Darknesses, Into the Straits, Solstice, and Come the Sabbath) are phrases from the poems of Paul Celan. Come the Sabbath is from Celan's final poem.

Chapter titles, given in Latin, bear a resemblance to the structure of the Mass since they start with "Introit," end with "Benedictus," and have "Fractio" roughly at the center, as in the eucharistic liturgy itself. English translations of the titles are:

I. A Thousand Darknesses

Introit (introduction, a going in)
Confiteor (to confess, to reveal)
Peregrinatio (traveling)
Laceratio (tearing, mangling)
Lamentatio (weeping)
Fundus (ground, foundation)

II. Into the Straits

Deus (God)
Corpus (the body)
Laborare (to work)
Memoria Excidere (to leave memory, to be forgotten)
Artes Liberales (the liberal arts)
Delectatio (delight)
Latere (to lie hidden)
Requiescere (to rest)
Musica (music)

III. Solstice

Ars Magica (magic, magical arts)
Libertas (liberty, freedom)
Ignominia (shame)
Infirma (illness)
Fractio (a breaking, a breaking of the bread)
Poeta (a poet)
Pictura (the art of painting)
Credo (I believe)

IV. Come the Sabbath

Mobilis (movable)
Appetitus (appetite, longing)
Salvus (safe, unhurt, well)
Ratio (reason, cause)
Rosa (a rose, a garland of roses)
Benedictus (closing, blessing, a short hymn of praise)

B.

Celan's best known poem, "Todesfuge," or "Deathfugue" enters the novel in Chapter 2, "Confiteor." While other phrases that appear in the novel can be understood on their own terms, it is perhaps helpful to see the phrases from this poem in their original context.

What follows is the translation of "Todesfuge" by John Felstiner. It is noteworthy in many respects, not the least being that he does not translate all the words into English. Instead, a little of the German is left untranslated. And then that small fragment becomes a larger untranslated fragment the next time it appears in the poem, and so on, so that by the end a reader who knows no German at all has been taught a little German in a very natural and easy way, the way a small child learns from its mother or father.

The problem, and the genius of this translation, is that the words Felstiner leaves untranslated are words a person may wish not to know. One feels a sense of having one's own speech defiled. One feels repulsion at what one has just learned rather innocently. It is even possible to feel one's innocence, itself, robbed, i.e. the innocence with which one came to the poem. In this minute experience, one comes perhaps a little closer to understanding Celan's deepest predicament, feeling in some sense his profound ambivalence toward the language that was his true and only home, the German language, his mother tongue, which was, due to the recent events, both a murderous and a murdered language, a defiling and defiled language. Felstiner's most recent translation, found in *Selected Poems and Prose of Paul Celan,* is as follows:

DEATHFUGUE

Black milk of daybreak we drink it at evening
we drink it at midday and morning we drink it at night
we drink and we drink
we shovel a grave in the air where you won't lie too cramped
A man lives in the house he plays with his vipers he writes
he writes when it grows dark to Deutschland your golden hair Margareta
he writes it and steps out of doors and the stars are all sparkling
     he whistles his hounds to stay close
he whistles his Jews into rows has them shovel a grave in the ground
he commands us play up for the dance

Black milk of daybreak we drink you at night
we drink you at morning and midday we drink you at evening
we drink and we drink
A man lives in the house he plays with his vipers he writes
he writes when it grows dark to Deutschland your golden hair Margareta
Your ashen hair Shulamith we shovel a grave in the air
    where you won't lie too cramped

He shouts dig this earth deeper you lot there you others sing up and play
he grabs for the rod in his belt he swings it his eyes are so blue
stick your spades deeper you lot there you others play on for the dancing

Black milk of daybreak we drink you at night
we drink you at midday and morning we drink you at evening
we drink and we drink
a man lives in the house your goldenes Haar Margareta
your aschenes Haar Shulamith he plays with his vipers

He shouts play death more sweetly this Death is a master from Deutschland
he shouts scrape your strings darker you'll rise then as smoke to the sky
you'll then have a grave in the clouds where you won't lie too cramped

Black milk of daybreak we drink you at night
we drink you at midday Death is a master aus Deutschland
we drink you at evening and morning we drink and we drink
this Death is ein Meister aus Deutschland his eye it is blue
he shoots you with shot made of lead shoots you level and true
a man lives in the house your goldenes Haar Margarete
he looses his hounds on us grants us a grave in the air
he plays with his vipers and daydreams der Tod ist ein Meister aus
        Deutschland

dein goldenes Haar Margarete
dein aschenes Haar Sulamith

ACKNOWLEDGMENTS

The sea that washed *The Memory Room* to shore is a mighty thing and exists in the beauty of its vast particularities. There is little room here for that detail. So I must take you to that shoreline blindfolded, muffled, dressed in too–heavy a coat, only pointing out the waves that formed themselves at the horizon, bringing the bottle to our toes.

—My parents, who challenged me from an early age to consider the moral dilemma of the world and who offered me a biblical framework in which to think.

—My husband and our three children who provide a radical apprenticeship within a moat of safety. *Stabilitas.*

—Friends who brought me, late in life, into their love of poetry.

—Writing teachers who helped me decide to begin, and those, later, who taught me how to exist on the page.

—Members of my writing group who give rigorous critique alongside sturdy friendship.

—New friends, poets, who give me the gift of their scrutiny.

—Outside readers who found in my nascent work sufficient merit to open the door to the larger literary community.

—My agent, for her early and persevering enthusiasm.

—My publisher, in whom I felt, from the first meeting, complete confidence, as one gives over one's child to the perfect teacher.

—Friends, both visible and cloistered, who, by their goodwill and prayerful lives, insure the wresting of the world from oblivion, and give me, thus, a future in which to work.

To these, who know well the debt I owe them, I am deeply grateful.

See further www.CounterpointPress.com/The Memory Room/Acknowledgments